TRUE COLORS

By

K. R. RAYE

J-pad Publishing

TRUE COLORS

J-pad Publishing books may be purchased for educational, business, or sales promotional use.
For information about special discounts for bulk purchases, please contact J-pad Publishing Sales at
sales@JpadPublishing.com.

J-pad Publishing can bring authors to your live event. For more information or to book an event, please contact J-pad Publishing Events at events@JpadPublishing.com.

First Edition, March 2014
Hardcover Edition, March 2022
Cover Design by Nicole Hower

ISBN: 978-1-940361-09-3 (paperback)
ISBN: 978-1-940361-11-6 (hardcover)
ISBN: 978-1-940361-06-2 (e-book)

10 9 8 7 6 5 4 3 2 1
Printed in the U.S.A.

This is dedicated to Charles Rothacker.

*Now we know how Santa Claus successfully delivered
presents to all the children around the world.*

Acknowledgments

In everything, let me give thanks to God. He continues to bless me in beautiful, yet mysterious ways!

To Jacques, the most patient, loving, and giving husband a woman could ever ask for in life. Thank you for everything you do and everything you are.

Thanks to my mother, Alyce, whose strength and courage amaze me. TiMom, TiPop, and Sabrina keep providing love, support, good company, and good food! Home is where the heart is, and mine's in KC and CA with my family. For my sons, finally, let's start writing!

Thank you to the friends who stayed with me during the entire journey: Lauren Dervish, Kelly Russell, Heather Fischer, Kate Sutton, Nadia Krook, and Cecilia Gomez. I love you all so much!

To my classmates, the true basis for life-long friendships. Thank you for the love and support.

Along the way two super fans turned into beta readers: Shannon French and Marcia Williams, thanks for the fantastic feedback!

To my fellow writers, who teach and encourage. The Bay to Ocean pearls: Justine Cowan, Judy Reveal, Mindie Burgoyne, Ramona Long, and Melanie Rigney. BWG of MD provides camaraderie and awesome opportunities. My BDOT sisters: Sandra Bowman and Dee Lawrence. My other C3 Comrades in Crime: Monica Mathis-Stowe, D.B. Corey, Ann Arbaugh, Fay Moore, Weldon Burge, Larry Matthews, rock stars John Gilstrap and Jeffery Deaver, and Austin Camacho. And lots of love to

Deidre Berry, TaNisha Webb, Cherrie Woods, K. L. Brady, Angela Render, Chicki Brown, Curtis Bunn, Omar Tyree, Kimberla Lawson Roby, Susan Fales-Hill, DeVon Franklin, Karen E. Quinones Miller, Sadeqa Johnson, Sonica Jackson, LaShaunda Hoffman, Carl Webber, Pat Branch, Stephen King, and Tom Clancy (RIP).

From the professional side, I'd like to thank: my editor extraordinaire Christy Payne; Mary at Allen Design for the beautiful covers; my family at J-pad Publishing; Ella Curry, master marketer; Tony and Yvonne Rose, looking forward to BEA; Justina Pollard, WBAL-TV 11; Stephen McDonald, ESPN; ΔΣΘ Sorority, Inc. and my magnificent Sorors, Tracey Reynolds, Kim Knight, Carla Walton, and the ladies of HCAC; Oprah and Tyler Perry, always dream big; and Sara Camilli, the agent I wish I had.

Music soothes and inspires, here's to those that helped me compose: Jill Scott, Jamiroquai, Mary J. Blige, Dwele, Conya Doss, Robin Thicke, Al B. Sure!, SWV, Justin Timberlake, Earth, Wind & Fire, Stevie, Luther, Kirk Franklin, Toni Braxton, Faith Evans, Musiq Soulchild, Vivian Green, Mike Phillips, Will Downing, Jon B., 112, Sade, and new inspirations: Yolanda Johnson and Rogiers.

To the fans, wow, you inspire me! I am forever grateful to you.

As always, I would like to thank anyone I may have inadvertently missed who provided advice, support, and love during this long, crazy roller-coaster ride. Now, let's prepare for the next trilogy. Thank you and big hugs!

PIZZA DELIVERY – JULY 2006

"I love you, Imani," Marco Cabrette said as he adjusted his cell phone while he drove.

"You got the pizzas already?" Imani Cabrette asked.

"Check," he replied taking another whiff of the two large pepperoni and sausage pies sitting on his passenger seat. "There's nothing like Nino's authentic, New York style pizza."

"Well, too bad Nino's doesn't deliver because Melody and Chris just put up the movies and cracked out the Scrabble board. They said they're ready for their Scrabble butt-whipping."

"Oh, please, not likely," Marco heard Melody mutter in the background.

Imani chuckled. "How far away are you, Sweetie?"

"I'm turning onto the main drag now. I should be home in less than five minutes."

"Perfect. We'll be waiting," she said sweetly. "And Marco?"

"Yes, Baby?"

"I love you, too."

Marco disconnected with a big grin and tossed the phone on top of the pizza boxes.

Feeling relaxed, he drummed his thumbs against the steering wheel.

An erratic movement caught his full attention. His relaxed state dissipated like mist as he leaned forward in his seat.

Bright summer sunlight filtered across the usually busy, two-lane road. Even though it was a little before 6:00 p.m. on a Saturday night, traffic was lighter than normal. *Thank goodness for small favors!*

As he squinted then frowned, both hands tightened around the steering wheel.

About a quarter mile ahead, an oncoming white SUV left its lane and crossed directly into his.

The only other car in Marco's lane swerved out of the SUV's way and rattled past onto the shoulder while it honked wildly.

Marco honked and considered following the earlier car's path, but the Ford Explorer adjusted and now straddled both Marco's lane and the shoulder.

With the distance between them closing faster than he liked, options sprinted through his mind.

Taking the only valid choice, he veered to the left into the oncoming traffic lane. If he could just get past the SUV, there was nothing except open road ahead and he'd be back in his lane well before anyone else even came into sight.

"Please stay on the wrong side of the road," he prayed aloud as he bit his lip.

However a scant second later his prayers morphed into a moan.

The Explorer—whose driver seemed deadly intent on playing chicken—straightened up, back into his correct lane.

"Damn it!" he shouted as he smacked the steering wheel.

Only a few car lengths separated them from a head-on collision and with Marco clearly driving on the wrong side of the street, the cops would easily find him at fault.

Gritting his teeth, he floored his Honda in a last ditch effort and swerved hard to the right, scuttling back into his lane.

Too late he realized his mistake as the Explorer driver reacted…and steered towards him again.

"What the hell!" he yelled as the driver countered his every action, like some fool playing real life bumper cars.

In one heartbeat the Explorer smashed into his driver's side door crumpling his car around him.

Oddly enough, he didn't feel any pain. *Adrenaline*, he mused. The random thought fluttered away and he noticed that the still accelerating Explorer had their pinned cars hurtling towards a solid wall of pine trees off to his right.

Determined to slow their impact, he stood on the brakes while random memories flashed like light bulbs. His mother bustling about her Italian kitchen; his father laughing at a raucous joke he'd told; his sister, Maria, imparting her sweet wisdom.

Bits and pieces of the Lord's Prayer, Psalm 23, and Hail Mary flitted through his mind before it stuck on a simple children's prayer. "If I should die before I wake, I pray the Lord my soul to take, Amen."

Imani's face floated in front of him, warm and beautiful. "I love you, Imani," he whispered as the Explorer rammed them into the pines.

Metal screeched and wailed while glass shattered and rained down as his Honda melded around the biggest tree.

Blinding pain seared him for a millisecond while the smells of burnt rubber, pine needles, gasoline, and pizza co-mingled in his nostrils like some bizarre cologne, and then…nothing.

***

A cold, heavy hand of dread settled on Imani's scalp.

Its icy fingers slithered down her spine and chills ricocheted throughout her body. Without warning it slammed a fistful of lead into her gut. A scream died in her throat as the pain forced her to inhale a sharp, jagged breath.

Everything began to move in freakish, fun-house slow motion. And her vision telescoped out like the exits in horror movies that went from being just two feet away to yards away down a steadily expanding hallway.

Trying to steady herself, she never even realized that she'd leapt up from the dining room table until she saw the Scrabble board fly across it.

Scrabble tiles scattered and tinkled onto the floor

with champagne glass clinks.

Melody Wilkins and Chris Weaver turned their heads towards her in unison.

"Are you okay?" Chris's amber-flecked, gray eyes stared at her like she'd gone berserk. His normally cute, boyish features and wild blonde hair morphed into an absurdist painting with each light tan freckle highlighted.

Although they'd hung out a bit over the years as co-workers and even more after Chris and Melody became an item, she realized that Chris had never experienced her weird sixth sense. But Melody had.

Imani ignored Chris and locked eyes with her old college roommate.

"Imani, what's wrong?" Melody asked as she ran over in slow motion, each blonde curl bouncing like a protracted spring about her golden-tanned face. Her usually optimistic green-gray eyes shimmered with concern.

Although Imani felt her mouth moving, it took centuries before the words actually emerged. "Marco," she replied with her heart and mind racing. "Something's wrong with Marco."

"Marco?" Chris asked, visibly bewildered. "You just got off the phone with him less than three minutes ago."

Shaking her head slow as molasses on a cold wintry day, Imani grabbed Melody's shoulders. "You have to take me to him, please!"

"What?" Melody's eyes widened. "Where?"

Imani ignored Melody's questions. *Dear God,*

help please! Overwhelmed by premonitions more intense than she'd ever experienced before, she began to hyperventilate. Images whisked past at warp speed and she felt compartments of her mind closing like hurricane shutters protecting windows from the impending storm.

***

The little hairs on Melody's neck stood on end. Somehow in that instant she believed that Imani knew the unknowable. "Get your keys, Chris," she said before helping Imani outside and into the back seat of Chris's car.

Chris got in with a shrug. "Do you mind telling me where we're going?"

Imani rocked and mumbled to herself with her eyes cast downward.

Over the seven years they'd known each other, she'd never seen her strong, determined friend act like this. It was as if Imani were devolving into a catatonic state right before her eyes. Imani's beautiful walnut skin turned ashen, her sharp, brown eyes focused inward and muddy, and her entire athletic frame seemed to implode into a sack of bones and skin.

Melody looked at Chris unsure. "Just drive two minutes to the main road and turn left. Nino's is three blocks from there, about a mile down on the right."

"Okay," he muttered still skeptical.

Turning onto the main road, they saw emergency

lights blazing in the opposite lane. A fire truck and ambulance pulled onto the scene as they approached.

"No, no, no!!!" screamed Imani.

"It may not be him," Melody said trying to comfort Imani while starting to panic inside.

As they pulled near, an officer began directing traffic away from the accident.

Chris pulled up to him and rolled down his window.

"Move along, please," the gruff officer said, assuming they were bold rubber-neckers.

"I'm sorry, Sir," Melody said, "but our girlfriend here thinks her husband was involved in the wreck."

The officer leaned down and peered into the vehicle. "What?"

"My husband was in the navy Honda," Imani said eerily calm. Her eyes appeared eagle focused again as they beseeched the policeman to help.

"Um, pull over here out of the way," he said, pointing to a bit of median out of the path of traffic yet still distant from the accident. "I'll check your story out," he shouted, directing the other cars around.

Another officer came over to investigate the problem.

They talked for a moment and the first officer walked to their car. "Do you know your husband's license plate number, Ma'am?"

Imani sat catatonic in the back seat again.

Melody shuddered and covered for her. "Oh God, it was a personalized vanity plate with his name on it." She could feel Imani recommence rocking and it sent goosebumps sprouting along her arms. "The license plate was Marco, M-A-R-C-O."

"Did you get that?" the officer asked speaking into the two-way radio attached at the shoulder of his uniform.

"Roger," a scratchy reply emitted from the radio. Moments later the scratchy voice replied. "Roger, the rear license plate reads Marco."

Arctic chills coursed through Melody's body and Chris turned to stare at Imani like he'd just seen a ghost.

***

Imani flung open her rear passenger door and rocketed from the car like an ejector seat. "No! God, please, no!" she screamed running towards the accident.

A startled paramedic saw her first before the officer, Chris, or Melody could react. Quick on his feet, the paramedic grabbed her around the waist and swung her away from the carnage.

All Imani saw before the paramedic, officer, and her friends pulled her away was Marco's beautiful, wavy black shoulder-length hair, matted with blood and safety glass fragments, dangling around his limp neck. His little blue Honda sat unrecognizably mangled and fused together with a large, crumpled white SUV.

***

Melody sat shell-shocked in the passenger seat feeling completely drained while Chris drove them back to Imani and Marco's house in stunned silence.

After they'd wrestled Imani back to the car, the paramedics had pronounced Marco dead at the scene. Thankfully, the paramedics and cops spared them the horror of driving to the morgue to identify the body.

Melody sighed then glanced back at Imani, but Imani hadn't moved a muscle since they'd left the accident site.

As Chris pulled into the driveway Imani's cell phone rang, startling them.

In a flash, Melody unfastened her seat belt, jumped out, and answered it.

"Baby, what's wrong?" Imani's mother's frantic voice bellowed over the line.

"Hi, Mrs. Jordan," Melody replied not wanting to say more. "This is Melody."

Mrs. Jordan gasped, clearly taken aback by Melody answering her daughter's phone. "Melody? Melody, where is Imani? What's wrong with my daughter? I feel something awful, where is she?"

"She's here, Mrs. Jordan. She's okay…" Melody fibbed then hesitated, her mouth reluctant to speak the words. "There was an accident. It's Marco…Marco didn't make it."

"Oh my God, my poor Baby!" Melody heard Mrs. Jordan address her husband next. "Pack our bags, Honey, our Baby needs us." With tears choking her voice, Mrs. Jordan came back on the line again. "We're on our way up, Melody. Make sure my

Baby's okay."

THE NIGHT FALLS

Lance Dunn stood on Imani's porch, drawing strength before he rang the doorbell. It had been a long time since he'd last seen her—really only twice in the thirteen months since her wedding to Marco last June. That dreaded day when he severed all ties with her…six years of friendship gone in a flash.

Unfortunately, he remembered the night before Imani's wedding better than he remembered yesterday because it constantly replayed in his mind.

He had finally mustered up the courage to tell Imani how he truly felt, before it was too late. Before she married Marco.

He confessed his love and he knew Imani loved him, too. But then the unexpected happened.

Imani declared in no uncertain terms that she loved Marco and she promptly kicked him out. Out to return to his wife, Heather—the wife he filed for divorce from a mere three days later.

The whole ordeal crushed him, made him bitter.

However, Melody—their ever-optimistic friend— kept trying to undo what his pride wouldn't let him do. She lured him out twice under the pretense of catching up over dinner once, then lunch another time.

Lance smirked. What she failed to mention was that she'd also invited Chris, Marco, and Imani. So, he'd been forced to see how happy Marco and Imani were, which only ripped his heart to pieces further.

Now Marco lay dead on a cold, morgue slab. Fun, carefree, never-hurt-a-soul Marco.

Although he yearned for Imani, Lance never would have wished this fate on Marco. Marco was too young, only twenty-five, not even in the prime of his life yet.

His shoulders slumped. Even Marco's death couldn't dampen the longing he felt for Imani. And here he was, stalling on her doorstep, feeling guilty and depraved, yet wanting her. But she wouldn't want him, not grieving for Marco…a grief that might take ages to heal.

Sighing, he shook his head and looked down at his workout shorts and tank top. *I should have taken the time to change.* When Melody called, he'd been on his way to the gym to participate in a pick-up basketball league tournament with his co-worker, Bobby. However, like always, when his girls called—no, scratch that, when Melody called, he dropped everything to come running.

"Snap out of it," he muttered in frustration.

Taking a deep breath, he forced the tenseness from his body until each bundle of raw nerve endings felt numb. Out of habit his old, football pre-game relaxation techniques clicked in, and he rolled back his muscular shoulders, stretching throughout his entire 6'2" frame.

With his game face set, Lance rang the doorbell.

The door opened almost immediately.

"God, yes! Thank you for coming on such short notice, Lance." Melody greeted him with a quick hug before she pulled him inside. "Chris is weirded out by the whole thing and Imani…" Melody gave him a worried look and lowered her voice. "I've never seen her like this, Lance. She's in and out of reality."

"I just can't handle both of them," she said looking distraught. Melody gestured her hands to elaborate, then wrung them together. "It's only been two hours since…the accident. And already it feels like a lifetime."

"Hey, hey, it's okay." Lance held Melody tight until he felt her calm down.

His normally perky friend looked haggard and run through the ringer. Her shoulder-length, curly blonde locks seemed wild and tussled as if she'd literally sat pulling her hair out. Her gray-green eyes were red and puffy from crying and her beautiful, natural tanned-looking, peaches and cream skin appeared blotchy and sallow.

"You should have called me immediately. You know I'll always come whenever you need me," he said, feeling her relax in his arms before she finally stepped back.

Melody managed a faint wisp of a smile, took his hand, and led him back into the dramatic yet inviting family room.

A tan brick fireplace acted as the centerpiece on the back wall with striking African masks flanking it as accents. The contemporary, mahogany wood coffee and side tables complemented the honey-colored hardwood floors. In the corner sat the requisite big screen TV. And the chocolate, suede-like loveseat and couch invited you to sink into their rich hominess. Everything exuded warmth and comfort except for one incongruent object…Imani.

Imani appeared to wilt under the thick, white terry cloth, spa bathrobe that cocooned her body. Oblivious to anyone else in the room, she rocked on the couch with her knees hugged to her chest.

However, Imani wasn't alone. Chris used every inch of his slender, 5'8" body to pace from the hallway to the family room and back.

Seeing the two of them, Lance understood why Melody needed help and he squeezed her hand.

Melody gave him another faint smile then she addressed Chris. "Honey, when did Imani finish up the phone call with Marco's parents?"

Chris quit pacing and noticed Lance. He nodded his head in greeting before answering Melody's question. "About three minutes ago. She hung up when they all started crying hysterically and she hasn't moved from that spot since."

"Okay, thanks, Honey," Melody replied although Chris had already recommenced his pacing. Looking exhausted, Melody rubbed her face and it seemed like she was trying to prevent an untimely breakdown.

Unsure if he should tend to Imani or comfort Melody with Chris pacing nearby, Lance simply held Melody's hand. Evidently it was enough as she gave it a grateful squeeze.

After a minute, she focused on Lance. "I can't imagine what the Cabrettes are going through. It's bad enough that Imani's mother employed that freaky sixth sense they both possess and called as soon as we pulled into the driveway."

"She insisted on coming up tonight, but we called them back and begged them to wait until tomorrow morning." Melody shook her head. "I couldn't let them drive. Not tonight, not in the dark, not after one accident…although Mrs. Jordan vehemently protested."

"That sounds like Mrs. Jordan," Lance replied. "Speaking of the accident, do the police know the cause?"

"From what we could assess at the…scene, with all the empty beer cans and the few comments we overheard, it appears that the other driver was intoxicated."

"Is he okay?" he wondered aloud, wanting to beat the guy to within an inch of his life for killing their friend.

"No." Melody shook her head. "He wasn't wearing his seatbelt and his head met the windshield with nasty consequences."

"Oh-kay." Lance felt a momentary bit of joyful retribution followed by guilt at yet another senseless loss of life.

"I'm sorry." Melody sighed. "It's just that Marco was going out to get the pizzas. We were supposed to be playing Scrabble now," she said gesturing to the game on the dining room table. Scrabble tiles inexplicably littered the floor.

Chris's pacing grew more frantic.

Melody threw Chris a worried look. "Lance, could you sit with Imani for a moment? I really should look after Chris."

"Of course," he replied. "Take as long as you need. You know I'm here for the long haul."

"Thanks," she said giving him a big hug. When she withdrew to go comfort Chris, Melody appeared stronger.

Unable to put off the inevitable, Lance sighed and walked over to Imani who still sat rocking in her own little world.

The shrunken, forlorn sack of a person before him did not even remotely resemble the self-assured, walnut-skinned, sexy beauty he knew and loved.

Careful not to alarm her, he sat and placed his left arm around her shoulder.

Imani glanced up at him, noticing his presence for the first time. Her eyes brimmed with tears for the longest before she simply said, "thank you," and continued rocking. Then a minute later, her upper body teetered towards him in slow motion and fell over sideways like a tree succumbing to the whims of the wind.

Stunned but working on automatic, his quick wide receiver reflexes took over. He caught her head with his right hand and cradled it down for a delicate landing on his lap. Unsure of what to do next, he waited for her to speak. When she didn't, he began stroking her soft, full curls with his right hand and her arm with his left.

Imani remained motionless.

Minutes later, Lance heard Chris crying and Melody promptly reappeared in the family room.

"I hate to ask," Melody said looking pained. "But is it okay if we leave for about thirty minutes? I just need to get Chris out of here for a while."

"Take as long as you need, Melody. An hour or two's more than fine," Lance assured her.

"I'll turn off the ringers on all the telephones so she won't be interrupted. And I'll check the voicemail later…" Melody hesitated.

"Anything else?" he asked wanting to help.

"Well, I was about to draw Imani a bubble bath and put her to bed with a cup of tea." Melody seemed torn between staying and helping her friend or keeping her fiancé sane. "Could you manage that, too, or would you prefer if I stayed?"

Although her requests set his nerves on edge, he didn't pause one nanosecond. Marco and Chris had been really tight, and he could tell that Marco's death devastated Chris. The thought of being alone with Imani under such circumstances bothered him, but his girls needed him and he couldn't disappoint them, not again. "I got it, Melody. Take care of Chris. Come back whenever you're ready."

"Thank you so much." Melody breathed a sigh of relief. "I'll be back as soon as possible."

Lance heard the door close soon thereafter and exhaled. Not wanting to disturb Imani for tea or a bath, he continued to stroke her head and arm for another half an hour until she stirred.

"Ready to go to bed?" he asked.

She rolled over onto her back and looked up at him. "Just don't leave me," she whispered.

"Oh, Imani…" His heart broke at the sight of her. "I promise you, I won't leave."

"Then, okay." Slowly she sat up and held out her hand waiting for him to get up first and lead the way.

Lance glanced around quickly to get his bearings; he'd never been in Imani and Marco's house before, no less her master bathroom. He scanned the bottom floor in two seconds. Next to the entry lay the dining room, behind that the kitchen, the stairs spilled into the middle of the traffic patterns, then across the back of the house were the family room and a powder room. That meant the bedrooms were upstairs.

Slow and steady, they climbed the stairs and proceeded down the hall, allowing him to check out the first of four doorways as they moved past.

Behind door number one, the slightly formal office boasted an old, Italian-styled green leather chair and cherry-wood furniture: two bookcases, a computer desk, and a futon. A treadmill sat tucked against the far wall.

Further down the hallway, they passed the guest bathroom. Next came the beach-themed getaway guest bedroom with its white and sand-colored decorations and whitewashed mission bedroom set.

That meant the last door at the end of the hallway had to be the master bedroom.

Lance paused at the door then entered with Imani silently in tow.

The dark yet soothing room felt like a forest retreat with its hunter green and sage colors and queen-sized sleigh bed.

Leaving Imani beside the bed, he entered the lighter, sage and tan, attached bathroom. The vanity was on his left, then the separate toilet. On the right were the shower stall and a soaking tub. Imani's bubble bath oils lined the back rim of the bathtub.

Kneeling by the tub, he drew the bath water and poured in a large amount of one of the pearly liquids. *The more bubbles, the better.*

Imani ambled daze-like through the bathroom door, stopping in the doorway to hold onto the frame. With the long, terry-cloth robe belted tightly around her, she looked small and lost.

Lance waited for her to approach, but she remained transfixed in the doorway, grasping it like her last lifeline. He stood and walked over. As he extended his hand, it appeared that she noticed him again for the first time.

Gratefully she clenched his offered hand with her right hand and reluctantly released the doorframe with her left.

He led her to the bathtub where the water still flowed. A thick curtain of bubbles lay on top. "Can you manage from here?" he asked praying that she'd snap out of it.

Her blank expression told him she couldn't.

"Do you want to wait for Melody to return?" He

took a step backwards, but she wouldn't release his hand.

His breathing slowed to shallow gasps and he tried to reason with her again.

"Please, you've got to do this, Imani, unless you're expecting me to bathe you." Uncharacteristic nerves evaded his body and he felt overheated; sweat threatened to break out along his forehead and neck. *Please God, she needs to wake up and do this for herself!*

Imani didn't answer at first, appearing to be just one breath away from collapsing in a heap. "Don't leave me," she finally whispered, eyes pleading for his strength and certainty in her unstable world.

However uncomfortable this felt, he knew he had to do this for her. Imani needed a friend tonight more than ever.

Her eyes stayed locked on his until he felt something click inside his head and his heart. His breathing stuttered and hitched as the realization hit him; their lost friendship meant more to him than his wounded pride or her earlier rejection.

Slowly, he nodded, feeling ready to take a genuine step up to the plate. "I'm here, Imani. I won't leave you."

Her head dropped in relief and she unbelted her robe, letting it puddle around her feet.

Lance inhaled sharp as a knife. She was even more beautiful than he remembered. He knew Imani and Marco were diligent about their workouts and it showed. Averting his eyes, he helped her step into the bathtub.

To his immense relief, once her body slipped under the cover of the bubbles, his tumultuous emotions disappeared. However, her tortured face still haunted him.

In business mode, he grabbed a washcloth and placed it in her right hand. "Here you go, Imani. Use this to clean yourself."

As soon as he released her hand, it dropped like a limp fish back into the tub. Never once did she move, remaining eerily still up to her shoulders in bubbles. To him, she seemed like an empty husk, a wooden replica where his friend once roamed free. Her fiery spirit snuffed under a broken shell.

Rubbing his hand across his face and head, he forced his emotions down. *You can do this!* He took a deep breath, swallowed hard, and fished around the bathwater until he found the washcloth.

Using a generous amount of soap, he lathered it into huge foaming bubbles and began to gently scrub her back.

Silent tears fell from her eyes and Lance cleared his throat in an attempt to repress his own sorrow. "I'm so very sorry, Imani," he repeated while he continued to wash her body.

By the time he finished, her tears had stopped falling. Carefully, he rinsed her body and helped her up.

Glancing around, he spotted a set of towels hanging nearby and he snatched one and wrapped it around her beautiful, glistening body. Once she stood on the solid bathroom floor, he engaged her again. "Can you dry yourself from here?" he prayed aloud.

Imani stood stock still and unblinking and he knew she could not.

Brisk but thorough, he dried her and kept his mind preoccupied with unpleasant thoughts so that it didn't wander to the task at hand. After years of friendship, he knew that she relished her lotions, so he conducted a quick search until he found her stash.

Grabbing a creamy, cocoa-butter lotion, he lotioned her body in a hurry and finished right before he reached his breaking point. Even with Marco's death looming large, it was almost too much to ask the lustful part of his mind—the part that enjoyed smoothing the silky lotion across her beautiful body—to remain completely platonic, not after all this time of wanting her.

Saddened by the situation, his shoulders drooped as he returned the lotion and hung up her towel. With the bathroom looking presentable, he took her hand and led her into the bedroom.

Remembering her college habits, he reached under her pillow, found her nightgown, and pulled it over her head.

She made a half-hearted attempt to assist him by putting her arms up enough so that he could dress her.

With that task complete, he began to turn down her bed.

In a flash she halted his hand and shook her head. "I can't sleep in here. Not without my Marco." Imani's bottom lip trembled and tears threatened to fall again.

Trying to protect her from painful thoughts, he captured her in a vise-like hug. "It's okay, Imani, it's okay. You don't have to sleep in here. Come on." With his arm draped around her shoulder, he walked her to the guest bedroom. "Is this okay?"

She nodded then withdrew into her shell once more.

With a heavy heart, he turned down the bed and helped her under the covers. "I'll be right downstairs. Just call me if you need me, alright?"

Imani never responded, so he turned to go.

Quick as lightening her hand appeared from under the covers and clenched his right arm, her grip hard as granite. Tears brimmed in her eyes again, but her voice sounded as firm as her grasp. "Don't leave me." It was not a request.

"Okay, Imani, I won't leave," he said tenderly as his heart wrenched in his chest.

For a few seconds he tried to get her to relinquish his right arm.

When she wouldn't, he kicked off his Nikes and climbed over her into the bed. After he assumed the spooning position, she finally released his arm and settled down.

Laying this close to Imani under the circumstances felt uncomfortable. Feeling restless and not at all tired, he stared at the wall past Imani, then five minutes later he looked up at the ceiling. Another five minutes passed and he glanced around the room until he located the television remote control on his nightstand.

Afraid to rouse Imani, but dying of boredom and discomfort, he finally asked, "Is it okay if I watch TV?"

Imani didn't answer.

After waiting a minute for her response, he switched on the TV and turned the volume down low. He sighed as he flipped through the channels, nothing really catching his attention. Nothing on CNN, TNT, SciFi, or TBS, especially nothing on the local channels. After cycling through all the channels twice, he gave up and left it on Cartoon Network in the midst of a *Scooby Doo* marathon.

About an hour later with Imani fast asleep, Melody returned to check on him.

"Everything okay, Lance?" she asked looking less harried than earlier.

"Yep, how's Chris?"

"Better. He actually agreed to sleep over here tonight. So, he's getting ready for bed now. We'll be in the next room," she said pointing down the hall. "The one that doubles as an office."

"Sounds good. Um, hate to ask but could you get me a glass of water?"

"Sure," she replied although her expression displayed her confusion.

"Every time I try to leave," he said while moving his arm away from Imani.

Immediately Imani groaned in her sleep, snagged his errant arm, and then snuggled it back around her.

He shrugged his shoulders as if to say, 'see.'

"No problem." Melody chuckled then got serious again. "Any changes at all?"

Lance shook his head no. "She was a zombie up until she fell asleep. The only thing she actually said was, 'don't leave me,' so I haven't."

"Well, I'll be right back with your water." Melody took a step out the door and then turned back. "Will you be okay staying the night?"

Managing to grin, he nodded his head. "I'm fine, Melody."

"Alrighty then," she replied as another faint smile flickered. "Do you need anything else? Anything at all?"

"Just the water."

"Okay, and Lance?" she said looking relieved.

"Yes?"

"Thanks again for coming."

"Be quiet with that nonsense. You know I'm always here for my girls."

THE MORNING AFTER

Trevor Mathis parked in front of the Cabrette house. He still couldn't believe that Marco, cool-ass Marco was dead. Marco and Imani had just visited his house last weekend for a barbeque. They all played dominos and spades, and the Cabrettes and Trevor and his wife, Erycah, took turns beating Chris and Melody soundly.

Damn, when he called Imani last night for their twice a week chitchat and the call rolled into her voicemail, he should have figured something was wrong. But knowing that Chris and Melody were coming over for movies, he'd assumed Imani simply couldn't come to the phone.

This morning Melody called him back after checking the voicemail and she broke the horrible news. He told her he'd come over immediately and now here he was.

As he exited his car and walked along the sidewalk, he took a mental inventory of the vehicles parked either in front of the house or in the two-car driveway. As expected, he recognized Chris's sporty Infiniti, Imani's silver Toyota Camry, and the Jordan's Cadillac from visits to Imani's parents down in the Bronx near his mom's place. Visibly missing was Marco's navy blue Honda Accord.

A shudder coursed through his body.

One other car, a sleek Mercedes, sat parked in the driveway. He didn't recognize the car's owner, however, with all the friends the Cabrettes had, they were in store for lots of mourners sending their condolences.

Ready to pay his own respects, he hurried to the door and rang the bell.

A tired-looking Melody answered the door. "Hey, Trev," she said, giving him a hug. "Thanks for coming." She led the way into the normally cheery-looking kitchen.

Today the yellow walls seemed artificially sunny.

Chris stood by the island looking drained and Melody went to comfort him. Meanwhile, Mr. Jordan sat at the dinette set, sipping a cup of coffee.

"Hi, Sir," Trevor said coming around to embrace Imani's father.

"Hello, Son," Mr. Jordan replied while clapping him on the back. "Nice to see you again, Trevor…although not under the best circumstances."

"I know, Sir." Trevor looked at Melody. "Where's Imani?"

"Well, her mom just went to check on her. Why don't you go upstairs as well?"

"You sure?" he asked.

"Yeah, she'd love to see you."

***

Lance thought he heard voices, but sheer exhaustion pushed the sounds from his mind and he almost succumbed to sleep's melodic pull.

However, sleep wouldn't quite return as an eerie sensation spread over him, as if he were being watched. His heart began to race. Needing to catch his bearings, he rolled from his right side onto his back and slowly blinked until the room became familiar.

Imani!

Before he could sit up, he heard and felt her still sound asleep beside him on his left. His heart skipped a beat and then slowed again as the sense of uneasiness diminished. *There's no one else here besides us.*

Relaxing again, he yawned and the uneasy feeling disappeared. Ready for more sleep, he rolled onto his left side into a spooning position behind Imani— when he realized someone actually *was* in the room.

Startled, he pushed back from Imani as her mother shot him a very suspicious scowl. "Mrs. Jordan," he stuttered.

"Lance." Her displeasure to find him lying in bed snuggled next to her not-even-widowed-for-a-day daughter shone through with extreme obviousness.

Embarrassed, he sat straight up and covered himself with the sheets. Although he still wore his tank top and gym shorts, he intuited that Mrs. Jordan would think it wasn't nearly enough clothing.

She stood in the doorway, glowering at him as if he'd done something wrong.

His blood started to boil. Why did she insist on turning something innocent into something sordid? He put on his game face and answered her unspoken question. "Imani didn't want to be alone last night and she refused to let me leave. Nothing inappropriate happened in the least."

"I never said it did," she replied snidely. "How's my daughter doing?"

He looked at Imani and his voice softened. "She slept soundly throughout the night, but she was pretty out of it before then." He returned Mrs. Jordan's cold, steady gaze. "As expected, she's taking it very hard."

***

Trevor made his way upstairs and down the hall, following the sound of voices.

As he headed towards Imani's bedroom, he spied Mrs. Jordan standing just inside the guest room doorway. Eager to see Mrs. Jordan, he entered the room with a big smile and then he turned towards the bed to greet the other voice, which he assumed was Imani. That was until his subconscious realized the voice sounded way too deep.

"What the…?" he stopped just short of cursing in front of Mrs. Jordan when he saw Imani sound asleep and Lance sitting in bed beside her looking guilty as hell.

Mrs. Jordan stepped forward and hugged him. With her lips by his ear she whispered, "my sentiments exactly." Smiling as she pulled back, she reached up and fingered one of his shoulder-length dreadlocks. "I see you still have your dreads."

He chuckled and rolled his eyes. "Yes, Mom, I do."

"Well, let me know when my daughter wakes up." She patted his shoulder and left.

Trevor managed to plaster on a smile until Mrs. Jordan disappeared from earshot. However, when he turned back to Lance, the smile disappeared in a flash. "Lance."

"Trev," Lance replied even-keeled although Trevor could tell Lance fumed.

"What are you doing here?" Trevor crossed his arms. Lance had another thing coming if he expected him to back down. *Please! Imani needed protection from this crazy-ass fool.*

"Who do you think you're talking to Trev?" Lance's back stiffened. "You know it's always been Imani, Melody, and me. The triplets, the trio, the Three Musketeers. You were around us enough years as the fourth wheel to know that." Gaining steam, Lance shot back. "What are you doing here anyway? You make the trip up from the City with the Jordans?"

"See, Negro," he replied with a smirk. "You just played yourself with that ignorant ass comment. Erycah and I moved up here from the City damn near a year ago. If you were any real friend to Imani or me, like you used to be, you would have known that."

Lance appeared stumped for the briefest of

seconds, before he narrowed his eyes. "Just because I don't spend my time talking about you, doesn't mean that Imani and I don't talk."

"Really?" Trevor tried not to snort. "Funny thing is Imani told me more than once that y'all haven't talked since, hmm…" Trevor uncrossed his arms and tapped his index finger against his chin three times in faux contemplation before he pointed at Lance. "Your ass filed for divorce the week after her wedding." He crossed his arms again and dared him to reply. "If I recall correctly, you've only seen her like what…two or three times over the past year?"

"Yo, Trev." Lance all but growled. "Step off."

"Niggah, please!" Trev flung his arms down to his sides, fists balled. "Don't come in here acting like you run things when you haven't been here for Imani in over a year."

"I was here last night when she needed me most."

"Whatever, Fugazie! That don't explain why your ass is sleeping in bed with her."

Lance looked ready to jump out of bed to try and beat him senseless. Although they were about the same height, Trevor knew Lance outweighed him by about 30 pounds of pure muscle. Regardless, he had no intention of backing down.

"Yo, Trev, we've never had any beef in the past. So I don't know why you're suddenly tripping. Therefore, I'm guessing Marco's death made you temporarily lose your mind."

Lance's voice took on a low, menacing tone. "Because I'm not being fake or shady and I know you're not crazy enough to call me or anyone else a faggot. So if you got something to say—"

Imani stirred and it stopped them both dead in their tracks.

***

The room felt way too bright meaning she had probably overslept. Still not wanting to get up, Imani covered her head with the comforter.

Wait, if it was so late, why didn't Marco awaken her with a sweet kiss?

Waking more, she noticed all the background noise and smiled; he was probably making her a cup of coffee and grabbing them both croissants or muffins. She slid the covers under her chin, stretched, and grinned before fluttering her eyes open.

As her eyes adjusted to the bright, white and tan room, she frowned. Why was it so bright and why was the bed facing the wrong direction? Her eyes widened. And when did Trevor come over? "Trev?"

As Trevor raced over to hug her she felt someone else behind her in bed. Twisting around, her eyes bugged out of her head when she saw Lance. "Lance?" her voice cracked and fragments of yesterday hit her hard from every direction like a prizefighter's punches.

Marco wasn't downstairs because Marco wasn't here. Marco would never return because Marco was dead.

Suddenly she couldn't remember how to breathe.

Air came in harsh shards and she began to hyperventilate.

"Imani take deep breaths, Baby," Lance pleaded as he rubbed her back.

"It's okay." Trev knelt by the bed and held her hand. "We're here, Boo. We're here."

"Get her mother," Lance snapped at Trev.

"Yo, you get her mom!"

Imani grabbed Trev's arm and sobbed. "My...mommy's...here?"

"Yeah, she's here," he replied, his head bobbing in the affirmative, dreads rustling.

"Please...get her...for me...Trev." Iron fingers gripped her heart and it became even harder to breathe. As her vision tunneled out into a welcoming blackness, Trevor raced downstairs to get her mother.

THE FUNERAL

Imani glanced behind her and scanned the large gathering of mourners. Scattered amongst all of Marco's massive extended family, New York City friends, and old family neighbors, were quite a few of their college friends and coworkers. Surprisingly, most of her and Marco's GE colleagues had made the almost three-hour drive down from the Albany area to the City.

As she spotted Lex and Tommy—Marco's two best friends, Lance, Melody, Trevor, Erycah, John and Krystal, Sophia, and Carmen, it felt like a college reunion…minus the crying and black attire. Even Big Tony had made the trip up from Tampa Bay, although she knew the Buccaneers training camp started soon.

Her father squeezed her right hand and she gave him and her mother a weak nod. Meanwhile, to her left, Mrs. Cabrette's sobs picked up again.

Feeling somewhat stronger surrounded by family and friends, Imani prayed she could provide a modicum of support to Marco's mother.

Poor Mrs. Cabrette or Mama, the nickname she begged Imani to call her, sat beside her, struggling to understand why she was burying her baby boy.

As Mama's sobs worsened, Imani released her

dad's hand and linked arms with Mama, who clung to her for dear life.

Mr. Cabrette draped his right arm around his wife's shoulders. His left hand entwined with Marco's older sister, Maria, who had flown in with her new husband from their residence in Italy.

While they consoled each other in their hot, metal chairs at the graveside, Imani studied her mother-in-law. They had just visited Marco's parents less than two months ago, and the change in Mrs. Cabrette's appearance from then until now still shocked her.

The once pretty, vivacious, little Italian spitfire had aged twenty years over the past few days. And come to think of it, poor Mr. Cabrette wasn't fairing much better. The strong, humorous man seemed to have shrunk a few inches in stature.

Father Bartelli stood up and began the service as Imani's mom passed her a fan.

The oppressive July heat hung heavily over everyone, wilting all under its humid intensity.

Imani fanned herself and Mama with her right hand while she stared straight ahead. Even though she didn't want to see anything, her eyes fixated on the beautiful floral arrangements. The blossom-filled bouquets failed miserably in their attempts to brighten the atmosphere; rather the fragrant flowers cloyed and contributed to the overall oppressiveness.

Unable to focus, she fidgeted and fanned.

Heat radiated from her left hand and she stared at the source. Painful pulsations emanated from her wedding ring. She twisted the ring around her finger.

'Til death do us part. The words echoed through her grieving heart like a desolate cavern.

She twisted the ring again. The physical pain subsided, but the emotional agony grew exponentially. And the service droned on.

Only after the priest uttered the words, "from ashes to ashes, dust to dust," did the finality of the situation sink in. Panic gripped hold as the priest stepped back.

With a nod of his head, the lovingly-hewn, mahogany coffin—too beautiful to bury under the cold, uncaring earth—descended into the ground.

Pull it together, she prayed as Father Bartelli nodded for the family to pay their final respects. With a collected sigh, Imani and the family rose as one, their arms still linked together for strength.

As they prepared to step forward, Mama emitted a grief-stricken wail and fell back into her chair pulling Imani down with her.

Mr. Cabrette rushed to their aide while Imani's parents, Maria, and Maria's husband covered for them.

A long sixty seconds later, Imani and Mr. Cabrette finally calmed down Mama.

Reluctantly Mrs. Cabrette released Imani's arm, and motioned for her to go towards the gravesite without them.

Imani glanced at the gravesite. She didn't want to go, but she needed to. Mustering every last ounce of willpower, she forced her legs to stand. After taking a deep breath, she took three strong steps towards the gaping maw in the ground where her husband had disappeared.

Silent tears wet her cheeks. *How is it physically possible for my body to produce any more tears?* She closed her eyes. *Please God, help me.*

After a minute she reopened her eyes and stared at the sunken casket. Although her belief in God stayed strong and she knew He had a reason for everything, she couldn't fathom any possible reason for Marco's untimely demise.

With a trembling hand, she removed a yellow rose from the family bouquet.

The rose looked too perfect to bury, too bright and sunny. It's bloom just starting to unfurl, the petals too young and fragile.

Kissing the rose in her hand, she inhaled its sweet, pure fragrance and tossed it onto the top of the coffin—then her legs buckled.

***

Trevor saw Imani go down and he made a move to rescue her even though he knew he could never make it in time from their spot five rows back. Out of the corner of his eye, he noticed Lance make a similar gesture, and Trev's hands balled into fists.

Luckily for everyone, Mr. Jordan expected Imani's reaction and he caught his daughter and helped her back to her seat without a hitch.

Trevor wanted to help Mr. Jordan, but a strange, fluttering motion around his left hand attracted his attention and he glanced down.

Erycah held his fist between her hands trying to ease it open.

As their eyes locked, she gave him a faint smile, and the anger building inside him dissolved.

Taking both of her hands in his, he composed himself enough to return his beautiful, pregnant wife's smile.

That was the reason why he wanted to talk to Imani last Friday. They were pregnant again with their second child. Although he knew you weren't supposed to disclose a pregnancy so early—bad luck and all—he always told Erycah and Imani everything.

Erycah still held the early pregnancy test in her hands when he dialed Imani with one hand while he balanced Trev, Jr. on his left hip. Meanwhile Marco lay dead in his car.

He stared at Marco's gravesite. *Strange how with every death there was a new life out there somewhere. God's cosmic balance.*

Somehow, Lance popped into view again and Trevor's eyes narrowed although Lance didn't look his direction.

Good idea, he fumed remembering the last time he saw Lance's scandalous ass. Saturday morning, after the Cabrette's doctor friend came over and medicated Imani, Melody had explained in her sweet, innocent way why Lance was there. Everyone else bought it, but Trevor had seen Lance's guilty expression at being caught in bed with Imani. And basically, he didn't trust Lance as far as he could throw him. Why was the fool back now after over a year's absence?

Lance disappeared from view into his row of mourners and Trevor refocused on the family recessional, his eyes locked on Imani.

Mr. Jordan braced Imani as he escorted her back to the limousines.

Yes, Imani's family would take good care of her while she stayed in New York City. But once she returned to Albany, he would support her. It was his responsibility as her friend.

GUILTY FRIEND

Melody checked her watch. Excellent, she had a couple of minutes before she needed to leave for work. With deliberate movements she grabbed her cell phone off the kitchen counter and placed her thumb on the shortcut button for Imani's home. She waited as her thumb wavered, hovered, and wavered again, before her resolve crumbled under a bundle of nerves.

Frustrated, she shoved the phone in her suit jacket pocket.

Normally, she and Imani called each other at least once a day. Now, they'd only talked about four times in the two weeks since Marco's death. And each time had been excruciating and awkward.

In the past their easy conversations revolved around two main topics: their love lives and careers. Talking about their love lives, well, that was definitely out now. Seriously, what exactly could Imani say with the love of her life buried six feet underground? Fresh tears sprang into her eyes and threatened to fall.

Plus, whenever Melody even mentioned Chris, well that just seemed heartless. Every topic hurt because it refreshed their memories of them as double-dating couples or reminded them that Chris and Marco were best buds, and at the end of each conversation, she still had Chris and Imani had no one, except an empty bed.

The list of cruelties seemed to go on and on. Melody shook her head as she gathered her briefcase, purse, and keys.

Come to think of it, their jobs weren't a safe conversation topic either.

With Melody spending more and more time at the television station vying for an anchor promotion, she'd used it as an excuse for not calling or visiting. And conversely, Imani hadn't even returned to work yet. Plus, with Marco and Imani both working for General Electric—although in different areas—they all knew Imani would experience double the well-meaning condolences when she finally returned to work Monday.

So no, work was off limits too, and that just didn't leave much else to talk about.

With a sigh, Melody locked up the house and jumped in her yellow Volkswagen Beetle convertible, praying the stink of guilt that seeped from her pores would cease soon.

As the car's engine jumped to life, she put it into gear and headed for work.

Maybe she could call Imani later? Or maybe she'd finally go over Imani's after work like she promised? Then again, Lance and Trevor ate dinner at Imani's every single night. Realistically, Imani would complain of overkill with so many of them "babysitting" her.

Melody shook her head; forget it, she would call Imani tomorrow. She nodded as her decision released a flood of relief through her limbs and she relaxed a bit.

Beautiful, with that settled, she looked in her rearview mirror and checked her patented daffodil and sunshine smile. If her authentic, empathetic smile helped her career—allowing her to follow in the footsteps of her role models, Katie Couric and Diane Sawyer—hopefully, it could help her now. Help ease her underlying guilt for not being there for Imani.

But it didn't succeed; the reflection of her smile faltered and a small shudder escaped down her back. *How can I be so selfish?* Images from the past threatened to take hold...all the times when Imani stood by her during some of her worst experiences...

With a concerted effort, Melody shook off the bad memories and forced her smile to shine through again. *Damn it!* Imani would understand, she was strong, things would work out fine, they had to...she hoped.

OTHER RESPONSIBILITIES – AUGUST 2006

Trevor watched from the wings of his family room as his pregnancy-glowing wife bounced Little Trev on her knee. In one deft move, Erycah swung their one-year old bundle of mischievous, house-wrecking joy into the swing and fastened him in while he spit bubbles at her and tried to pinch her nose.

Trev chuckled under his breath.

That trick appeared to be Little Trev's latest torturous amusement, seeing how wet he could get people while making them breathe through their mouth. Little Trev laughed and clapped his hands animatedly once Erycah started the swing.

"Hey, Sweetheart." Trev glided in and landed a juicy peck on his beautiful wife's lips. Her gentle, chestnut brown, bohemian style always put a smile on his face. He twirled her in a circle then held her hand as he hovered over the swing trying to time his kisses on Trevor, Jr.'s cheeks while the baby swung back and forth.

After successfully landing two good-bye kisses, but now brandishing wet cheeks and a sore nose, Trevor headed for the front door.

In a flash, Erycah blocked the door, hand planted on her hip. "Exactly where do you think you're going?"

"What do you mean?" he asked caught off guard as his eyebrows rose.

"You're not going to Imani's again," she said leaving no room for an argument.

His eyes shot open. Rarely did his wonderful wife ever put her foot down, but when she did, Lord, look out!

"Trev, you've gone there each and every night since she returned from Marco's funeral."

Trying to appease his wife, he relaxed and smiled. "Sweetheart," his voice took on a Jamaican patois lilt, a gift that he inherited from his father. He could turn it on and off at will and he knew Erycah loved it, especially when he seduced her with it.

Erycah held her hand up to stop him, clearly not amused. "Look, I know you and Imani aren't doing anything—"

"Not a chance." He shook his head in vigorous denial. The mere thought of cheating on his sexy, pregnancy-glowing, wonderful queen, tore him apart. "You have to know I'd never—"

She waved off his protests and repeated herself in a calmer manner. "Look, I know there's nothing going on. I love Imani like a sister, I really do." Erycah stepped towards him and dropped her hand off her hip. "And if anything ever happened to you..." she said, touching his face with her soft, warm hands. "God forbid...I would want the same support you're giving her."

"Then, what? Are you jealous?" His brow

furrowed at that foreign possibility. Erycah had always been trusting and low-key over their three years of dating and three years of marriage.

"No, boy!" She sucked her teeth, appalled that he would even think that. Her arm flew back to her hip. "What I am is tired!"

"Damn, Trevor! If you hadn't noticed," she said sweeping her arm in Trev, Jr's direction, "you have a son. A little, adorable, one-year old monster and—" her hand dramatically came back and showcased her belly like one of Barker's Beauties on The Price is Right. "I'm pregnant with another one of your rascals now. I need your ass here, not over at Imani's."

He started to speak, but his mouth hung open as he stared at her.

"Look, I felt it was real sweet of you the first few days, but seriously, Boy. She's got no kids to take care of and plenty of other friends to help her mourn." Her finger wagged around accentuating each point. "You've been over her house every damn day for the last thirty days! That shit is ridiculous!"

Finally finding his voice, he took her hands in his, just wanting to soothe his fiery wife. *Why hadn't he noticed how much this upset her earlier?* "I...I had no idea you felt that way, Sweetheart," he stammered. "I was trying to be a friend not realizing..."

Like sunshine peaking from behind a cloud, her natural easy-going demeanor made a welcome reappearance.

Relieved, he pulled her to him and kissed the top of her beautiful, braid-crowned head. "Baby, I'm sorry for not understanding. Please forgive me."

After squeezing him tight, she relaxed in his arms. "You're forgiven." She smiled, and then kissed him for one long minute until her sweet lips whisked away all his worries.

"I'm sorry for going off on you, Baby." She looked down and rubbed her barely there baby bump. "But between Trev, Jr. and these damn hormones, I don't know which way is up sometimes. And all I want to do is get lost in your arms or have you massage my feet, and you're never here."

Tears brimmed up and threatened to spill over. "It'd be different if you invited us along, but you don't. You just leave me here alone with your crazy, little boy. And I'm strong but c'mon, I need some help." She tried to blink them back, however, the tears fell anyway. "I need you, Trev."

"Oh, Sweetheart!" His heart ached while he kissed her wet eyes. "I promise I'll never leave you again." There didn't seem to be enough hugs and kisses in the world that he could offer to lessen the pain he felt for neglecting her. "Why didn't you say anything before?"

She shrugged, her face a mask of sad regret.

"I would have stayed next to you and only you if I would have known, Sweetheart." He cupped her chin and stared into her soulful, mocha-colored eyes. "I love you more than life itself, Erycah. You know that, right?"

A shy smile broke out across her face, "I know."

"Let me call Imani right now and tell her I gotta

take care of business here at home."

Erycah snuck a peak over Trev's shoulder at Trev, Jr. who slept soundly in the swing. With a seductive smile, she took his hand and led him into the dining room across the hall. "Maybe you can take care of some other business first?"

"What kind of business do we need to take care of in the dining room, Sweetheart?" he asked, his eyebrow arched up on its own accord.

Lifting herself up onto the table, she pulled him between her skirted legs. "The kind that will take about fifteen to twenty minutes. The same amount of time your son will be sleeping in that swing down the hall." Her lips devoured his.

"You know," he said coming up for a quick breath, "I'll never be able to think about our Thanksgiving dinners the same way anymore. I'll only remember the feast I'm about to partake of right now."

***

"Yo, Trev, where you at?" Imani asked after picking up the ringing phone.

Lance stared at her from across the dining room table with an indignant look on his face.

"You know Lance is so hungry he's about ready to eat the table."

Lance picked up his fork and knife and started pounding the table with them, "I want food. I want food."

Imani shushed him with her hand as she focused

on Trevor's lengthy explanation. When he finished his story, she almost fell out of her chair laughing. "I wondered when Erycah was going to throw down the law on your ass."

"She threw it down hard," Trev replied.

Imani chuckled again. "Hell yeah, she should be mad with you spending all your time over here. I don't blame her one tiny bit."

Lance smirked, gathered their plates, and disappeared into the kitchen.

"It figures you'd side with her," Trevor replied with a moan.

"Well, come on now," she said, fussing. "And why exactly didn't you invite her over? You know I love seeing her and even that beautiful, little, bad-assed boy of yours."

"See, that's why I didn't bring him over!" Trev laughed. "I didn't want to hear your mouth when he tore apart your non-childproofed home. That's why married folks with kids don't have any single or childless friends. Too complicated."

She laughed again. "How about a compromise? Why don't y'all come to my house this weekend for a barbeque? That way the little angel can only tear up my backyard."

"Oh, so you're suggesting we keep the animal outdoors in the wild, huh?" Trev chuckled.

Laughing, she tried not to guffaw. "You said it, not me."

"Well, regardless, I'm sure Erycah would love your invitation, no matter how wrong and foul." Trev laughed again and she could imagine his long, toothy grin and his dreads flying as he shook his head. "We'll catch you then, Boo."

"See 'ya and definitely wouldn't want to be 'ya," Imani sang out, ready to hang up.

"Hey Imani, one last thing," Trevor's voice became dead serious.

Feeling his concern translate through the telephone, she sat up straight, brows furrowed as she listened. "Yeah?"

"Watch Lance, okay?"

Imani glanced up as Lance returned with their food-laden plates. "Will do, Trev, thanks," she replied and then disconnected.

The pork chops, green beans, and applesauce played delicious melodies for her nose as Lance set down her plate.

"Mmm, perfect timing," she said. "Everything looks great!"

"Enjoy," he replied with a smile as he took his seat.

They both bowed their heads in prayer, and then they dug into dinner.

Lance chuckled. "I wonder how long Trev will be in the doghouse?"

A slow smile worked its way across her lips. "I have a feeling he's already out again," she insinuated before eating a bite of applesauce.

"Go, Trev!" Lance saluted a forkful of pork chop and green beans. "I understand where he's coming from, though. Bobby's complaining that I don't work out at the gym with him anymore."

"Bobby?"

"You remember the tall, dark, close-shaved brother I hang out with at Chase."

"Yeah, sorry, brain fart. Your crazed pack of four co-workers consists of you, Bobby, Nate, and Darryl, right?" She took a bite, but didn't really taste the food.

"How in the hell do you remember odd, random facts like that? It's not like you ever really met them or we talked extensively over the past year."

"I guess I just remember things that are important to my friends," she replied not so subtly.

"Well, just so you're up to speed," Lance continued either not picking up on her sarcasm or choosing to ignore it. "Nate got fired for sexual harassment and Darryl left for some small investment firm in NYC. So, it's just Bobby and me now."

"And he misses his workout buddy," she said stalling as she prepared herself for what she needed to say.

Lance nodded as he chewed.

"Seriously, though," she said, taking a deep breath. "It has been a month since…" She stopped, unable to continue without choking on the words. Imani gazed at Lance.

He stopped chewing and his eyes locked on hers, concern flooding his chiseled, caramel features.

Closing her eyes, she took another deep cleansing breath and bowled through the heart-wrenching words. "Since Marco died."

Somehow by stating the words aloud, she felt herself gaining strength from an indefatigable well within. "And I'm okay now." With the worst of it over, she even managed to find her sense of humor as her sarcastic side took over. "You don't need to come over here every doggone day," she said cracking a smile. "Eating all my food and shit."

"Oh, no, no, no," Lance replied waving his fork at her as he smirked. "Did you conveniently forget Trev and I both went to the store and brought groceries for the last two week's worth of meals?" Lance stabbed his fork her direction.

"Yeah but y'all Negros eat mad food," she said trying not to laugh. "I'm cooking way more now than I ever did before."

"Correction, *we're* cooking." Lance shook his head and laughed. "You're so sad."

Letting her chuckle fade away, she played with her food. She didn't want to ask, but Trev's warning rang through her ears like a siren, 'Watch Lance.' Sighing out loud, she narrowed her eyes and studied Lance. "Why are you here?"

With a grimace Lance's jaw stopped mid-chew. When he swallowed his bite, he sawed off a cut of meat but left the fork and knife on his plate. "You mean Trev wants to know why, huh?"

Shaking her head twice, she kept her eyes trained on him. "No, it's not just Trev. Everyone who knew that you disappeared wants to know why you've suddenly returned after a year," she stopped and gave him an out. "Everyone that is, except for Melody."

"Good old Melody!" He smirked and toasted the air with his stabbed pork chop before ripping into it. "I can at least count on one person."

"Yep." Imani set down her silverware. "She tends to envision the dormant, freshly fertilized rose bush transplant about to blossom into vibrant flowers whereas the rest of us simply see a dead stick in a pile of steaming pooh."

"Ohhh-kay," Lance gasped, almost choking. "Tell me how you really feel."

She felt her nostrils flare as she placed her hands on the table. "Look, Lance, I'm too emotionally bereft to try and sugarcoat this for you."

"Oh, please be honestly blunt, that's what we've always loved about you." Lance threw his fork down and pushed his chair away from the table.

"Fine, I will!" Her arms crossed on their own volition. "Are you truly trying to resuscitate our friendship or are you some ambulance-chasing vulture using any tactic available to get into my pants?" Once she voiced her concern, the anger subsided and curiosity replaced it. She just needed to know where he stood.

Lance flinched, pain shot across his features. Closing his eyes, he rubbed his hands over his face and head. "Is that what you seriously believe?" When he finally reopened his eyes extreme sadness took up residence there.

Empathy ate at Imani but not before she spoke. "You didn't answer the question."

"What am I supposed to say after that?" he shot

back, waving his hands. "I mean, did you ever consider maybe I needed resuscitation, too?" He glared at her for a moment before his shoulders crumbled and his head dropped.

Imani wanted to comfort him, but she couldn't move.

Lance spoke again, his voice barely audible. "Excuse me for thinking that the best way to regain a friend, was to be a friend."

Hearing what she needed to hear, she sat up, shrugged, and forked another bite of food. "Okay, sounds good."

"What?" Lance's head shot up and he stared at her like she'd lost her ever-loving mind. "Sounds good?"

She stopped with the fork halfway to her mouth and her eyebrow rose. "What did you expect me to say?"

Indignant, he shrugged. "Hmm, maybe, sorry for attacking your integrity there, Buddy."

"Look Lance," she said setting her fork down. "You need to know that people are watching your every move." She didn't want to lecture him, but he needed to understand the seriousness of the situation. Her tone became direct, blunt, but not heartless. "If you're toying with me, it's not just me you'll need to deal with. Lots of folks will come hunt you down."

Lance nodded once almost imperceptibly, his wounded feelings emanating from every pore. "I know."

God, she wanted to give him a hug. Instead she played with her napkin, twisting it into knots. "Look,

I miss our friendship, too," she confessed. "If you're really here to renew that relationship, then please, come over as much as you want. Okay?"

Without a word, Lance pulled his chair back up to the table and picked up his fork.

They both resumed eating in an uncomfortable silence.

REMOVING GHOSTS – SEPTEMBER 2006

Imani awoke and stroked her hand across the empty side of the bed. Nothing. Her fingers wrapped around the sheets and dug into the mattress. Nothing. She buried her head into his pillow. Nothing. No matter how hard she tried, she couldn't feel Marco.

People always talked about feeling the presence of their departed loved ones hovering over them or their homes. But she didn't sense Marco anywhere. Not even one tiny hint or twinge of him remained after the accident.

Marco was simply gone.

The familiar heartbreak and confusion settled around like a shroud of despair. *Why can't I feel him?*

Hoping for any sensation, she stared at her gorgeous one-carat, princess-cut diamond solitaire wedding ring. Not even a sparkle.

She twisted the ring around her finger wanting to trigger even the slightest essence of Marco. Anything. Anything at all.

Nothing.

In fact, the bauble burdened her finger like a leaden weight.

She glared at it.

It hadn't felt right since the funeral. Instead of reminding her of Marco, it behaved like a black hole that consumed its surroundings. Squelching all energy and life. *How could such a beautiful piece bring such ugliness?*

Fighting back the all-encompassing guilt and grief, she wrested off the ring and tossed it on her nightstand.

It bounced against the bedside lamp and clattered onto the nightstand top with a dull clink. The diamond mocked her with its glittery brilliance that promised undying love.

Frustrated and on the verge of tears, she got out of bed, showered, and dressed in sweats.

Today of all days, she wanted to feel Marco; make everyone realize that this was too soon. But she felt nothing. And her mother and Mrs. Cabrette would arrive any minute. Ready to help her remove almost every trace of Marco from the house.

She'd argued against it. *Why the rush?*

However, they'd quoted the so-called "experts" who insisted that survivors needed to move on after tragedy. Clean out the bad memories and start fresh.

Nothing but a damn bunch of hokum!

Yet her mother and Mrs. Cabrette seemed to think it was a good idea. And now she had played right into their wild theories by removing her wedding ring.

The doorbell rang and she took her own sweet time going downstairs to answer the door.

"Hey, Baby," her mother said almost bowling her

over as she embraced her. After her mother let her go, she moved inside so that Imani could greet Mrs. Cabrette.

"Hi, Mama." It took everything in her power not to comment on Mrs. Cabrette's haggard appearance as they hugged. Only two months had passed since she'd seen her last at Marco's funeral and the woman seemed to have aged another ten years!

"Thank you for allowing us to come up here, Imani," Mrs. Cabrette replied.

"Thank you for coming, Mama. I don't think I could do this without your help." She closed the door and ushered them into the kitchen. "How's Papa?"

A spark ignited in Mama's eyes for the briefest second before grief extinguished it. She did however manage a feeble smile. "He's doing fine. You know he sends his best; he truly adores you."

Imani smiled, "I adore him, too. Give him a big hug tonight."

Mama nodded.

"And Maria?"

"Ah, she's well. She enjoys her husband and Italy, although I don't think she'll ever give me any grandkids."

Imani steered clear of that conversation since she couldn't provide any grandchildren now either with Marco buried six feet underground. "Where are my manners? Do you want me to get you anything to eat or drink?"

"Actually, if you don't mind, I'd like to use your bathroom?" Mama asked. "My bladder's not what it used to be.”

Imani smiled and pointed to the powder room down the hall. “You remember where it is. Please, take your time, Mama.”

Once Mrs. Cabrette walked away, Imani’s mother started in. “So, are you alone?”

“Excuse me?” Imani frowned, not liking her mother’s tone or insinuations. “What exactly is that supposed to mean?”

“Well, you said Lance still comes over every night, right?”

“Yes, he does—to eat dinner; nothing else.” She glared at her mom. “And then he leaves. What the hell, Mom?”

“I’m just making sure the boy’s acting on the up and up. Especially since he’s been hanging around you tighter than snot on a booger. I’m just concerned, that’s all.”

“Really?” Imani huffed. “He’s just helping me get through a rough patch, Mom, it’s totally innocent.”

“Look, I’m not going to beat around the bush. You know I think it’s odd that he’s back all of a sudden out of the blue like this.”

Imani didn’t like lying, especially to her discerning mother, but she couldn’t let her throw out accusations. Unrefuted accusations quickly became truths in her mind’s eye. “Although we didn’t hang out like before, he stayed in contact.” Which technically was true; they maintained contact through Melody and hung out a couple of times. “Regardless, you always liked Lance."

"Girl, I liked him until your wedding when the boy stomped around acting all ignorant, not speaking to people trying to ruin my baby's big day. I was absolutely delighted when his evil ass left early. Then the next time I see him, he's all snuggled up on you in the bed the day after Marco died. And you wonder why I have issues with Lance? Seriously?"

Imani knew when to concede defeat and she remained silent although she still held her mother's stare.

"Anyway, I don't want us to remove all of Marco's things today just for Lance to think he can move right on in."

"Oh, my God, Mom! Is that what you really think?" Imani crossed her arms and fumed. "Give me a little credit here—"

They both heard the toilet flush and the water turn on in the sink.

"I'm sorry, Baby—"

"Don't, Mom," Imani interrupted her. "Just leave it alone before I really get pissed and call this whole thing off."

Her mother looked hurt, but Imani walked off to greet Mrs. Cabrette, who already appeared grief-stricken and teary-eyed.

"Hey, are you sure you want to do this?" Imani asked while she put a comforting arm over Mrs. Cabrette's shoulders.

Mama gazed at a picture of Marco hanging on the wall. "I think I need this even more than you do," she whispered.

And with that they spent the day alternating between tears and laughter as they packed up Marco's clothes for donation and placed his trinkets, and all but three photos, in boxes for Mrs. Cabrette.

WEDDING PLANS

"Are you sure about this?" Melody asked Imani after their café waitress set down their drinks and left with their lunch orders.

"Are you kidding me?" Imani gave her an incredulous look. "Let's see, you don't have any sisters to perform the Maid of Honor-Wedding Planner duty. And last time I looked, I'm still your best friend, so, ah, hell yeah!"

"I could get my mom to do it—"

"Oh please!" Imani scoffed. "One, that's not even proper etiquette. Two, every single thing we show your mom, she breaks down crying. Talking about, 'My little Melody is getting married,' and 'I'm so proud of you,' then she starts pinching your cheeks. I love your mom, but I'm sorry, she's absolutely no help." She crossed her arms and sucked her teeth. "Plus with your overly romantic behind, you know you need someone to make sure your dress isn't overwrought with ruffles, bows, pearls, or the like!"

"Oh, you're so wrong!" Melody couldn't stop giggling.

Imani snorted and shrugged. "I'm just being honest. And it's September, the clock's ticking. Sorry, but contrary to the fairytales you subscribe to, weddings don't plan themselves!"

Instead of laughing, her heart dropped. "You know I can change it."

"What?" Imani frowned and leaned into the table. "The wedding date?"

Melody nodded knowing how hard this had to be for Imani.

"Girl, please—"

"Hear me out, Imani," she said as she reached across the table and took Imani's hands. "Back in June, when you celebrated your first anniversary, and Chris and I celebrated meeting for the first time at your wedding—"

"And Chris proposed marriage to celebrate your one year meeting anniversary." Imani added while she rolled her eyes and played with Melody's engagement ring.

"I planned on saying that next, thank you!" Melody squeezed her hands and continued. "I know we decided then to get married not on the same day, of course."

"Of course, because luckily Saturday didn't fall on the same damn date either year!"

"Could you please stop interrupting?" She popped Imani's hand then held it again. "But we decided to get married during the same week in June. So, we could always celebrate our love together; take joint, week-long anniversary vacations…" Her throat closed shut and her eyes got misty.

"Hey!" Imani hit her hand. "I already told you, I cancelled our portion. The deposit is back in my savings account collecting interest."

Melody smiled in spite of herself. "Look, I'm trying to be serious here!"

"I know, but I'm okay. In fact, I'll get pissed if you change the date. Let your wedding date be a reminder of the love Marco and I shared. That would make me happy, okay?"

"I'll feel guilty about leaving you. Knowing we should be honeymooning together."

Imani pulled back to sip her strawberry daiquiri. "Don't. Mom and I already made plans."

"What?" she gasped and searched Imani's eyes.

"Damn, this daiquiri is good!"

Shooting Imani a disbelieving expression, she frowned. "Are you serious?"

Imani nodded and laughed. "Of course, I'm serious." She waved her hand dismissively. "Trust me, I'll be fine."

God, she wanted to believe her crazy, strong-willed friend. She even felt one of her daffodil and sunshine smiles attempt to sparkle, however, it faltered and disappeared under somber clouds of guilt and shame. Before Imani could ask her what was wrong now, she spoke. "I want to apologize—"

Imani started to interrupt, but Melody held up a hand and halted her. "Please, Imani, I need to say this or I'll never feel right. This guilt's been weighing on my chest and I'll die if I can't apologize and explain."

She paused until Imani nodded. "I'm sorry I wasn't there for you when you needed me most." Her hands automatically reached across the table and covered Imani's. "Especially considering everything you've done for me."

Imani squeezed Melody's hands. "Girl, I understood why. And I knew you felt bad."

"It sucks because you've always been the strong one in our relationship. And I know it's rotten, but I couldn't handle both you and Chris breaking down. It was just too much." She bit her lip and hesitated while Imani waited.

Somehow Imani's silent strength encouraged her to continue.

"I know you guys rely on me to always find the silver linings in the clouds, make lemonade from lemons, or take the positive spin...however, I couldn't. Not this time." She shook her head and prayed that Imani would understand.

"I'm sorry, Imani. When you were counting on me the most, I just couldn't fathom one single positive reason for Marco's death." Melody sighed and powered through. "So, although I wanted to be there, I kept hoping and praying that Trevor and Lance's constant presence sufficed."

"Actually, I probably owe my speedy recovery to you." Imani chuckled much to Melody's surprise. "When you're surrounded by all that testosterone, you tend to, for lack of a better phrase, 'man up' pretty quickly. Guys just can't deal with crying women, so I stopped crying."

"Great, now I feel even worse!" Melody withdrew her hands and covered her face.

Imani took the opportunity to sip more of her

daiquiri before she recaptured Melody's hands. "Look, I'm not going to lie, there were instances when I would have loved to have an understanding, sympathetic woman there who would just let me ball my eyes out."

Surprising emotions bubbled across Imani's face. She sniffed in an attempt to squash the waterworks although her eyes still shimmered. "It helped when my mom brought Mrs. Cabrette up Saturday and we went through Marco's belongings together." Imani grunted. "They insisted on striking a healthy balance between maintaining a mausoleum—leaving each item exactly as Marco left it—and totally removing every single trace of him."

Even if Imani could keep her own tears at bay, Melody couldn't and she rubbed Imani's hands as a few drops slid down her cheeks. That's when she realized Imani wasn't wearing her wedding ring. She gasped in shock.

Imani caught her gaze and her face saddened. "They didn't take my ring. It's safe at home." Imani stared at her ring-free finger. "I just couldn't wear it…they understood. Surprisingly, it helped; talking about the ring, sharing the stories, reviewing the pictures as we packed most of them up for Mrs. Cabrette. Mama also took all of Marco's high school and college things. And my mom donated his clothes." Imani hesitated. "All except one shirt." She stared at Melody. "Is it wrong that I kept his shirt?"

Melody wanted to break down and cry for Imani,

but she simply shook her head. "No."

"I couldn't part with it; this sage green dress shirt I brought for his birthday." A solitary tear escaped and Imani seemed to struggle as she swam through a sea of memories. "He hated wearing anything except white dress shirts, and I wanted to show him that he could pull it off."

Imani's eyes dropped to their intertwined hands. "The color made his eyes pop, and Lord, it looked so damn good against his gorgeous, olive skin." She looked up and smiled. "Marco loved that shirt as much as I did. So I kept it."

Although relief seemed to seep throughout Imani's soul, Melody couldn't take the guilt anymore. She retracted her hands and dropped her head. "God, I'm so sorry I wasn't there, Imani. I could have just sat and listened."

"But you just did." Imani grabbed Melody's hands and swung them over the table until Melody lifted her head. "That, right there, was exactly what I needed. Thank you."

Tilting her head, she studied Imani.

Imani beamed back, all traces of sorrow gone. It was like a storm had blown past and cleared out all of the sadness.

If only she could bottle some of Imani's strength… she frowned, still uncertain. "Are you sure?"

"I'm positive!" Imani smiled, then dropped Melody's hands and drummed the table. "Now where's our food? We're going to need our sustenance if we're hitting five bridal stores for their

Labor Day sales."

And just like that, everything was back to normal.

Melody laughed in disbelief and shook her head as she pointed to their plate-laden waitress. "She's coming now, hold your horses."

FOOTBALL

Lance readjusted the two grocery bags in his left arm and unlocked Imani's front door with his right hand. Imani supposedly gave him the key last month for "safety" reasons, but he figured she simply needed to assuage her guilt. Twice she'd gotten caught up at work and raced home to find him patiently waiting in her driveway. Not that he minded, but he much preferred the key.

Heading into her kitchen, he set the bags on the island and then put the groceries away. Curious. Normally Imani dashed over when he arrived. Then again, it was Saturday; maybe she hadn't heard him. "Hey, Imani, where are you?" He followed the faint sounds of a TV playing to the family room.

"In here," Imani replied with barely a glance in his direction. Her focus locked on the television…and the players running onto the field.

Lance stalled mid-step, anxiety mounting. "What? What are you doing?"

"What does it look like? I'm watching the game. Now quit yapping and grab a seat."

"Why?" he asked never moving an inch as his pulse escalated.

When Imani cocked her head sideways to better

see him, she looked mildly annoyed. "Hel-lo, it's Notre Dame and Penn State, only the best match-up of week two!" Frowning, she turned around to study him closer. "Yo, are you okay?"

An immense boulder of dread rolled into his gut.

"Lance?" Imani came over and put her hands on his shoulders. "What's going on, Boo? Talk to me."

How could he explain when even he didn't understand why his innards churned and his limbs remained frozen? Inexplicably his eyes focused on the game playing on TV.

In an instant his stomach performed flips like Cirque du Soleil and his legs quivered. His inhalations only resumed when Imani forced his head away from the TV to face her. "I can't...I can't watch football..."

Imani's eyebrows knitted fast and furious while she fought to understand. "Since when?" Her eyes burrowed into him and then she knew. "Since your injury?"

Lance gulped and flashed back to the 2003 NFL Draft. The NY Jets selected him as the fourth overall pick and he, in return, immersed himself in the only sport he truly ever lived, breathed, and loved. Playing professional football used to stand as one of the highlights of his life, but it had all come crashing to an end during the last game of his rookie season.

After his injury, he never watched ESPN or football games again. He had no idea which colleges were ranked where or who played for what teams. It hurt too much. Basically he treated football as if it didn't even exist. Football meant loss and pain.

As that realization flooded through him, his legs strengthened and he could finally breathe like normal. Yet how could he put into words this dark secret that he kept hidden even from himself until now? He stopped.

Why exactly did he need to share? In fact, what was Imani trying to do to him?   He glared at her. Wasn't it bad enough that she tortured him with wanting her? He'd promised a plutonic friendship, however, deep inside his yearning and intense desire for Imani loomed and lingered. And now she wanted to torment him further, dredging up old football wounds that were long since dead and buried!

Defensive instincts kicked in.   Spiteful words came to mind, ready to roll off his tongue, and just as his mouth opened, she touched him.

Imani's warm, sympathetic hand stroked his cheek and he nestled into it against his will. For two torturous years, he'd dreamed about her hands, longed for her touch, desired physical contact that she initiated.

"You never told me," she said her soft, concerned eyes drew him further under her spell.

As she caressed his face, the words tumbled out. "Soon after the injury, I married Heather and she never watched sports. Then after the divorce, well, it's easy to hide when no one else is around to notice or care."

God, he hated what she was making him say and feel. No, he had to resist falling deeper for Imani. He closed his eyes determined to shut out her hypnotic pull.

Yet she seemed hell-bent on breaking through his defenses. Her stealthy fingers found their way to his tense neck muscles. Gentle yet firm, she massaged him into submission. Anxiety melted like butter under a hot summer's sun.

"You love football, Lance, always have." Her talented fingers found their way to the base of his head, sending delicious chills throughout his body. "Accident or not, you're alive and cutting off an integral part of your life."

It bothered him that she was right, that a certain part of his life felt dead afterwards. That she could still reach him through all the walls he erected.

Imani's loving voice brought him back from his reflections. "Don't you miss it?"

He studied her cocoa eyes and found warmth and comfort; a wonderful place to unload all his deepest thoughts and most frightening feelings. "I do but…"

"Don't let that one bizarre moment, although scary and career-ending," she said before her teasing smile brought a slight grin to his face. "Don't let that define your experience. Don't let it ruin your life-long love of the game."

Frustrated and sad, he dropped his head. "That's much easier said than done."

"Hey, come sit down." Imani took his hand and led him to the couch. While he slumped onto it, she grabbed the TiVo remote and hit "Pause" to freeze the football action on the screen. For some inexplicable reason that helped although he would have preferred if she turned it off completely.

However, without the television's distraction, her siren-like powers increased ten-fold. Sitting down next to him, she draped her arm around his shoulder and massaged his neck.

Wanting more of her massaging hands, his body betrayed him. He shifted until she sat behind him, his entire back exposed to her magical mitts. She didn't speak again until his body flowed and moved like pure putty.

"If your injury never occurred and you played out your entire NFL career, where did you see yourself headed after retirement?" Imani's voice soothed.

His answer came without a moment's hesitation. "Coaching."

She waited for him to elaborate.

"I love…loved the strategic maneuvering of the game—point, counterpoint, offensive bombs, defensive attacks, trick plays." Weird sensations overtook him as his heart raced. It annoyed him how animated he felt during that simple description.

"That doesn't sound like someone who believes in his heart that the sport is dead."

"I guess not," he said, admitting it more to himself.

"If you were to start coaching, have you considered where to begin?"

"It's complicated. I'd need to get into a good, high school program or maybe get on as an assistant college coach to one of the disciplines, like an assistant wide receivers coach." *There was no way,* he shook his head in defeat. "But that takes connections and a record."

"You're telling me you didn't make any connections during your college and pro careers?"

"Imani, I've been out of the game for over two years! That's a lifetime in sports." Agitated by her prying and his conflicting emotions, he moved from between her legs and ran his hand over his head. "Things change. I've been passed by."

"Please. It hasn't changed enough to nullify almost twenty years of knowledge." She took his head in her soft, warm hands. "Lance, I know that dealing with the past is hard. A life-changing injury. A career over too soon. Never forget them, but don't use them as a crutch." Her right hand commenced its hypnotic stroking of his cheek. "You're physically fine now. You can live your life again."

He shook his head free from her inviting hands and sat back. He wanted to believe her, but this was all way too much, too soon. "Seriously, what will people think with me returning out of the blue after two years away?"

"They'll think you're just like any other professional athlete that comes out of retirement or walks away from a career-ending injury to go on to an even better career in coaching or broadcasting." Her hand movements emphasized her words. "Look at your idol, Michael Irvin, he suffered the same injury and he's on with Boom and T.J. on ESPN."

Life sparked through him and he grabbed her arms. "That's it Imani! You're a genius!" She answered with her patented raised eyebrow and skeptical expression which made him laugh as he tried to explain. "Broadcasting."

"Yes?" she replied, waving her hand in a tight circle to get him to clarify.

"I know you think I can just step out onto the field and coach, but I can't. Not yet." Memories of his injury flashed for a second and he shook his head. "The sounds and sensations of that last game, that final hit, still linger."

Maybe this really was too much, too soon. He rubbed his hands over his face and head. When he dropped his hands, her patient eyes gave him the strength to continue. As his thoughts switched gears, the anxiety decreased. "But with broadcasting, you're up in the booth or in the studios and I can do play-by-plays or pre-game and post-game analysis. I might even have to report from the sidelines, but that's still not the same level of engagement or emotional investment as coaching. I could wean myself back into the mix."

"And I know your agent mentioned broadcasting the last time you talked to him," she said with an encouraging smile.

"Exactly." He sounded sure at first, then the overwhelming possibilities engulfed him and he slumped back on the couch.

"Hey, hey." Imani shook his shoulders worried by his reaction. "It's going to be fine." She took his face between her hands and locked onto his eyes. "We'll take this slow, at your pace. No pressures, no worries, right?"

He barely nodded. Why couldn't he siphon off a smidgeon of her confidence?

"I promise to walk each step of the way with you. You won't face this battle alone, okay?"

When he didn't immediately respond, Imani straddled his lap and hugged him tight. With her mouth so near to his ear, she whispered, "You helped me deal with losing Marco and showed me life goes on. Now I'll do the same with you and football. Let's bring you back to life."

Each of her words clicked a switch inside him and as he returned her hug, a floodgate opened. Fears and emotions threatened to drown him, but Imani remained like a life preserver holding him aloft and eventually, it passed. As the first flicker of hope sowed its seed in his soul, he smiled and released her. "Thank you."

"That's what friends are for, Boo." Imani flicked his nose, flipped off his lap, and landed back onto the couch in one smooth move.

"Oh Lord," he replied with a chuckle. Taking another deep breath he relaxed further, excited and optimistic about his future. Just knowing that Imani planned to stay by his side, helped ease his anxiety.

Grabbing the TiVo remote, she hit "Play" and the football players flew back into action. "Now, take notes because you've got two years of catching up to do," she said slapping his leg.

"Oh no," he groaned. "What did I just get myself into?"

LIKE OLD TIMES – JANUARY 2007

Melody sank into Imani's overstuffed chair and clapped her hands with glee. "This is so cool! It's been forever since we've hung out, just the three of us. Cooking dinner together, drinking wine," she said waving towards the uncorked Chardonnay, "listening to jazz. It's—"

"It's perfect just like the good, old days," Imani squealed, mimicking Melody.

Lance popped Imani with one of her couch's decorator pillows. "You're so wrong."

Melody ignored Imani's teasing. "Well, it is! And I, for one, miss our times together."

Lance grabbed his glass and toasted her, "I miss them, too."

"Yeah, yeah," Imani waved their sentiments away like pesky gnats. "What do y'all want to talk about?" Imani settled back and sipped her wine.

"Anything as long as it doesn't concern weddings," she replied with a sigh, the mere thought felt exhausting. "I'm about fed up with Emily Post and—" she noticed Imani smirking and Melody pointed a threatening finger. "Don't you dare say, 'I told you so,' Imani!"

Imani merely shrugged and continued to sip her

wine in smug silence.

"Fine, I admit it. Wedding planning isn't the easy little fairytale I thought it would be."

"That's why they skip that part in the movies," Lance replied with a chuckle. "So, no wedding talk, what else?"

"God, it's been so long since we've all been together like this, I don't even remember what we used to talk about."

"That's easy," Imani replied, "our love lives, our families, and our career goals."

"Um, speaking of careers, Lance," Melody said as she felt a mischievous desire to get Lance and Imani riled up. "Imani mentioned that you're in contract negotiations with ESPN and the NFL Network."

To her surprise Lance blushed while conversely Imani beamed with pride. "We're only in talks," Lance admitted, "but after all the meetings, interviews, and test screenings, it looks promising. If all goes well, I might be on the air as a guest analyst by training camp. Then we'll see what happens after that test period."

"Outstanding!" A surge of pride compelled her to applaud. "And if for some reason that doesn't work out, I might be able to pull a couple of strings at the station."

"Here, here, Miss Noon Anchor," Imani cheered. "First you were but a lowly summer intern, then a cub reporter—"

"Ah, it's called a general assignment reporter." Melody rolled her eyes and blushed.

"Yeah, yeah, one of those, and now you're the noon anchor at WNYT NBC 13! Next stop AM anchor or maybe the evening anchor." Imani laughed. "All I know is Katie Couric, Diane Sawyer, and Barbara WaWa better watch their backs!"

"You are too crazy," she said as she set down her wine glass.

"Crazy like a fox." Lance chuckled and shook his head. "See, you're making jokes about Melody, but what about you, Imani?"

"Yeah," Melody piped up. "How's General Electric treating you?"

Imani answered with a satisfied shrug. "Pretty well, I can't complain. I'm busy in Quartz, working on cool stuff—"

"That you can never tell us hardly anything about," she replied with a pout.

"I already told you, if I mentioned some of our company's top secret projects, I'd have to kill you." Imani grinned and winked. "Just remember our logo, 'GE, we bring good things to life' and you'll never go wrong."

"You guys are very diversified," Lance said. "Locomotives, healthcare, light bulbs, appliances, airplanes. I can't imagine you ever getting bored."

"No, although I might consider making a move." Imani drank some more wine. "Our Ceramics and Metallurgy Technology organization and the Coating and Surface Technologies Lab are both developing some really innovative products."

"Well, it sounds complex and exciting—" Melody

began until a vibration emanating from her front jean pocket stopped her mid-thought. "Excuse me a moment," she said as she set her wine glass on the coffee table and dug out her cell phone.

The phone showed a new text message. "Ahh, Chris texted me." As she read his sweet message, her smile erupted.

"Let me guess." Imani smirked. "He loves you and misses you, oh so very much."

"Yes!" Even Imani's teasing couldn't dampen the warmth encompassing her heart and she beamed brighter. "That's pretty much the gist of it."

"Well, did you finally give that boy some putang?" Imani asked point blank.

"Imani!" Lance sounded as shocked as Melody felt and he reprimanded Imani with a swat on her leg. Turning towards Melody, he leaned forward on the couch, cupped his hands around his mouth, and asked in a shushed tone, "Well, did you and Chris get busy?"

Melody's jaw dropped even further and Imani's eyebrow arch into a 'what the—' look as her lips pursed into a scowl.

Lance ignored Imani and waited for Melody to find her voice.

All she could manage was a stunned, "et tu, Lance?"

"Well, inquiring minds want to know," he replied.

She shook her head in disbelief. "How many times do I have to tell you two that we're waiting until the wedding?"

Imani frowned. "Why? It's not like either of you are virgins."

"No, we're not." Melody felt her cheeks blaze. "But that doesn't mean we can't rededicate our lives to Christ and do the right thing now." Her arms crossed on their own accord. "You do realize that the Lord kind of frowns on that pre-marital sex stuff. And I could have sworn you were sitting beside me in church a few weeks ago when Pastor preached about this very topic." A tinge of sarcasm crept into her voice. "Hmm, I think he called it…adultery?"

"Yep, I was there." Without batting an eye or a moment's hesitation, Imani continued nonplussed. "And I get the whole spiritual symbolism thing." With unbridled audacity, Imani looked up to the heavens, her hands raised in mock surrender. "Sorry, Lord—"

"Uh, uh." Lance scooted away to the other side of the couch.

Imani glowered at him. "What is your problem?"

Lance shrugged. "Hey, I'm not getting struck by lightning."

"Please!" Imani pointed her finger at Lance. "With as much pre-marital and adulterous sex that you've had, I should move."

Lance gave them a weary sigh. "That was in the past," he said rubbing his hands over his face and head once. "I haven't been with anyone since my divorce."

Melody's eyes widened although she didn't say a word.

"What?" Imani made a stop gesture with her hand. "Okay, I already did the calculation in my head, but I need to vocalize this to make sure I got it right."

Lance crossed his arms and awaited Imani's assault.

"I know you filed for a quickie divorce right after my wedding. And Marco and I celebrated our one-year anniversary last June. It's January now. Are you really saying that you haven't had sex with anyone in…nineteen months?"

"That's what I said." Lance's voice sounded flat and emotionless.

"Humph, impressive!" Then abrupt as a snake strike, Imani redirected her attention to Melody. "Look, I'm not being snide. I get what you're trying to do. I'm just saying that Marco and I were aligned spiritually, mentally, and emotionally." Imani's eyes smiled at some unseen memories, then a split second later they narrowed and refocused on Melody. "But if we didn't add in that physical attraction—and this may sound harsh—well I don't think I would have married him."

Melody let out an annoyed breath. She'd witnessed how taken Imani was with Marco well before they ever became intimate. *"Really?"* she stated more than asked, letting the sarcasm ring through. *Who did Imani think she was fooling?*

"Well, c'mon! Marriage in and of itself is hard. Add in the interracial dynamic and that compounds the effort more." Imani smiled as she thought about her statement. "But I don't need to preach to you.

You've lived your entire life as a byproduct of an interracial marriage."

Uh, no duh, she wanted to roll her eyes and scream. Every single time Imani referred to Melody's Caucasian mother and African-American father lineage or talked about race relations, it made her blood boil. She wanted to smack Imani upside the head for the way she always harped about race, but instead, she gave her a curt nod.

Lance shook his head and chuckled at Imani's comments.

At least Lance didn't harbor any such racial hang-ups. Hell, as long as you were a beautiful woman with a pulse, he was ready to go. Melody suppressed a giggle. Well, maybe not in the last nineteen months!

"Anyhow," Imani continued. "Since marriage is forever, especially for you, Melody—" Imani gave her a curious look. "Don't you want to make sure the chemistry works where it counts?"

Exhaling a big sigh, she explained her position for the umpteenth time. "Sue me, Imani, but I believe that love conquers all. Even if we didn't already have great chemistry, Chris and I love each other. Look, when you're in love, the chemistry's a given, it just comes about naturally."

She tried another tactic. "But if you don't believe me, Imani, just ask Lance. He understands my viewpoint." She turned towards Lance to garner his support. "Especially considering you and Heather abstained before your wedding."

Lance shook his head slow and solemn. "Normally I would agree with you, Melody," he shrugged. "However, if you recall, waiting didn't work too well for me." He rubbed his mustache and goatee like an absentminded professor. "Even though my virgin bride claimed she liked sex after our first time, we only did it a handful of times in our nine months of marriage." Glancing at Imani, he frowned. "So, unfortunately I have to agree with Imani on this one."

Imani nodded and shrugged as if to say, 'see.'

"No, I'm not buying it," she replied as she retrieved her wine glass from the coffee table. "You and Heather had to have some semblance of chemistry." Melody sat back and then leaned forward in her chair. "Seriously, weren't there times where you practically died from anticipation waiting to see her again?"

Shoot if Chris walked in this instant, she'd leap up and scream as she covered him with kisses. When Lance continued to look nonplussed, she explained further. "Did the world stop when Heather walked into a room? Or didn't your body ever tingle just from her touch or the sound of her voice?"

"No. I never felt that way." Lance rubbed his head.

While she waited for him to expound, she sipped her Chardonnay. Its tropical fruits floated across her tongue, leaving oaky-vanilla, honey trails in their wake.

Lance's voice softened to a whisper. "At least not

with Heather anyway."

Melody wasn't sure she heard him correctly and she couldn't tell if Imani did either because of the way Imani stared at Lance. *Funny, it wasn't her usual scowl and raised eyebrow.* No, on second glance, Imani looked almost quizzical as if she were trying to unearth valuable, hidden clues.

Somehow Imani realized that Melody was watching her although she never made eye contact. In a flash Imani jumped up to refresh her empty wine glass.

"Anyone want some more?" Imani lifted the bottle of Kendall Jackson without glancing their direction.

"No, thanks." Lance shook his head.

Placing a hand over her glass, Melody shook her head and watched Imani. "No, if I drank any more, I couldn't drive home and I'd have to spend the night here." She waited for one of Imani's snide remarks.

Instead Imani topped off her glass with the remaining wine and downed half her drink.

Concerned, she looked at Lance to gauge his reaction.

Rather than watching Imani, he sat patiently waiting for Melody to continue the conversation. "So, are you sure you don't want to reconsider your vow of abstinence?"

Chuckling, she dismissed Imani's oddness for a moment as Imani took her seat again. "No, and despite what you two believe, I'm not a prude, and Chris and I have outstanding chemistry."

The thought of Chris's kisses made her hug herself. "Yes, I admit there are times where I just want to jump Chris's bones on the spot. But I know that while we're waiting, we're getting closer, learning more about each other, and increasing the passion and desire between us." She leaned forward and continued in a conspiratorial whisper. "Don't worry, unlike you and Heather, our wedding night will be well worth the wait."

Lance smiled and finished his wine. "Yeah, you're right. The two of you will be fine."

Imani muttered something under her breath that sounded like, "I sure hope so for your sake," before she drained her glass.

Truth or Dare – March 2007

Imani studied Chris from across her family room.

Although she knew and liked Chris enough to introduce him to Marco, and then later, set him up with Melody, she realized with regret that she didn't really *know him*, know him. She had left the real connecting up to Marco since he and Chris had clicked so effortlessly. She bit her lip.

What a big mistake! Although Chris enjoyed everyone's easy banter, he missed some of their internal references.

The six of them—Melody, Lance, Trevor, Erycah, Marco, and Imani—had formed lasting bonds attending college together while Chris studied nearby at Rensselaer Polytechnic Institute. And now Chris evidently wanted to bridge that gap, because she couldn't think of any other reason why he would suggest playing the adult rendition of Truth or Dare, minus the Dare.

She glanced around the room. Unfortunately, everyone else seemed deluded enough to believe that this sounded like a good idea.

Humph, and to think that the cold, March afternoon had started out so well. To celebrate their ability to dig out from all the ridiculous amounts of snow they'd received, everyone decided to get together at her place.

After feasting on a winter picnic potluck, they commenced a full onslaught barrage of Pictionary. Boys against girls. Chris and Trevor sat on the couch and Lance claimed the overstuffed chair while the girls, except for a ridiculously pregnant Erycah, sat on the floor in front of them. Melody sat between Chris's legs; Erycah on the couch wedged between Trevor and Chris; and Imani, by default, next to Lance. Even with the unfair seating arrangements, the girls won handily while the boys dogged each other over their horrible performance.

But now all that camaraderie was about to head the way of the dodo bird and Imani didn't like it one bit. Truth or Dare? Please! If she wanted others to know something, well hell, they already knew it. And if she didn't want something known, then there was a damn legitimate reason for that!

No good could come from them playing this game! Why did white people insist on playing crap like Truth or Dare anyway? While she sat and fumed, Chris got the others excited.

"I don't know if this is fair, though," Chris said. "You guys already know so much about each other, I'm just trying to play catch up."

"Yeah," Erycah agreed. "Joining this group can be a little intimidating. They," she pointed to Melody, Imani, Lance and Trevor, "share some weird kismet. They know absolutely everything about one another."

"Not everything," Melody replied almost with an

accusatory tone.

Imani glanced at Melody. Something about Melody's attitude gave her pause.

Trevor lit up, apparently seeing an opportunity to get some answers, too. "We could always find out more, right?"

"Fine," Lance stated dryly. "At this point in our friendships, what do we have to lose?"

Plenty! Imani frowned at Lance. Sometimes the truth needed to remain cloudy and hidden. Damn, she didn't want to play this game, but she was outnumbered. Screw it, better to take control and try to steer things to safer waters. "Chris, since you brought it up, why don't you go first," she suggested sweet as sugar.

"So, we can ask each other anything?" Chris looked around the circle of friends. "And you have to answer honestly, correct?"

"Yep," Trevor replied.

"That's right," seconded Melody.

Erycah grinned, looking thrilled at the prospect of getting some real insight into the group while Lance simply nodded.

"Okay then. Since I don't want to ruffle any feathers right off the bat, I'll go for an easy ice-breaking question." He surveyed the group. "This one's for everybody. How did you get your name?"

When no one volunteered, he spoke again. "I guess I can go first. My maternal grandfather's name was Christopher, my paternal grandfather's name was Edward. Hence Christopher Edward Weaver."

"Oh no," Erycah said with a groan. "You two can't get married. Melody Weaver is too damn sing-songy."

Everyone chuckled.

"I warned her about that." Imani shook her head. "But she likes not having to change her initials, Wilkins to Weaver."

Sounds beautiful to me." Chris smiled at Melody. "Why don't you go next, Honey?"

"Alright, sure." She nodded. "This is an easy one. See my parents had difficulty conceiving. My mom had a miscarriage in her second trimester with what would have been my older brother."

"Oh, my God!" Imani placed a comforting hand on Melody's arm. "You never told me that."

"Wow, this is working already," Erycah whispered.

Melody gave Imani a weak smile. "I've never told anyone that before." Her patented sunshine and daffodils smile returned. "I don't have a middle name. However, when my parents finally had me, they always said I was the Melody created from the beautiful music they made together."

"Damn! No wonder you're always so romantic and consumed by fairytale stories." Trevor tsked.

Lance shrugged. "That does explain a lot, huh?"

"Yep," Imani replied. "Your turn, Trev."

"Well, my mother heard my names over the years and they always stuck with her. So I'm Trevor Xavier Mathis."

"Xavier," Melody repeated with a nod. "That has

a nice ring to it."

"I think so, too." Erycah stroked Trevor's leg. "My turn, right?" She paused while everyone agreed. "My folks bought into the whole creative Black phase. My mom loved the name Erica, spelled E-R-I-C-A. So, add in the funny twists and you got it." She looked towards Lance whose turn came next.

"Uh, not so fast," Imani said. "You forgot your middle name."

"Ohhh, no!" Erycah wagged her finger. "I never disclose my middle name."

"Wait a minute. You wanted to play this game," chided Melody. "Full disclosure and complete honesty, right?"

Trevor nudged Erycah. "You asked for it, Sweetheart."

"Alright, alright fine. But this never leaves the room." Erycah took a deep breath. "My middle name is Albertalene."

"Wow," exclaimed Chris.

"What?" Lance asked, frowning.

Imani managed to keep a straight face, but she swore Erycah said, 'Alberto VO5 Vaseline.'

"Remember, creative parents, right? Combine grandmothers Albertine and Magdalene."

"Nice," Lance replied with a chuckle. "Well I never knew where my mom dreamed up Lance until I found my birth certificate and my real father. My real dad's middle name is Lance. My middle name, Joseph, comes from the Bible." He smiled at Imani; her turn was next.

"Like Mary and Joseph, Joseph?" Melody asked.

"Yeah," replied Lance. "My mother mentioned it was more for him than for the Technicolor coat guy."

"Like Jesus' father, Joseph?" Trev caught on, as well and he saw it click on Imani's face.

"Except Joseph wasn't really Jesus' father." Imani filled in the blanks.

"Just like the other guy wasn't really your Dad either," said Erycah with a gasp.

Lance shook his head in disbelief. "Maybe my mother really tried to tell everyone the truth the whole entire time with something so innocuous."

Imani laughed. "We always knew your mother was a trip." She patted his foot and winked, then turned to the rest of the group. "My folks were proud of their African-American heritage. Imani Nia means Faith and Purpose in Swahili."

Trevor thrust his fist in the air. "Power to the people!"

"You are so silly," said Melody laughing.

Imani shot Trev a look, but she couldn't keep a straight face.

"Okay, who's next?" Chris seemed impatient for more revelations.

"Why not continue around clockwise like we just did?" asked Erycah.

Everyone else besides Imani shrugged, nodded, or agreed in some fashion.

"So that means me." Melody sighed. "Do we really want to get serious?" Melody studied each person for assurance.

"Ask the hard questions." Trevor smiled. "If you dare."

"Alright. You asked for it." Melody focused in on Erycah. "How did you really feel when you found out that Imani and Trevor kissed?"

"Whew!" Lance ducked his head.

Imani threw Melody a stunned glare. *What the hell?*

Trev finally closed his open mouth. "Since when did you go for the jugular?"

Chris leaned down and asked Melody, "When did Trev and Imani kiss?"

"Well, I asked for it, didn't I?" Erycah exhaled and glanced at Trev; then she turned to Chris. "Here Chris, let me clue you in. See, Trev used to have a thing for Imani." Erycah shrugged. "I kinda jumped in sophomore year and asked her if I could take a shot with him—"

"Since Imani wasn't interested," interjected Melody.

Imani shot Melody another puzzled look while Erycah continued.

"We went out for a few months and then right after he dropped me off for the summer break…"

"Imani *accidentally* kissed me." Trev arched his eyebrow.

"When did you wind up telling Erycah and did you ever consider going back with Imani?" Lance asked.

Melody threw up her hands. "Hey, she didn't finish answering my question!"

"It's alright," Erycah replied. "I was pissed off at

first, but my relationship with Trevor immediately improved. We became much tighter." Trevor hugged her close and Erycah gazed at Lance. "He told me that very night."

"You did?" Imani gasped at Trevor.

"He did. We've never kept secrets from each other." Erycah patted Trevor's hand. "I don't feel the need to mark my territory. I've always had complete faith in Trev and Imani. That kiss was past history."

"Up until that kiss, I would have jumped to be Imani's boyfriend. But what she said afterwards put life in perspective." Trev gave Imani a genuine smile. "Thank you again."

"You're welcome, I guess." Imani rolled her eyes and grinned.

Chris looked elated at the turn of events and apparently, he couldn't wait for more. "Trevor, your turn. That is if you're finished Erycah?"

"Oh, I'm quite done," Erycah replied as she patted Trev's leg.

Trev rubbed his hands together and looked around for a victim. "Let's see here…" His eyes settled on Imani. "Don't be mad."

"Ah, no." She shook her head, moaned, and held her stomach while anxious nerves jangled inside as they prepared for the worst.

"You told me once about your Top Five Kisser list."

"Oh, shit!" She covered her face with her hands.

"Who's on the list, in what order, and short answer of why?" Trev sat back delighted to see her squirm.

"Ooo, yeah!" Melody clapped her hands together. "The infamous Top Five list."

Chris leaned forward on the loveseat, ready for something big to explode.

"Trev," she wailed. "I thought you were my friend."

"Spill the beans already woman." Lance adjusted his position in the overstuffed chair.

"Fine!" Feeling defeated, she leaned back against the ottoman that lay next to his feet. "Number five was my first boyfriend in high school."

"Darling Ricky," Melody said, fluttering her eyelids.

"He scored so low because we both were young and inexperienced. But let's just say his stock improved dramatically the more we practiced over the two years we went together."

"Ahh," said Erycah with one of Melody's romantic sighs.

"Next." Lance pretended to yawn.

Imani dropped her head and mumbled the name of number four so soft that they could barely hear it. "Trev."

"Whoa, I made the list?" he asked both shocked and impressed.

Erycah smiled and kissed his cheek. "You know you're numero uno on my list, Baby."

"Alright now," he replied with his toothy grin.

Melody snuggled between Chris's legs. "You didn't say why, Imani."

"Despite the Lo Mein breath and the obvious

wrongness of the situation, it was nice," she replied before daring to look up again. "Julian was three."

Lance chuckled. "DJ strikes again."

"Who's Julian and was he a DJ?" Chris asked confused.

"I heard lots about him, but I never met him," Erycah said.

"He was cool," replied Trev.

Melody leaned back and filled Chris in. "D.J. stands for Dexter Julian—"

Imani kicked Melody in the leg. "It's Demetrius, Cow," she scoffed. "When are you ever going to get that right?"

Lance doubled over in a fit of laughter. "She's never going to get that right."

"Dexter, Demetrius, whatever. Anyhow, a mere two weeks after Kissahontas here laid one on Trevor, she meets fellow General Electric intern, DJ Jones and they enjoy a wild, passionate summer together." Melody continued the story with extreme theatrics. "Then she decides to let him play the field during the school year. He finds his one true love back at UT Austin and the rest they say is history."

"You dated DJ Jones?" Chris leaned back in shock.

"You knew him?" Imani asked.

"I do work at GE, too, lest you forgot where we met!"

"I thought he was before your time there?"

"Nope. I met him and Chantal. Nice couple. Heard they got married." Chris made a quick face, eager to joke around.

"Whoops, did you hear that juicy nugget, Lance?" Melody bounced with glee.

Lance tried to rein in his laughter as he patted Imani's shoulder.

"So, not funny, Chris!" Imani mock rolled her eyes. "Anyhow, Marco was number two."

An abrupt hush fell across the room at the mention of her deceased husband.

"The white thing never mattered." Memories of some of their better lip locks flashed through her head. "He was an excellent kisser."

"Evidently way more than you ever let on before," Melody said almost as a complaint.

Imani studied Melody again trying to decipher what in the hell was going on with her.

However, Chris wanted to move on from the sadness. "So, who's number one?"

Embarrassed, Imani leaned away from Lance and dropped her head again. "Lance."

All eyes turned to Lance who sat stunned.

"Am I the only guy in this room that she didn't kiss?" Chris asked no one in particular.

Erycah reared around to Trevor who sat with a knowing smile on his face. "When did she kiss Lance?"

"After Spring Break our junior year."

"Was that the only time?" Melody asked with a haughty tone and a shocked expression.

"Yes." Imani sighed before glaring at Lance. "We clicked for one magical moment." Sadly, she realized her sarcastic tone didn't quite mask the underlying pain. She turned to Erycah eager to move this train wreck along. "Next question, please."

"Okay. Uh, Chris, Darling, we don't want you to feel left out," Erycah began. "Have you ever hit a woman and would you ever?"

Melody turned beet red. "Erycah!"

"Inquiring minds," Lance replied.

"Yes, of course I have," Chris answered honestly, almost chipper-like.

"What?" Lance damn-near knocked over the chair he pushed off it so fast. Standing at his full, imposing 6' 2", arms crossed over his muscular chest, Imani finally, for once, understood how white folks could be so scared shitless by a passing black man that they would cross the road to avoid contact.

Melody moved from between Chris' legs, her face in anguish at his unexpected response.

Even Trev leaned in looking ready to pounce.

"Whoa!" Chris shrank back into the couch, hands up half in surrender, half for self-defense. "I have two older, obnoxious sisters who have picked on me since day one. They slap, kick, punch, and wrestle. I always fought back and will continue until the day I die."

"Oh, good Lord," Erycah said with a large exhale.

"You don't know how close you were to getting your ass kicked," Trevor said to Chris.

"What?" Chris asked, clearly missing something. His arms finally dropped to his sides.

Imani enlightened him. "Melody used to date a

guy—"

"Imani, please," Melody pleaded not wanting to dredge up old ghosts.

"Full disclosure, Melody," Lance warned her getting comfortable in the chair again. "Honesty before marriage, trust me on that point."

Melody held Lance's gaze before relenting. "Fine, I had an abusive boyfriend that beat me twice, once pretty severely. Then, when he felt he couldn't control me any longer, he drew a gun on me. Only after Imani and Lance intervened, did he turn the gun on himself."

Erycah gripped Trev's arm. "Damn, are you serious?" She shook her head. "Kudos to the college and you three for keeping everything pretty hush-hush. I mean…there were a few rumors about an accidental discharge, but…nothing even vaguely close to that."

"I'm so sorry." Chris's face fell. "I didn't know." He embraced Melody and stroked her hair, afraid to let her go.

"You seem like a good guy, but that's why we need to know," Lance replied. "My question to you, Melody. "Why did you stay with him after he beat you, and would you ever allow that to happen again?"

"Let's back off Melody for a while," said Chris as he protected her in his arms.

Melody pushed back a bit. "It's okay, Chris." She gave him a faint smile. "Lance has a right to know." Remarkably, Melody faced Lance, expression set strong. "I loved him. I understand now that love doesn't hurt physically. That I should have left after the first occurrence. But in that moment I would have done almost anything to please him, to keep him happy. You just want to believe that you can change people, save them, fix what's wrong." Melody shook her head with regret. "I know that's not true now, Lance."

Lance nodded in appreciation. "Thank you for your honesty, that helps me understand what happened better."

"Well, I forfeit my turn," Imani said, trying to short circuit this disaster. "I already know more than I need to know about all of you."

"Oh, that's such a cop-out," Erycah wailed with disappointment.

"Her prerogative though, and I already went," Lance replied happy to escape the hot seat.

"Fine, I'll go," Chris said although he looked unsure of what to ask now.

"Actually, Baby," Melody interrupted. "Do you mind if I jump ahead of you in line?"

He threw up his hands only too happy to surrender. "No, please go, I can't think of any other questions."

"Thanks," she replied as she patted his leg. "This is addressed for my two best friends."

Imani's breath caught and her heart dropped. She exchanged a quick, concerned glance with Lance who looked just as puzzled, then she eyed Melody with extreme caution.

"We always told each other everything. Why didn't you tell me about Spring Break?"

Lance licked his lips deep in thought. Then he stared down at Imani and waited for her to take the lead.

If only the floor could open and swallow her whole, make this dreaded scenario or her disappear. "Damn it, Melody." She had carefully buried the memories of that day for a reason, never wanting to relive those confusing and painful emotions. She closed her eyes. Everyone wanted full disclosure, right? Screw it! It was all ancient history now.

With a resigned sigh, she reopened her eyes and answered. "Look Melody, I felt like a stupid whore the day after it happened. Not something I wanted to announce proudly. Oh, lookie here," she said, waving her arms around. "I'm the latest stop on the Lance mobile!" She threw her arms down in disgust.

"So you two slept together?" Melody gasped as the pieces fell into place.

Trev nodded. "It finally comes out."

"You knew?" Erycah asked.

"I always had my suspicions." Trev gave Imani a sympathetic smile.

"Well come on people," Chris spoke like they were little children. "Kisses are wonderful, but they're not generally considered the *magical moment.*"

Erycah smirked. "That just means you haven't done it right, then!"

"Alright, now!" Trevor nodded his head in agreement.

Melody stared at Lance with equal parts shock and

hurt. "After all of our talks, and you never once mentioned this?"

"Imani and I made a pact to never, ever discuss it." Lance squirmed in his seat, wanting to hug Melody but knowing better. "I'm so sorry."

Imani snapped her head around to appraise him. "I take that back, I do have a question and Lance, this one's on you." As her jaw flexed, Lance deflated back into the chair, his wary eyes never leaving hers. "Why did you marry Heather?"

"Oh, snap!" Erycah slapped Trevor's thigh.

"Complete disclosure, right?" Lance smirked then he locked eyes with Imani. "Because of that one magical moment you mentioned."

Imani frowned. *What kind of B.S. was he selling?*

"Care to elaborate?" Chris asked hoping he wasn't the only one in the dark here.

"Obviously I never got over Imani." Lance's nostrils flared. "After I let Imani slip through my fingers, I hoed around." He stroked his goatee, lost in thought. "After my injury," he gestured at Trevor and Erycah, "their wedding, and Marco's surprise proposal to Imani, I knew I had to settle down."

Lance rubbed his face and head. "I went for the first woman I ever had to chase. Someone completely different than anyone I'd dated in the past."

He grunted. "Stupidly, I proposed after only two months of dating and we got married three months later. The reward, I guess, was what I thought would be a picture perfect life. You know the dream, the two kids and the white picket fence." He grimaced.

"Unfortunately, it was just as shallow as a picture; it looked good from the outside but absolutely no substance, no depth."

"Did you know all this?" Erycah asked Trevor astounded.

Trev shook his head slowly.

"No," Melody replied. "No one knew." Melody squinted at Lance then frowned. "Not so fast, Buddy. You told us that you loved Heather."

"I thought I did, but in hindsight, you two were right." He shrugged. "It was more the thrill of the hunt. Under normal circumstances, Heather and I would have never been friends. We didn't really talk or communicate. Our aspirations lay in different directions. She wasn't there for me through thick and thin, the good and the bad."

For some reason, Lance's voice dropped and Imani turned to see him more clearly. He smiled at her. "But you were there, Imani, you've always been there." Lance leaned forward, honing in on her. "I still love you, Imani."

Imani's breath caught in her throat and she couldn't respond. Her bottom lip quivered as she held his intense gaze. With Lance's sandalwood cologne caressing her in its soft, fragrant embrace, her heart thumped wildly, wanting to believe him, wanting to reciprocate his feelings.

Then a shift occurred.

Guilt and sorrow clouded her vision and she squeezed her eyes shut. This was way too much, too fast. Marco just died eight months ago and inside she still physically ached for him.

When she reopened her eyes, she pleaded with Lance to understand. "I…I can't."

His hurt expression forced her to look away and she scanned the room for her friends' reactions.

Melody sat with a stunned expression on her face as if Lance had just slapped her. Chris, on the other hand, looked ready to grab a tub of popcorn to accompany their thrilling, action movie. Trev's mercurial face changed from smug to skeptical to…pissed? While Erycah borrowed a move from Melody's overly romantic playbook and bounced on her hands, barely containing a squeal of happiness.

"Forget them, Imani." Lance's deep voice compelled her to focus solely on him. Somehow he'd captured her left hand in his. The warmth and strength of his hands eased her nervousness. His eyes never wavered from hers. "I understand that you can't now, but could you ever?"

Something about his insistent stare that burned deep into her soul, made the walls around her heart crack just a fraction. She gave him an almost imperceptible nod yet her reply lacked conviction. "Maybe?"

However Lance saw through her defenses and ignored her verbal response. Gently, he squeezed her hand and nodded once, satisfied. "Take your time, Imani. I'll wait."

Chris exhaled aloud, breaking the mood. "Wow, I like hanging out with you guys! Never a dull moment."

LUNCH WITH LANCE

Melody sat at the café table fuming at Lance. "Why didn't you ever tell me about your feelings for Imani?"

Lance leaned back and rubbed his head. "How much longer are we going to go over this?"

"Until I feel satisfied that you didn't take advantage of my friendship," she said ready to smack him. Just as she prepared to say more, Imani entered the restaurant.

In an instant, Melody's blood boiled and she turned on Lance again. "Why is she here?" she hissed wanting to work this out with him first before including her defensive girlfriend.

Apparently, she didn't speak quietly enough because Imani overheard her and reared up, attitude at the ready.

"Oh, I can most definitely leave if I'm not wanted!" Imani's eyes blazed into hers, arm poised on the hip, creating the exact scenario Melody didn't want to deal with.

Before she could reply, their poor waitress made an unfortunate mistake in timing. "Do you need another chair?" she asked as she approached.

Imani glared at her. "Now's not a good time.

We'll call you when we need you."

Lance wanted to soften the blow, but the waitress scurried off like a frightened rabbit before he had a chance to react. Instead, he gave Imani a warning glance, then sighed.

"Look, Melody, it's my fault," Lance replied trying to break the tension. "I invited Imani thinking we were all going to chill out over dinner like old times. I didn't realize you wanted to speak to me privately."

"Although I don't get what the big ass deal is," Imani snapped. "I thought you ferreted out all your answers during your fiancé's stupid Truth or Dare inquisition last week."

Imani's unexpected appearance, her attitude, and now her unwarranted attack on Chris, all combined to push Melody's last button. Her mouth tightened and her back arched. "Look, if you're going to stay, fine; but don't you dare utter a single, negative word about Chris!"

"What is your problem?" Imani asked as she grabbed a chair from a nearby, vacant table.

"Like it's not entirely obvious!" Melody slammed her hand down on the table. "My two best friends lied to me! You screwed behind my back or right under my nose, take your pick. And it evidently meant enough that he's uttering proclamations of love." She shook her head as the outburst brought her close to tears. "Here I'm supposed to be this ace reporter and instead I feel like such a complete and ridiculous fool!"

Imani became uncharacteristically quiet and calm. "So, let me get this straight. You're saying you never once lied to either of us?"

Melody couldn't quite sense the trap. "Of course not. I always told you both everything!"

Rather than exploding, Imani chuckled. Even Lance looked cautious.

"You really don't remember that whole abusive period? The lies about what happened..."

Melody winced as the low blow connected. *What...how...why would she bring that up?* Her mouth moved, but the words took a second to follow. "That was different," she replied trying to keep her voice from shaking.

"Why?" Like an acrobat, Imani flipped directions again with ease. Her voice, tone, and mannerisms soothed. All traces of animosity vanished. Now she was just a friend asking another friend a simple question.

"Because..." Melody struggled to find the right words. "I was in love and I felt stupid."

"And how's that any different from the situation with Lance and me?" Imani asked. "I thought for a split second that I was in love and I felt incredibly stupid for falling for his lines. Embarrassed because you and I always joked about the dumb broads he bedded."

"Uh, thanks, Ladies!" Lance threw his hands up. "I am sitting right here you know."

Imani rolled her eyes and ignored him. "Do you understand why now?"

Although she hated to admit it, if the tables were turned she would have done exactly the same thing Imani did. She nodded. "Yes, I'm sorry for being a pain about this."

"No worries." Imani reached across the table and squeezed her hand. "This brought out the worst in all of us."

"True," she replied although something still irked her. Turning towards Lance she stared at him until her thoughts cohered. For some reason, she couldn't let him completely off the hook yet. "I still don't understand something, Lance."

Cautious and tense, he sat back and watched her while she held his steady gaze.

"After Imani's wedding, you stopped calling her, correct?"

He nodded.

"Yet you still called me two to three times every week? Just like nothing happened. It wasn't until after Marco's death that I realized the discrepancy. Why?"

Lance looked perplexed, seeming to wonder where the pitfall lay in wait. "I kept calling you because nothing ever happened between us. Our friendship never changed. So why would I bring that mess up and let our relationship suffer?" His hand waved the suggestion away. "If you never noticed or brought it up, why would I?" He chuckled. "Plus, it's not like I'd ask you to choose sides; that's just not my style."

"That's because he knows I would have easily won that battle," Imani said.

Lance snickered. "Yeah, probably."

While they joked, Melody's shoulders relaxed and she leaned back in her chair, however something kept nagging at the corners of her mind. She tried to utter a logical question, but stopped before her mouth opened. She needed time to reflect alone tonight.

However, Imani and her doggone intuition wouldn't relent. "So, what's wrong?"

Lance turned and gaped at Melody. "There's more?"

"I really don't know—"

"Are you wondering if Lance would be here now if it weren't for you keeping the lines of communication open?" Imani asked.

Dumbfounded at how Imani knew, when even she didn't, Melody frowned and nodded. "Yes, that's it. And it's making me feel used."

Imani turned to Lance. "So, what's your answer? If Marco died, and you had quit speaking to Melody like you quit speaking to me. Would you be here now?"

Lance sat back and pondered for a moment. His voice rumbled deep and slow, like an approaching train still a quarter mile down the track. "Yes." He leaned forward and rested his elbows on the table.

"After seeing Marco's obituary in the paper, I would have come over pronto. Regardless of what you both may think, I always liked Marco and I never held it against him when he married Imani. He just did what I wanted to do."

"However, once I saw Imani in pain…mourning,

my hurt pride didn't matter anymore." He turned to face Imani and reached over with his left hand and held hers. "It felt like old times, protecting my girls. Innately I knew I needed to be there to help you through."

Lance turned back towards Melody. "And when I saw you," he said reaching across the table with his right hand to capture hers. "Struggling to keep Imani, Chris, and yourself sane, how could I not help?'

Between his warm, caring hand and his passionate, brown eyes, Melody could feel the door to forgiveness unlock. Damn, she couldn't stay mad at them if she tried!

"I love you both," Lance said squeezing her hand.

Imani reached across the table with her free left hand and patted Melody and Lance's intertwined hands. "Cool," Imani said abruptly as she looked at Melody. "So are we good now? Are you done interrogating us?"

Melody smiled and nodded.

"Excellent!" Imani withdrew her hands from both her and Lance and drummed them on the table. "Because I'm seriously hungry and I *will* go somewhere else if y'all don't plan on eating anytime soon."

Melody giggled at Imani's ridiculousness. Some things just never changed.

Special Delivery - April 2007

"Are you sure we should be in here?" Lance asked Erycah and Trevor as the nurse prepared Erycah for another push.

"Of course," Erycah said with a tired sigh as Imani took her place at Erycah's bedside.

"We go au natural," Trev replied, "and how much more natural can you get then this? Plus," he added with a wink, "it might just make the two of you real men."

"I don't know how manly I need to be," Chris replied looking nervous.

Melody chuckled while she rubbed Chris's back.

"We can have everyone removed," the nurse rudely suggested, "it is a bit crowded."

"There won't be a need for that," said the doctor. He looked up at Erycah from his perch between her legs. "Are you ready?

Erycah nodded and grabbed both Trev and Imani's hands.

Lance watched Imani although not too carefully, trying to honor her request for time and space. In the month since he'd confessed his love in front of everyone, things seemed both promising and frustrating. Their relationship hadn't progressed like he'd wanted, but they hadn't regressed either which, when it came to Imani, was a victory in and of itself.

Actually, there was one regression that he enjoyed. Back in college, they used to greet each other hello or good-bye with an innocent peck on the lips before…well before that 'magical moment.' Now, although they hadn't regressed that far, at least it was back to their post-Marco dating times, when he could sneak in a kiss to her forehead or cheek each night in greeting and again when he said his goodbyes.

"We're almost ready," the nurse said interrupting his thoughts.

The doctor nodded to the nurse and then nodded at Erycah. "Give me a big push on the count of three. One."

Lance noticed that both he and Chris leaned forward in spite of themselves.

"Two."

Trev and Imani braced Erycah's legs.

"Three!"

Erycah pushed, the baby's blood-slicked, hairy head crowned, and Chris and Lance reared back in unison.

"That's just not right," Lance muttered under his breath.

"Eww," Chris said turning green. "I don't want to see *all* of the crowning glory."

Melody giggled and nudged in front of Chris to get a better view.

Lance glanced at Trevor and frowned. Maybe the dreadlocks and half-Jamaican genes somehow made

Trev a more carefree, enlightened man. Because if the tables were turned, he definitely wouldn't want everyone else in the room seeing all of Imani's most secret areas.

Appalled and shocked by their nonchalant openness, he nonetheless leaned forward again, bracing for the next push. Against his better judgment he had to admit that the whole experience seemed spiritual and beautiful—in some strange, convoluted way.

"You're doing wonderful, Sweetheart," Trevor encouraged Erycah, then he kissed their entwined hands.

The doctor and nurse readjusted for the next push.

"Ready, Erycah?" the doctor asked.

Erycah nodded, determination set on her face.

"One…two…three, push!"

With a strange "slurp" sound and the help of the doctor's nimble hands, the baby's head emerged. The doctor performed a quick, deft hand twist which dislodged its shoulders, and the baby practically spurted out. "It's a boy!"

Chris almost passed out and Melody grabbed and hugged him to keep him steady.

What a miraculous yet disgusting thing to behold. Lance backed away stunned as the nurse and doctor flew into their post-delivery flurry of action. Crying baby, Trev cutting the umbilical cord, weighing, cleaning, testing, afterbirth, a swaddled baby nursing on his mother's breast, it all whizzed by in a blur and strange sensations streamed through his body.

Struggling to understand what he felt, he backed against the wall trying to distance himself from the whir of activity and complex emotions. He stared at Trevor, Erycah, and Imani. Then it hit him like a sucker punch.

He frowned at the realization.

Not normally prone to bouts of jealousy or covetous thoughts, his eyebrow lifted in disbelief and he stared at Trevor. It was true. Right now he'd give anything to stand in Trev's spot. But not with Erycah laying there in bed. No, he imagined Imani, with a soft sheen of victorious sweat, returning his gaze of love and pride. The two of them staring in awe, beholding their little gift from God. A beautiful baby featuring a mix of their genes, characteristics, and looks. A precious life full of potential, possibilities, and dreams.

With eyes too damp for his liking, he looked at Imani.

And she smiled at him.

For a moment, he basked in the warmth of her loving gaze. It radiated like the sun to a man emerging from a cave. Then, too soon, it was gone as she returned her focus to Erycah, Trev, and their new baby boy, Xavier.

MELODY'S WEDDING – JUNE 2007

Melody stared up at the ceiling of their room in the Hilton Garden Inn Albany Airport, listening to Chris snore softly at her side and wondering what happened.

The day went even more perfect than she ever dreamed. Imani could seriously consider another career in wedding planning. Not only did she act as the perfect Maid of Honor attending to all Melody's needs, but in addition, she planned one breath-taking wedding. Plus, it hadn't cost them a fortune either. Go figure—cheap, on schedule, and still a complete fairytale.

Melody smiled as she recalled her reflection in the mirror. With her voluminous tulle-skirted wedding dress, translucent glass-looking heels, understated yet elegant tiara, and her golden curls swept up into a classic French twist, she looked like a princess. The four-piece orchestra played like angels, Pastor Thomas performed a reverent yet hilarious ceremony, the doves and horse-drawn Cinderella carriage added a romantic touch, and the 105 guests enjoyed the classy, delicious, party-filled reception.

After the too good to be true wedding and reception, the white limo whisked her and Chris away to this beautiful hotel room. And like the gentleman that he was, Chris carried her over the hotel room threshold.

Inside their hotel room, they kissed once nervously before accidentally bumping heads.

That's when Melody decided to change in the bathroom while Chris removed his tuxedo. Safe inside the bathroom, she concentrated on erasing her nervousness. Between deep breaths, she glanced in the mirror and whispered a quick thanks to Imani for helping choose the wedding gown.

The bridesmaids had detached the overskirt, 100 yards of billowy tulle, after they finished taking the numerous wedding pictures, leaving Melody looking stunning in this sleek, satin column dress that lay underneath. She sashayed at her reflection. The same dress that moved with her as she danced the night away. The same dress which she easily unzipped solo. She lovingly hung it up with a proud smile for Imani to retrieve from the hotel tomorrow after they left for their honeymoon.

Taking one more deep, calming breath, she freshened up and donned lacy, white, baby doll lingerie—a present from her beaming mother. With a nervous exhale, she turned off the bathroom light, and opened the door.

Somehow Chris still stood in a state of undress. His tuxedo jacket, tie, cummerbund, and pants were gone. Packed away in the Men's Wearhouse suit bag that hung inside the closet. His remaining shirt, underwear, and socks brought to mind her own personal, blond version of Tom Cruise from *Risky Business*. Chris's appraising smile beckoned her to come hither.

They kissed even more tentatively than their first time and then Chris scooped her up and carried her to the king-sized bed.

"You look so beautiful, Mrs. Weaver," he murmured as he set her on her feet. Before she could reply, he kissed her again and this time all nervousness and trepidation disappeared.

Her heartbeat quickened as his passionate kisses intensified. His breathing picked up and he pulled away, ripping off his shirt and underwear, his eyes burning with desire. They traveled down her body and back up again, resting on her breasts. His hands followed suit, freeing them from behind the skimpy lace. But then he squeezed them a bit too hard until she almost cried out in pain.

However, Chris didn't notice, his mouth now engulfed her breasts.

Ow! Melody frowned as she tried to figure out what he was doing with his tongue or lips or…teeth? Just as she was about to stop him, he was back up kissing her again.

Eyes closed and breathing heavy, he maneuvered them onto the bed and his hand slipped between her thighs. "You are so hot. I love you, Melody."

Melody trembled with anticipation. And then somehow without warning, Chris was inside her. Surprised, she jerked and he began thrusting. By the third thrust, she recovered and moved with him.

"Oh God, yes! Right there," he almost screamed in her ear. His body arched and two thrusts later he exploded while emitting some strange guttural noises.

Spent, he rolled off her, smile wide as the Grand Canyon. "Mmm, what a perfect way to end the day." He popped up on his elbow, leaned over and gave her a quick, albeit appreciative peck. "I love you, Mrs. Weaver." His expression looked so joyous she couldn't help but return it.

"I love you, too."

With that, Chris lay back, got under the covers, and not two minutes later he started snoring.

Melody stared at him both stupefied and amazed. With a sigh, she slumped back on the bed. Five minutes later, she shook her head and returned to the bathroom to clean up, brush her teeth, wash her face, and change into her normal nightgown. When she finished, she slipped under the covers next to Chris and stared up at the ceiling.

Maybe, he was too tired after such a long, exciting day. Or maybe he was too excited with it being their first time and all; neither one of them had made love in years. Or maybe…

Melody couldn't come up with any other possibilities that she liked. Whatever just happened, next time would prove better. Seriously, five strokes and done, left a lot to be desired.

WEDDING ANNIVERSARY

Brilliant yellow sunlight filtered through Imani's half-drawn bedroom curtains, signaling the start of a beautiful June day. Imani sighed and pulled the pillow over her head. She wasn't fooled. Today wasn't a beautiful day. It would have been her second wedding anniversary if Marco were still alive.

A paralyzing pain threatened to leave her lying numb in bed all day. *Lord, please help me snap out of it.*

Two seconds later, the phone rang and she jumped. She glanced at the caller ID and shook her head before answering. "Hey, Mom."

"Hey, Baby, how 'ya doing?"

"I'm about to get up and get ready for work."

"Good, it'll help take your mind off everything. At least that's the excuse you used two weeks ago when you cancelled our trip," she said not hiding her displeasure.

"It's not an excuse, Mom. I really do have a lot going on at work right now." Imani shook her head, sat up, and kicked her feet over the side of the bed. "Plus, we were only going to Atlantic City for a few days and you know neither one of us really gambles."

She stifled a yawn and stretched. "I really wish

you and Melody would quit coddling me, pretending like I need company this week. What she needs to do is enjoy her honeymoon without calling me every damn day and you and Dad should go do something fun together…like Atlantic City! Trust me, I'm fine."

"If you insist," her mother replied sounding skeptical. "If you need me, you know how to reach me."

"I know. Thanks, Mom."

"Oh, and one last thing."

"Yes, Mom?" Imani rolled her eyes expecting her to take another jab at Lance.

"Are you calling the Cabrettes today?"

Imani's body tensed. Forcing her voice to remain normal, she replied. "Yes, Mom, they're next on my list." Her free left hand rubbed her temples and she prayed it would keep the paralyzing pain from recurring. "Tell Dad hi and I love him," she said rushing to get off the phone.

"Will do, Baby. You take care of yourself today," her mom's concern rang through the phone lines. "I love you. Talk to you later."

With a sigh, Imani disconnected and looked at the alarm clock. She could call the Cabrettes now or…on second thought, life might look better after a refreshing shower and a cup of coffee. The latter option won.

After she finished getting ready, Imani sat at the kitchen table with the cordless phone and her second cup of coffee. Grabbing a napkin, she wiped the last crumbs of Danish from around her mouth, sighed, and dialed the Cabrettes.

"Imani, Bella," Mr. Cabrette answered. Although his voice sounded frail, Imani could still hear the underlying joy from her calling.

"How is everything, Papa?"

Mr. Cabrette hesitated for so long before answering that Imani's heart stuttered. Just when she was about to cry out in concern, he replied. "To be honest, Imani… things aren't so good. Mama, well…Mama says it's unnatural to lose a child, even an adult one. Her health, it's not so good now. The doctor says she has high blood pressure, diabetes, and depression."

"Oh, no!" Imani shook her head, trying not to cry.

"I don't know how she can have high blood pressure and diabetes when she doesn't even eat anymore. She's lost over thirty pounds." Mr. Cabrette's voice hitched. "You know that she's my heart, Imani. If she goes…well, I don't know how much longer I'll stay here either."

"Papa, no!" Her heart twisted in her chest, she couldn't lose all of them. "What about Maria and your future grandkids?"

His voice reclaimed some of its jovial nature. "Ah, Imani, don't worry about us old people. You and Maria, you're both young and strong. Such strong beautiful women, you make me very proud. There won't be any grandkids, but please, please go on and live your lives to the fullest. Continue to make us proud. Lei capisce?"

"I understand. But don't you dare give up, Papa."

"Ah, I said too much. I didn't mean to worry you, Bella. We'll be fine. I'll tell Mama you called. You take care, Imani."

"You, too, Papa." After disconnecting, she sniffed back the tears. Today wasn't going to be easy.

Despite her initial reservations, and primarily because she worked on automatic, the rest of the day flew by. Lab tests, computer analysis, a couple of meetings but nothing too taxing. As she sat back down at her desk, her phone rang. Distracted by work, she half-answered it.

"Hey Imani," came Lance's smooth, booming voice.

"Hey, Lance." A small smile emerged as she stopped working. "What can I do you for?"

"Just wondering how late are you working tonight?"

She glanced at her watch. "I'll probably leave at 5:00. What's up?"

"If you don't have any hot plans, I wanted to try out a new recipe on you."

"So you need a guinea pig, huh? Should I stop off at the pharmacy and grab some more antacids?"

"Yeah right, very funny. Just wait until I catch you licking the plate, begging for more."

She kicked back and smiled. "Oh, you think your cooking's all that?"

"I know it is," he boasted.

"Alright, bet." Her eyebrow arched. "Just promise me one thing?"

"Yeah, what?" he asked, waiting for the jab.

"Please promise me that you'll stay by my hospital bed, after they pump my stomach for food poisoning."

"Oh, please!" Lance chuckled. "You sure do talk a lot of smack. I'll see you at 5:30."

"See ya!" Imani chuckled as she disconnected and went back to her analysis.

When Imani returned home at 5:15, her carefree mood evaporated like rain droplets on Phoenix asphalt in July. She set her purse and keys down on the entry table and stared at the empty house. Each second that ticked past she expected to see Marco's devilish grin as he surprised her for their anniversary. However the house sat lifeless and devoid of Marco.

With a heavy sigh she placed one foot on the first step. *Might as well change and get comfortable.* Before she started up the stairs, she reared back and stopped. *Music!* Maybe listening to something easy and mellow might just lighten the mood.

Making a detour into the family room, she selected a couple of smooth jazz CDs—Diana Krall, George Benson, Fourplay, and Michael Franks—to play on the stereo. With the tunes playing, she unfastened her suit jacket buttons while she walked upstairs to her bedroom.

Inside the closet, she kicked off her heels and paused half undressed, scanning for something to throw on. Spotting a J-Lo inspired, lightweight, black sweat suit with white piping, she began to undress again. As she stepped out of her skirt, her foot caught on the waistband and she lost her footing.

Flailing, her hand grasped at anything to catch her balance. With her face only three feet away from hitting the floor, her hand connected.

Startled shitless by her almost imminent face plant and breathing hard, she managed to pull herself upright as her heart hammered in her throat. With both feet planted solidly on the floor, she finally noticed what saved her.

A rattled exhale escaped her lips. The object still remained captive in her grasp.

It was the sleeve of Marco's sage green, dress shirt.

Imani cried out as she tried to let the shirtsleeve go, but next thing she knew the shirt was off the hanger and snuggled against her body. Amazingly, after laundering and hanging in the closet for close to a year, the shirt still smelled like Marco mixed with remnants of Eternity for Men cologne.

She closed her eyes and inhaled the beautiful scent again. Before she realized what she had done, she found herself shed of all clothing except Marco's shirt and her panties.

However, she still didn't feel enveloped enough in Marco's essence despite the fact that she stood there shrouded in his shirt. Acting on automatic, she padded into the master bathroom and picked up the nearly full bottle of Eternity for Men.

Memories of Marco opening this cologne, her first anniversary present to him a year ago today, flooded through her mind. Marco wore the fragrance religiously, ever since college when she first told him how good he smelled in it. The recollections brought tears to her eyes and she sprayed the cologne on the nape of her neck and at the back of her wrists.

But it wasn't enough.

Desperate, she pulled his shirt far enough away from her skin to get between her breasts. It felt like Marco showering her with love. She smiled and pumped out another spray. It tickled her chest like Marco's sweet kisses. Wanting to get lost and disappear in the scent of him, she sprayed some up in the air and relished in the fine mist that rained down.

***

Lance rang the doorbell a second time, but when Imani still didn't answer, he used his key. Strange, her car sat parked in the driveway, so she was definitely home. Closing the door behind him, he announced his presence. "Imani, I'm here," he shouted.

Her keys and purse sat on the table by the door, but beyond that, there was no sign of her on the first floor. "Imani," he called out again as he followed the sounds of Diana Krall crooning about the moon into the empty family room.

Where was she? His heart beat faster as he tried not to worry or think the worst.

Faint noises sounded upstairs, so he took the steps two at a time. With his heart in his throat, he made a beeline for her bedroom and called out once more. "Imani?"

The empty room mocked him. *Where was she?* Frowning, he turned around ready to check the house room by room when he heard faint sounds coming from the master bathroom. He snuck over to the doorway...and screeched to a halt.

The smell and image combined for a one-two punch that paralyzed him. Dumbfounded, he stared, unable to speak.

First came the overpowering, caustic smell. It took him a second to recognize the stench of too much perfume, in too small an area. Then secondly, came the visual. Imani stood in the middle of the reeking room wearing nothing but a man's dress shirt.

He swallowed hard and tried not to stare at Imani in the shirt. The sight of a woman in a man's dress shirt always imbued one of the sexiest visuals he could imagine. Then the truth hit him. It wasn't his shirt. The shirt belonged to Marco. That realization made him snap into action.

"Imani?" he coughed trying not to inhale the fragrant fumes.

***

Imani spun around to face Lance. She wanted to make the cologne not remind her solely of Marco. She needed the scent to lose its debilitating effect. She walked over to Lance, arms down at her side. "Doesn't this smell nice?" Without warning, she reached up and sprayed his neck with the Eternity before he could react.

***

Shirking back, Lance's hand flew to his neck. *What the hell?* His fingers came away wet and then his brain processed what happened. Imani had tagged him with the cologne. His eyes narrowed as he caught sight of the offending bottle in her hand.

"I think you've used more than enough, Imani," he said through gritted teeth. With a concerted effort to be gentle, he pried the cologne from her hands and set it on the counter.

The cloying smell in the confined space seeped into his lungs and almost nauseated him. Unable to take any more, he pulled her out of the bathroom into the fresher air of the bedroom.

Kneeling over, he took a few deep breaths to clear his lungs and he stared at her immensely concerned. He wanted to ask if she was mentally all there, but he settled for an easier, less loaded question. "Are you ready for dinner?" he asked as he finally managed to stand upright.

Imani seemed to come out of a haze once she emerged from the all-encompassing smell of Eternity.

Shaking her head slowly, she gave him a doleful look. "Oh God, I'm so sorry, Lance." Completely embarrassed, she dropped her head. "I know how bad this must look. I feel absolutely ridiculous and pathetic."

Lance smiled to himself, *yes you are*. However, he hooked a finger under her chin and raised her head until her eyes met his. "No. You're not."

"Nice try, Lance." Imani managed to half smile. "I really don't know what happened. I came home to change and kick back with you, then I almost fell, but I caught myself with Marco's shirt. Next thing I know, I'm dressed in it and spraying his cologne all over God's green earth."

Lance couldn't keep from laughing. Luckily Imani laughed with him, too.

"I'm fine now," she said, squeezing his arm. "Go start dinner and I'll be right down…in my sweats this time."

He grinned. "You can wear whatever you want, just no more cologne, please."

"Go!" she replied, swatting him out of her bedroom.

***

"Alright, I really owe you an apology." Imani suppressed a belch and scooted back from the dining room table. "Dinner was absolutely delicious."

"I don't know why you front like I can't cook." Lance collected their dirty dishes with a knowing smile. "But thanks for the compliment." He paused to kiss the top of her head, and then he proceeded into the kitchen.

As soon as Lance disappeared from view to scrape off the dishes and load the dishwasher, her melancholy mood returned. She got up and grabbed the half-empty wine bottle. "Do you want a refill on your wine?" Imani poured herself another large glass while she waited for his reply.

"Sure, but not too much, I need to be able to drive home tonight."

Imani shrugged, filled his wine glass up halfway, and then she walked into the family room while taking a long sip. Not really knowing where to go, she wandered over to the French doors and stared out into her lushly landscaped backyard.

A few minutes later, she heard Lance enter the family room. But instead of joining her at the patio doors, he plopped down on the couch.

"Is the music okay or would you like me to change it?" she asked with her back to him.

"I got it." She heard him set his wine glass on the table; then he padded over to her stereo. "I feel like the old jazz greats, if that's cool with you?"

"Mm-hmm," she replied as she watched a squirrel scurry across the yard and scramble up a tree. Another one followed behind it. A butterfly flitted past. Then a robin alighted on the deck.

"How about some Coltrane, Sarah Vaughn, Miles, Billie Holiday, and Etta James?"

"Sounds fine." Realistically she couldn't care less. Her mind kept battling back the sorrow that crept in like a cold she couldn't shake.

Somehow, Lance exchanged the CDs and snuck up behind her. "Anything interesting to see?"

She wanted to say, 'all the live things that keep

mocking me, reminding me that Marco's dead,' however, she doubted that would play very well. So, she took a long swig of wine and turned to face him. "Just admiring God's beauty."

He gave her a funny look although he didn't say anything.

Taking another long swallow, she drained her glass. "We can sit down if you want." She gestured towards the couch.

Lance shrugged and led the way.

After he sat down, she parked beside him. This was probably pretty awkward for him and she felt crappy. No matter how much she bluffed to her Mom and Melody, she realized now that today was not the day she should have tried to go it alone. At least Lance was here. She gave him a big smile, grateful for his presence, no matter how awkward.

He returned the smile and patted her leg.

"Thanks for keeping me company," she said, resting her head against his shoulder.

"My pleasure." Lance readjusted and wrapped his arm around her shoulder.

For thirty wonderful minutes they sat there relaxed, listening to musical maestros perform. Their conversational silence felt so comfortable that she hated to break it. However, inklings of sorrow threatened to reemerge and she wanted to ensure they stayed subdued.

"Would you like a refill?" she asked as she swished over to the dining room table with her wine glass in hand.

"No, I'm still good."

"Good," she replied with a chuckle as the last of the wine filled her glass. She waved the empty bottle as she walked back. "Because I seemed to have finished the vino." She set the exhausted bottle on the family room table and toasted her full glass his way. "Guess, you'll have to share mine if you want some more."

She took a long, slow sip letting the grapes caress her tongue. The cinnamon and pepper chased the sharp bite from the tannins before everything smoothed out to silk. The sorrow retreated further.

"You know what's so sad?" she asked abruptly.

"What?" Lance raised an eyebrow.

"How so many of our artistic greats succumb to the evils of drugs," she said walking towards him. "I mean look at Bird, Lady Day, Dorothy Dandridge, hell, even Richard Pryor." She set her glass on the coffee table and dropped onto the couch beside him.

"It's not just our people, not by a long stretch." Lance's eyes seemed to sparkle. "So many musicians, actors, and even athletes—who should know better—partake."

"I know. It's like some twisted prerequisite to becoming a member of the artistically gifted club. To tap into this highly creative state, it's essential that you're a tortured soul who can barely exist in the real world." Her hands dramatized her words. "The pain of life's burdens must cripple you to the degree where you can't function sober."

"Should I be concerned about you?" Lance's eyes

twinkled with a mischievous glint.

"Hell, no!" She hit him and gave him a playful glower. "I'm just commenting on some of the musical artists *you* chose to play."

"Yeah, remind me to put on Dizzy Gillepsie and Duke Ellington next time." He chuckled, then turned and leaned back, enjoying the music again.

Wanting to stretch out, too, she lay down with her head resting on his lap.

***

Unconsciously, he started to stroke her head. He didn't even notice until her silky, hair tickled his fingers. Long gone were the twists and knots that she used to wear. Now she sported two-inch locks of soft, natural looking curls or rocked the hot, short styles that Halle Berry, Nia Long, and Eva Pigford made fashionable. Not everyone had a face designed to pull that off, but Imani easily made the styles sizzling, strong, and oh so very sexy. "Do you ever wear your hair like you did in college anymore?"

She chuckled. "No, I finally surrendered to Corporate America."

"Say it ain't so," he replied giving in to her frequent use of slang.

"Yep, strong sista girl assimilated. I be's one of them now." She rolled onto her back to look up at him, semi-serious. "You know as long as I wanted to stay in the lab running compounds and testing, my hair was fine. But start wanting to interact with customers and other Big Wigs in the company and you get funny stares or comments about your hair."

"You ever compare notes with Trevor?" he asked thinking about Trev's shoulder-length dreadlocks.

"Oh, yeah!" Imani giggled. "He quit his first job because he was so unhappy with the lack of advancement opportunities."

Lance considered his own short, wavy fade haircut. His grooming had never come into question at JPMorgan Chase. Then he thought about all the brothers who emulated the sports stars and rappers with their big fros one minute and intricately braided cornrows the next. Try as hard as they might to make it part of the American lexicon, it would never become acceptable in the boardroom. Even Jay-Z and Diddy were clean-shaven. The most successful ones in business always were.

Billie began *Good Morning Heartache* and Imani popped up. "Please dance with me, I absolutely love this song!" She pulled him to his feet and into the middle of the family room.

In a second they rocked comfortably together to the music. Imani sang a soft accompaniment to Lady Day.

"Wait a minute," he said, giving her a solemn look after most of the song had played. "Are you trying to say something about me with that song selection?" He smiled and waited for her smart aleck response.

Her eyes rested on his. They were a little too serious, intense yet sexy beyond belief. "I guess it's partly true since you never left me in the middle of the night." She closed her eyes and nestled back into his body without missing a beat.

Thoughts of their one night of passion entered unbidden into his head. His voice softened, full of regret. "No, I guess I didn't."

Surprisingly, Imani failed to notice his mood change.

***

Etta James' husky powerhouse voice began *At Last*.

Imani smiled. Weird how the wine, Lance's comforting arms, and the song mixed together, leaving her feeling safe and grateful. She raised her head off Lance's chest to thank him for coming by again.

"I'm," she paused to take a deep breath, but the cleansing exhale never came. With the deep inhale, her nose so close to his neck, she could smell Lance's natural aroma mingling exotically with the Eternity.

How could the same cologne smell so differently depending on who wore it? On one person a fragrance could smell delightful, the next person just okay—nothing to write home about, and on a third it could smell downright putrid.

Eternity always made Marco smell strong, confident, and in control. When she wore it, the scent took on a softer, warm cinnamon undertone. But on Lance—who already possessed strength and confidence in bucket loads—the cologne embodied pure, natural sexuality.

An overwhelming desire to swim in his sexiness overtook Imani. His very pores seemed to dare her to devour every single inch of him. As her heart raced, she glanced up into his beautiful, concerned eyes and wanted to drink him in. Slowly she brought her lips to his. She saw his hesitation, but she pushed further, needing to lose herself in him, to escape from the crushing pain of loss, to feel alive again.

***

Lance responded against his better judgment, wanting to believe Imani wanted him. Although he knew on today of all days, she was merely acting out and he couldn't lead her on, not like this. At the last minute he managed to hold her at bay. "No, Imani. Don't."

"Please, Lance," she whispered in a soothing, seductive siren call. "Please."

Somehow her lips found his. He tried to push away from her heavenly, vanilla-cinnamon-Eternity concoction again, but her hungry lips sucked all doubts from his mind. Voraciously, she stole from his body all the emotions he kept pent up for the last two years. Tired of fighting it, he succumbed. This was the moment he prayed for and dreamed about. His heart-wrenching desire to hold, taste, smell, and feel her took charge.

Their kisses couldn't convey their yearning fast enough. Oh God, he missed her, he missed this. He didn't know how she managed to undo his tie, but it was gone, and her fingers toiled on his shirt buttons. He wanted to help her however, he couldn't pry his fingers off her body. At some point in time his hands slipped under her zippered sweatshirt and caressed a soft, tone waist; a graceful, arched back; and the supple swells of her breasts.

She broke his connection to her beautiful body when she managed to unfasten his buttons and cufflinks. Pulling—almost ripping—his shirt off, she tossed it on the couch and led him upstairs to her bedroom.

Unable to tolerate the loss of body contact, he swept her up into his arms so that the kissing and touching could continue unbridled as he carried her up the remaining stairs and down the hall.

Gentle as a summer breeze, he set her down by the bed. As soon as her feet touched the ground she set to work removing his pants.

***

Imani took a moment to admire Lance's muscular body, his spectacular form, and the crowning glory bulging from his black, cotton boxer briefs. She could almost see the electric current surging through his physique. Every muscle rippling, ready to pounce.

Employing a slow, deliberate pace, she unzipped her sweatshirt and Lance's eyes followed the zipper with an insatiable desire. She slipped off the jacket and let it land on the floor near his pants. With a few seductive moves, she wiggled out of her pants and kicked them off so that they landed by his feet. Confident in his gaze, she proceeded to unhook her bra when he came forward, powerless to resist her tempting striptease any longer.

Lance's fervent kisses burned her skin and made her breath come in ragged gasps. Gently, he lowered them onto the bed and her bra disappeared before they hit the soft, down covers. His loving lips wandered over every inch of her body, a long, languorous walk of exploration and discovery. Finally her body screamed for release and she managed to open her nightstand drawer and remove a condom from the dusty, unused stockpile under her latest John Grisham book.

Lance hurriedly took it from her and unrolled it and she guided him home. Pulling him close she smelled the Eternity again and Marco's face appeared. Not mad, sad, or disappointed, just a beautiful memory that faded into her subconscious like the jet entrails that dissipated into the bright blue sky. Then Lance's delicious, sexy aroma overtook her and she forced him to thrust longer, deeper, and fiercer in a desperate need to lose herself completely with him.

***

Imani's body fueled something primal inside him and he wanted to, needed to claim her until he felt like they truly coexisted as one. The intensity of their coupling drove him wild, made him want to stay locked together forever. Thirty-odd minutes later, he felt her ramping up. He didn't want this to ever end, but the vise-like clamping of her walls around him sent him to his release.

As he came, Lance watched Imani enjoy their simultaneous climax. It commenced with her murmuring his name, continued into a sweet lilting giggle of satisfaction, and then transformed into soft cries and tears of joy.

Moved to the core, he kissed each salty tear that fell from her eyes. He understood her reaction because he felt like she'd breeched every pent-up physical and emotional dam he contained, and released it in an immense watershed.

Feeling protective, he stayed beside her, kissing and soothing until her heaves evened out, regulated, and turned into faint, rhythmic breaths of sleep.

With a smile, he snuggled into Imani, matched her breathing, and soon surrendered to a peaceful sleep with her locked in his arms.

Hours later, he heard strange noises.

Coming wide awake, his eyes tried to adjust to the dark. *Where the hell am I?* His body tingled.

It had been years since he found himself in a strange bed after a night of sex. Little springs of disappointment erupted until he recalled tonight's beautiful memories. *Imani!*

Feeling content, he relaxed once more until he

heard the noises again.

Without moving a muscle, he listened closely, ready to protect the house...until he realized it was just Imani talking in her sleep. He propped his head up on his elbow to hear her better.

"I love you," she murmured.

He smiled. *Finally! After all this time.* As he leaned forward to kiss her beautiful lips and respond likewise, she spoke again in her sleep.

"Marco."

What?!? He pulled back unsure of what he had heard.

As if to answer his request, her sleeping lips repeated it for his benefit. This time there was no confusing her words. "I love you, Marco."

Pissed and hurt, he launched out of bed and paced around. *Oh God, I knew better!* But he had wanted her so much that he foolishly kicked reason to the curb and fell hard...again.

In a huff, he located his underwear, socks, and pants and snatched them on. Half-dressed, he stomped out of her bedroom and down the hall.

For some odd reason thoughts of *Good Morning Heartache* trickled through his mind and he stopped cold at the top of the stairs. Although he wanted to get as far away as possible, he knew he couldn't leave her to awaken alone. But if he didn't release his building anger, he was liable to break something.

Work it off! Her exercise equipment beckoned from the bedroom closest to him. He pivoted and went inside. In twenty seconds flat, he removed his pants and socks and jumped on the treadmill barefoot in his boxer briefs.

Quickly cycling the machine up, he soon broke into a sweat. Pushing his body to its limits, he left behind the angry thoughts until he jogged along at full speed, thinking of nothing except the delicious feel of his body performing like the fine-tooled machine he had trained it to become after years of football.

After forty wonderful, cleansing minutes, he decided to take a shower in her guest bathroom. He redressed, leaving off the sweaty underwear which he stuffed in his pocket, and then he went downstairs to put on his shirt. After finding his tie and cufflinks, he slipped the cufflinks in his other pocket and let the tie dangle freely around his neck.

Checking his watch, he knew that even with breakfast, he would have more than enough time to journey home and change before work. He entered the kitchen, added a second cup to the coffeemaker, and set it to brew earlier. Next he scrounged around her cupboards and fridge until he found the ingredients to fry bacon and make pancakes from scratch. As he flipped the last pancake, Imani entered the kitchen doorway, dressed for work.

"Good morning," she said with an amused smile. "You're up early."

"Morning to you, too," he replied, making a deliberate attempt to keep his emotions in check.

"Smells delicious." Imani set the table for breakfast and poured two cups of coffee.

"Thanks." Lance focused on the pancakes again uncertain of what to expect. He turned off the fire, added the flapjack to the stack, and buttered it. Bringing the full plates of pancakes and draining bacon to the table, he set them beside the syrup. "Bon appetit."

He sat down across from her, prayed, and dug into breakfast, waiting for her to make the first move.

"Mmm, delicious," she moaned taking a bite after her prayer.

"Glad you like it." Their refusal to talk about the large elephant in the room killed him, but he continued to eat while studying her unabashedly.

Imani kept her head down and focused on her meal, almost attacking it. Only after she finished chewing her last bite did the facade crack and crumble. Then the tears fell.

The tears caught him off guard. Even as mad and conflicted as he felt, his heart caught in his throat at the sight of her crying. "Imani, what is it?"

"What are we doing, Lance?"

He sighed and rubbed his hands over his face. "I was kind of hoping you could tell me."

Sadness left her eyes and accusations settled in the vacated space. "How could you let last night happen?"

"*Excuse me?*" No way in hell was she going to pull this again! He shook his head in vehement protest. Back in their junior year—the day after they had experienced heaven together—she had shut down and he responded defensively, and they had lost out on love. It was not going to happen this time, not if he could help it.

But he sure as hell didn't plan on accepting full blame for last night either! "Imani, I tried to stop, but you refused." His eyes narrowed and his nostrils flared. "And you *know* how much I want you. I'm sorry, but that's asking way too much of me."

"So, it's *my* fault that on my anniversary to Marco, I somehow slept with *you*!" She slammed her hand down on the table making her plate and silverware jump with a crash.

"Don't do this," he warned, his deep voice filled with even more bass. He chewed his lip, closed his eyes, and took a cleansing breath. When he reopened his eyes he implored her. "I'll admit the timing wasn't the greatest, Imani. And it didn't help matters, hearing you profess your love to Marco last night while you slept."

"I did?" she asked, her trembling voice quiet as a whisper.

He answered with two, slow nods.

"See, Lance," she said, reaching across the table to take his hands. "I'm not ready for this yet. It's not even been a year since he died."

"It's been eleven months and I know I don't understand what you're going through, but when will you be ready, Imani?" he asked, growing frustrated with the situation. "How long am I supposed to wait?"

"There is no magic number!" She wrenched her hands back and covered her face.

Crap! His shoulders slumped as he walked over knowing that the words hadn't come out right. He stood before her unsure of what to do next. Instinctively, he wrapped her in his arms and hugged her to his waist. "I'm sorry for sounding insensitive."

Imani dropped her hands and pulled him down to his knees so that their eyes locked. "I'm not going to lie, Lance. Last night… well," she cupped his face. "I needed last night. It was absolutely beautiful, just like you."

Yes, finally! His heart almost exploded as she stroked his cheeks.

"And I do love you, Lance. I do." Her eyes pleaded with his and she removed her right hand from his face and placed it over her heart. "But Marco still lives here, too."

Oh God, could she dig the knife in any deeper? His heart filled with such sorrow and pain, that he wanted to roll over and die.

"No, Lance, please don't look away," her voice soothed again and she forced him to meet her eyes. "I feel guilty and horrible for trying to move on. Like I'm dishonoring Marco's memory or downplaying my extreme love for him. So, you must be patient with me. Please?"

He didn't want to give her any more time or any more chances. But his head betrayed him and it nodded. Hurt and disappointed, he turned away, but she pulled his head to her chest and kissed his forehead. Her magical hands rubbed his neck and back until he relented.

Imani would be his, but it would take more time.

At this point he wanted to give her all the time she needed just so they could revisit last night again and again and again. He wasn't sure, though, how much more rejection his heart could handle.

THE HONEYMOON'S OVER

Melody settled into Imani's kitchen chair. Now that her hands were no longer preoccupied with tossing the salad, she wondered if she should sit on them to prevent them from fidgeting.

She glanced at Imani, who multitasked with ease—preparing the jerk chicken for the oven and setting the rice and beans to simmer. At this rate Imani would finish soon, and no doubt, she'd finally grill Melody about her honeymoon.

And therein lied the problem, *what should I tell Imani?* Much to her dismay, the sex had not gotten any better, and it wasn't for lack of trying. She and Chris made love every day during the honeymoon and three times in the week they'd been back home. Regardless, the longest session lasted ten minutes, most averaged only five! Half of her wanted to get Imani's advice on what to do, but the other half…well she didn't want to hear 'I told you so' from Imani.

Too late, she moaned inside as Imani turned around looking deep in thought.

With a long exhale, Imani walked over and stood across the table from Melody. She opened her mouth to speak, paused, and then drummed her fingers on the table.

"Look," Imani said then she dropped her head and appeared to study her hands. "It's only because you made such a big deal about keeping secrets from you before that I'm even considering telling you this. If it were up to me, this would go with me to the grave."

Huh? Melody frowned. *What in the world is she talking about?*

"I have a confession to make." Imani's head snapped up, her eyes flashed with defiance. "I slept with Lance. On my anniversary…to Marco."

"What?" Melody's mouth fell open. She didn't know whether to feel shocked or upset. "Imani!"

Imani shrugged in defeat. "You and my mom were correct. That was not the time to attempt to go it alone." She raised her hand up in a stop motion. "And before you even go there, there was no way I was going to be a third wheel on your honeymoon. Please!" Imani shook her head. "But I shouldn't have cancelled my trip with my mother either."

"So what happened?" she asked, still unable to believe it.

"I basically had a meltdown in the bathroom when Lance found me—don't ask." She wagged her finger. "Then I felt melancholy and depressed, so I drank too much wine, and after moping around a bit more, I pretty much jumped Lance."

"Oh my God, and now you're regretting it."

"Actually," replied Imani, she looked up at the ceiling then her eyes met Melody's and they softened. "I don't. I'm not gonna lie, it felt *so good*. With all the emotions and junk I had bottled up inside…I guess I needed the release." The lust left Imani's eyes and despair took its place. "But our timing sucks!" She threw her hands in the air. "Seriously, of all the days for that to happen, my anniversary? It couldn't get much worse." Imani shook her head and sighed.

"So what are you guys going to do?" she asked wondering how she could help.

Imani looked even more depressed as she shrugged. "I don't know, Melody. I'm so confused." She put her hands on her head and groaned. "What are your thoughts?"

Hmm, that was a first. Imani never asked for advice. Melody managed not to show her surprise. "Do you love him?"

Perplexed, Imani knitted her eyebrows. "I guess...I don't know... sometimes I think I do, but..." Imani waved her hand in dismay. "This is Lance we're talking about."

"True," she replied with a side nod.

"I mean, the qualities we loved in school are back in full force. He's protective," Imani said, her hands emphasizing her words. "When he's around I feel like nothing can hurt me. He's a loyal and caring friend." Imani chuckled. "Plus his humor is as crazy as ever, so we're always joking on each other."

"But?" Melody asked, not hearing the downside yet.

"That's just it; I can't put my finger on the 'but' anymore." Imani sighed. "For instance, we always hated his womanizing ways. However, if we believe his claim of prolonged abstinence—which I can't say I doubt, then that's no longer a negative."

"I swear he's been over here practically every night since Marco…" Melody deliberately didn't finish the sentence. "Right?"

"Yeah, he's only missed literally a handful of times." Imani counted off on her fingers. "Tonight's one, the time Mrs. Cabrette and my mom came up to clean out Marco's things is two, and the three nights during his series of interviews."

"Well, come on, Imani! If you ask me, whenever a guy spends that much time with you—well, that's love." Melody smirked and crossed her arms. "Especially when that guy is Lance."

Imani cracked up laughing. "Yep, you got a point there."

Melody joined in Imani's laughter and then she decided to go for broke. "Well, since you were so forthcoming, I guess I'll do the same." A lump appeared in her throat and she found it hard to swallow.

Imani's eyebrow arched, but she didn't speak.

"Please don't say, 'I told you so' at any time during this, okay?"

"I promise—"

They both heard someone at the front door fumble with the doorknob.

Alarmed, she turned to Imani, ready to run or defend herself if needed. "Who has a key to your house or is somebody breaking in?"

"Lance is the only one with a key," Imani replied

while staring at the door with a look of concern.

"I thought you told him not to come over tonight?"

Imani shot her an annoyed look. "I did! I said you wanted a Girls Night and he said he planned on hitting the gym with Bobby and then going home to watch TV or a movie."

The door lock disengaged and the door swung open.

"I can always tell him to leave," Imani whispered.

Lance entered, shut the door, spotted them, and broke into a big smile. "Hello, Ladies. Mmm, smells good, what's cooking?" He bounded over and kissed Imani on the cheek.

"Jerk chicken, rice and beans, and salad." Imani shot Lance a perturbed frown, but he already headed over to greet Melody, so she took the opportunity to check on the chicken and stir the rice and beans. "Although there's enough food for three, we were only planning on dinner for two."

Evidently Lance didn't catch Imani's hint because he was too preoccupied encapsulating Melody in a huge bear hug. He didn't spin her around in circles like normal, probably because of the lack of open space, but he did swing her off her feet a bit and she held on for dear life. "And how are you, Mrs. Weaver?" he asked, his deep voice tickling her spine.

Just when she was about to run out of air from his unyielding embrace, he set her down. After taking a deep inhale, she answered. "Fine, when you're not suffocating me!" She smiled.

Lance chuckled then prepared to kick back and

relax. "So, what's going on?"

"Well, before you so rudely interrupted our Ladies Only Night, Melody was about to confess some deep, dark secret." Imani placed her free hand on her hip.

"D'oh," he said smacking his forehead. "I totally forgot that you told me to make myself scarce." He looked from one to the other, apprehension on his face. "Do you want me to leave? Because I could, no problem."

Imani looked at Melody. "It's your call."

"I don't know why I even bothered trying to talk to one of you alone." She shook her head as she sat back down. "I should have known better." She gave him a wink. "Of course you can stay, Lance."

"Whew," he wiped the non-existent sweat from his forehead. "Thank goodness."

Setting the serving spoon down on the counter, Imani cut right to the chase. "Now that that's settled, you were saying?"

With the spotlight focused on her, Melody wasn't sure how to proceed and she shifted in her seat. Small fires set her cheeks ablaze.

"Spit it out already," Imani said waving her hands in circles to indicate that Melody needed to move it along.

"Fine!" With a deep exhale, she stared at Imani. "Promise you won't say I told you so—"

"We already went through this," Imani fussed. "Yeah, yeah, I promise."

Lance chuckled and got comfortable in the chair next to Imani.

"Unfortunately, you were right," she said bracing for their response. "Sex with Chris has been, let's say, less than fulfilling."

"Come again?" Lance's eyebrow rose to precipitous heights.

True to her word, Imani remained silent.

"Each time, Chris is done in three to ten strokes. Our longest session was maybe five minutes of actual sex."

"Hm, that sounds like it could be a medical issue," Lance replied with a grimace.

"Yep, what do they call that, premature ejaculation?" Imani asked Lance.

"La la la la, not listening," replied Lance putting one hand to his ear and holding the other out in an effort to stop Imani from talking.

Imani sucked her teeth and rolled her eyes. "So much for hoping you'd matured." When she finished, she gazed at Melody. "Do you think it's medical, too?"

"Maybe," she replied with a sigh. "I just don't understand. It's not for lack of passion. His kisses are breathtaking, passionate, and perfect. But then it feels like an inexperienced adolescent plays body snatchers with my husband. And this poor kid doesn't understand the first thing about foreplay or making the moment last, he's just excited to get his rocks off. And literally five to ten minutes later, just as I'm starting to warm up, he's done."

"Actually, if that's the case, you might be able to train him," Imani said.

"How's that?" Lance asked before she could say the same thing.

Imani gave them an exasperated sigh. "When you first start running, you don't decide to run a marathon on your second day."

"Oh-kay," Lance drawled, seemingly as confused as she was.

Speaking in a tone that a kindergarten teacher would utilize when trying to teach a five-year old, Imani expounded further. "Build up his stamina and endurance just as a runner would. Practice and go further each day." She could tell that they were at least getting the analogy.

"For example, let him get worked up for a minute or two and then stop. Force him to settle down, regain his cool, lose his erection, and then go to work again. The more you tease and stop him before he comes, hopefully the longer you train him to go over time. If it works, he's learned to prolong the act."

"Wouldn't that give him blue balls?" Melody wondered aloud.

Lance chuckled. "It might increase his level of frustration initially. However, as long as he finally gets to, as you said, 'get his rocks off,' then he should be fine. In fact," he said turning to Imani, "it sounds like a fun experiment."

Imani glared at him and muttered what Melody figured were curses under her breath.

It didn't appear that Lance heard the words either, but he nonetheless laughed and returned his attention to Melody. "So when are you going to begin

Operation Extend?"

"Seriously, you're naming it!" Melody looked at him aghast and then she turned to Imani for support.

"Don't look at me; you wanted his ridiculous behind to stay." Imani crossed her arms.

"Ugh!" Melody gave up and decided to answer his question with a question. "How exactly should I approach this?"

"Well, you don't want to go home and tell Chris, 'sorry, but your lovemaking sucks!' That tact tends to demoralize a man. Attacking a man's manhood, not so good."

Imani hit him in the shoulder. "Of course, she's not going to do that." It looked like she held her tongue not to call him a name before she refocused on Melody. "Look, you've got the perfect excuse. You're still in the honeymoon phase for at least six more months. Plus, you even admitted that you two never went far past kissing."

Melody nodded. A strange tingle of excitement coursed through her body.

"So, exploration and adventure as you get to know each other is expected and encouraged. Let him know you want to try something new each time. Ask him where and how he wants you to touch him. And you damn well better tell him how and where to touch you! Don't be afraid to take his hand and guide him and vice versa. You understand?"

"Yes, ma'am," she said unable to suppress a giggle. Although the suggestions were well outside her comfort zone, she looked forward to…hmm, 'expanding her horizons.' But as Lance mentioned, guys interpreted things differently and she wanted to be sure this would work. "You agree, Lance? Will this fly with Chris?"

"Are you kidding me?" He gave her an incredulous smile. "Humph! Chris now has a hot, young wife that not only wants sex, but she also wants to get freaky-deaky? Yeah, I'm not seeing the problem here." He stroked his goatee and studied Imani. "You sound like you've done this a time or two before. Anything you'd like to share?"

"In your dreams," she replied through clenched teeth. Then she popped up and checked the food. "Dinner's done!"

DEATH ANNIVERSARY – JULY 2007

For whatever reason, the burden of oppressive sadness did not encumber Imani this morning. It should have. Today was the first anniversary of Marco's death. She frowned and wondered why she wasn't laying in bed comatose. As she reflected on the events of that dreadful day, her mind mercifully repressed the image of Marco at the accident site. Try as she might, only peaceful, loving warmth encompassed her from head to toe.

Annoyed, she finished getting ready for work and then decided to call the Cabrettes. When she picked up the receiver to dial, an icy tingle slid down her spine. With a shudder, she pushed down the unpleasant feeling and dialed their number.

Mr. Cabrette answered on the third ring, his voice weak and strained. "I was going to call you next Imani, Bella."

Imani tried to swallow the lump in her throat.

"Mama is gone, Imani." Fresh sobs caused his voice to crack. "Her heart gave out this morning."

Imani couldn't tell whose cries were louder.

"She woke up early and patted my hand, then she went back to sleep and never woke up."

"Papa, I'm so sorry." Words couldn't convey her

sorrow. *God what else can I say or do?*

"You know I loved Mama since the very first time I spotted her in the old country. I was seven and this beautiful, fiery four-year-old moved in next door. I always knew we would be together. And now almost sixty years later, I can't bear the thought of being without her."

"What are you saying, Papa?" Tears slipped down hot and fast as her hand gripped the phone so tight that her knuckles turned white.

"I was supposed to die first, Imani, not her. Then again, Marco was supposed to die well after both of us." His voice became stronger. "You know Marco would want you to be happy, Imani. It's no good for you to stop loving and living."

"Humph!" She couldn't believe his audacity. "Wait, you want me to move on and live, yet you're saying that you're not going to do the same? I'm sorry, Papa, but that sounds a tad hypocritical to me." Imani wanted to hug him and beat some sense into him at the same time.

Mr. Cabrette managed a small chuckle. "Ah, you got me there, Bella. However, the difference is that I am an old man—"

"Sixties aren't old," she interrupted. "Eighties or nineties maybe, but not now, you have so much life left." Tears of frustration followed their earlier sorrowful brethren.

"I've lived a good, long life, Imani. We did and saw everything we wanted. But you have not. Mama and I shared over fifty years of friendship and love.

Promise me you will try to find love again, Imani."

Imani refused to answer.

"See, stubborn and strong. Just like Maria." He chuckled again. "Both of you will flourish, of that I have no doubt." He hesitated, his voice lost in reflection. "Marco always said you had Mama's unbreakable spirit. Please honor her memory and his by shining your light and sharing it with others.

Imani nodded before the words followed. "I promise, Papa."

Five days later, she stood beside Maria and Papa as they buried Mrs. Cabrette.

One month later she returned to bury him.

SEX AND BABIES – AUGUST 2007

Candles flickered along the back of the bathtub and Melody sighed before she leaned forward and extinguished them. Things were improving but still too slowly for her liking.

She left the bathroom and joined a sleeping Chris in their bed. At least Imani and Lance were right about one thing; Chris loved all of the sex. He eagerly accommodated each request.

Melody gazed at him before she snuggled beside him. However, since she didn't want to control every single session, working feverishly to prolong the experience, she let him lead about half the time. So, although they accomplished a 100% improvement, going from five minutes to ten minutes, it still wasn't near enough.

With one last sigh, Melody closed her eyes and welcomed sleep. At least they were actively trying for a baby. Maybe all the extra effort would pay off someday soon.

GOOD NEWS – SEPTEMBER 2007

Lance fumbled the key twice before sliding it home in Imani's front door lock, the dozen, yellow roses in his hand hindering his progress. Anxious to share the news, he barely shut the door behind him in his eagerness to find her.

"Hey, there!" Imani welcomed him from the kitchen. A huge grin covered her face.

"Well, someone looks really happy. Hopefully these will make you even happier," he said handing her the bouquet.

"Yellow roses?" Imani looked surprised as she took the bouquet.

Lance swore he spotted a hint of sadness in her eyes and he thought he heard her mumble, "the last time I held one was…" But her voice choked off as she inhaled the bouquet.

However, when she looked up and placed the bouquet on the kitchen counter, Imani beamed from ear to ear. "To what do I owe this pleasure?"

"I figured red would be too presumptuous. Yellow means friendship and that's what you are to me," he replied as he came over for their customary hug. With Imani wrapped in his arms, he kissed her forehead. After their never again mentioned tryst two months ago, he'd begun to sneak in innocent kisses, without any protest from Imani.

She surprised him by kissing his cheek before pulling away. "I've got some great news."

"Hmm, okay, well so do I, but ladies first," he said with a slight bow.

"You sure?"

"Of course," he replied with a smile and a nod.

"Well, you know that big project I've been working on for months?"

"Yes, the one where you're using the new analysis software."

"Wow, you really do listen to me." She laughed. "Well, my boss called me into his office this afternoon. Not only is the project viable and getting the green light, but they want me as the Project Manager!"

"Get out of here!" He gave her a high-five. "So, how many patents do you expect to see your name on?"

"Oh, my God, you really do listen!"

"Alright, keep it up," he replied as he shook his finger and chuckled.

"Okay, okay, I'm sorry," she said with a mischievous smile. "So, what's your big news?"

"Well, I got a phone call from ESPN—"

"No way," she interrupted jumping up and down. "Did you get the job?"

He smiled. "You're looking at the latest college analyst."

Imani shrieked and then leapt into his arms. At

first he assumed it was for a congratulatory hug, but then her lips locked on his…and remained there for two seconds too long.

When she stepped back with a coy look on her face, he couldn't do or say anything.

"I'm ready," she announced.

Ready? His heart jumped in his throat at her words. But then he caught himself. *Ready for what?* Although he wanted to believe her kiss meant she was ready for them, this was Imani, and she could just as easily mean she was ready to eat dinner. He watched her enjoy his confusion, her smile sliding from coy to mischievous. She'd never make anything easy. No worries, two could play this game. "Ready for?" he asked, his voice steady.

"For us," she replied, her eyes sparkling like diamonds.

"Are you sure?" When things sounded too good to be true, they usually were. Instinctively, he felt like there was some hidden catch.

Imani shrugged and that gave him pause. "Yeah, I guess."

A frown creased his brows. "You guess?" He shook his head, his voice still calm. "Imani, Baby, I'm *sure* how I feel about you. I'd rather wait until you feel the same way instead of settling for a shrug and an, 'I guess.'"

"Fine," she replied. In a split second, she stepped forward and wrapped her arms around his neck. Her intense eyes locked with his. By the time she said, "I'm ready," her lips connected with his and then he lost all cognizant thought.

Automatically his body responded to her hot embrace, her tender lips that consumed him. Flames leapt within him as if she'd struck a match to his tinder box. A powder keg of explosives ignited. She became his fuel and like a greedy fire, he needed her. Her body responded to his and the next thing he knew his very essence stood alert.

Imani pulled back abruptly. "I'm not ready for that yet."

Lance could barely comprehend her comment. The sudden stop made him feel like a fish out of water gasping for air. All of his fire deprived of oxygen. He hated that her kisses made coherent thinking impossible and breathing so ridiculously difficult. Taking a concerted effort to inhale, his response came out sharp and ragged. "When?"

He realized too late that it sounded harsh even to his ears.

Livid flames shot into Imani's eyes. "I don't know when!"

His hands motioned for her to settle down. But now that they were on the topic, he needed to mentally prepare his little buddy for the long haul. "Are we talking days, weeks, months," he paused hoping that she didn't suggest the next option, years.

"There isn't a timeframe!" Her arms flew to her hips. "Or is there, Lance?" Imani's neck got in on the action, too. "If I don't tell you what you want to hear, are you going to cheat on me now like you did with Heather? Are my days numbered?"

"Heather?" Lance stopped listening once he heard his ex-wife's name. He only saw red. "So, what you're saying is that you're going to promise me sex and then withhold it?" His eyes narrowed as she crossed her arms. "Or worse yet, are you saying you're really a whining, nagging gold digger who plans to shop my wallet dry?"

"You know what, Lance," Imani replied, voice icy as a glacier, death beams shooting from her eyes. She over annunciated each word, extending the delivery for eons. "Fuck you!"

It felt like she slapped him and his head rocked back. Pissed, his mouth opened for an automatic retaliation, but just as quick he decided it was beneath him to even dignify her with a response. His tongue flicked across his teeth then his jaw clenched tight enough to crack walnuts. His right hand raised into a stop sign before his fingers clenched into a ball.

Imani knew how much he hated profanity. Growing up, his mother cursed like a sailor and even at a young age, he always believed there were better ways to express yourself. Especially when it came to that vulgar word, the one Imani knew he detested.

As he glared at her, she returned his stare ten-fold. Without uttering a word, her stance dared him to say or do anything.

Fine! If that's how she felt, he could take a hint. He was through fighting and caring. Done playing games. He took one step backwards ready to leave and never return when a quiet voice bubbled forth from deep within. 'Don't give up now, she doesn't mean it.'

Lance swore if the voice were coming from a tiny angel standing on his right shoulder, he would have taken his fingers and flicked it hard to kingdom come.

As the immense wrongness of that thought sunk in, it stopped him dead in his tracks. If he wanted to intentionally maim an angel, what further irrational behavior was he capable of in his current raging state?

Exhaustion flooded his body and left it drained. As his shoulders slumped, it took every ounce of his waning strength to look at Imani. He half-raised his arms in a resigned shrug. "What the hell, Imani?" he asked in a subdued plea.

Although she didn't answer, Imani's defensive stance softened. It almost looked like she wanted to apologize. However, he could tell that just one wrong word or move on his part, would send her straight back on the warpath.

Weighing the risks, he spoke again, hoping to gain some clarity. "When I came over, we were both thrilled. You even told me you were ready, and for one brief moment it felt like you were. Then somehow…" he gestured, "it devolved into this mess. What happened?"

"You basically called me a screeching, sniveling gold digger because I wouldn't have sex with you." Contrary to her inflammatory words, she spoke to him as if they were in the midst of a normal conversation. No accusatory tone, no dramatic head weaving or finger waving.

Careful to match her tone, he replied in a calm voice. "It's because you ridiculously compared yourself to Heather." His right hand rubbed his head. "I'm still perturbed that you put that wretched image in my mind." When his hand dropped, his eyes narrowed. "Why in the world did you even mention her at all?"

"Ah, because she was your wife." The sarcasm crept in and her hand readjusted on her hip.

"No, she's past history and I'd rather you not mention her name again."

"Are you kidding me?" Imani stared at him perplexed rather than pissed. "Marco's in the past, too, but I'm going to keep saying his name. I'll always cherish every single memory."

"That's different," he replied, almost cutting her off. Although her words stung and he wished she could one day get over Marco, he couldn't hold it against her. "You lost Marco in a senseless accident. I divorced Heather."

"Regardless, you married her."

"And I keep telling you that was a mistake!"

"What's to say that I'm not a mistake? And regardless, mistake or not, if you cheated on her why should I believe you won't cheat on me?"

Exasperated, he threw up his hands. "Because you're nothing like her!"

"You say that now, but what prevents you from saying that about me in the future?"

He glared at her. "I said, I won't!"

Imani let out a heavy sigh. "Look, Lance," she

said, her eyes beseeching him. "You understand that I could never forgive you, if you cheated, right?"

"Of course." His nostrils flared again. *What was with her constant questioning, accusations, and distrust?*

"Trust reigns supreme with me." She shook her head. "I don't do doubt and jealousy well, nor do I want to become accustomed to it in my life. If there's even an inkling of that side left in you, we need to end this immediately." Tears slipped from her eyes.

Man, those tears of hers get me every time! Immediately his defensiveness dropped and his body relaxed. "Is that what you think?" He tried to pull her into his chest, but she was having none of it.

He sighed in exasperation. *Why did she insist on dwelling on the past? Why couldn't they just move forward?* "Look, I admit I've experienced more than enough easy women to last two lifetimes. But you have to see that's not what I want now."

They stared at each other for the longest time. Imani's eyebrows knitted sweaters as she processed his words.

Finally, he reached out and pulled her over. "Why can't you get it through your thick skull that *you* make all the difference?" He caressed her face.

"How many times and ways do I need to tell you that I love only you? Yearn for only you. Need only you." He stopped and looked at her in disbelief. "You can't possibly be insecure?"

"Why not?' she asked, her eyes issuing a challenge.

"Imani, you're all I want. Please believe I'm never going to cheat on you." His hands tightened around her face as he pleaded. "You have to trust me on this one. Can you do that?"

"Okay," she replied soft as a whisper.

"So, are we good again?"

Imani nodded and he managed a faint smile before he gave her a peck. Neither of them seemed energized enough to take it any further.

"Good." Feeling completely drained, he dropped his hands and plopped down in the nearest kitchen chair.

Imani followed and sat on his lap.

Once she got settled he took her hand. "You know I hate all this drama and fighting."

"So do I," she replied as she played with his fingers.

"Then why do we do it?"

"I don't know."

"Did you and Marco fight?" He hated to ask because it meant yet another comparison that he wasn't living up to in her eyes.

"No, very rarely." Imani refused to look at him and her fingers increased their pace across his palm.

'What's the difference now,' he wanted to ask, but that would only take them further down this interminable rabbit hole. Regardless, if she lived peaceably before, that meant she could do it again. "Can we make a pact to never fight anymore?"

Imani snorted. "Never is a very long time, Lance."

When he didn't respond, she finally stopped

playing with his hand and looked him in the eye. "Are you serious?"

"Deadly," he replied, wanting the arguments to end.

"You really believe the two of us can quit arguing?"

"I promise to try my best, Imani."

Imani huffed out her disbelief and shook her head. "Then I'll try, too."

Lance smiled and held Imani tight. Deep down, he prayed that their best was good enough.

YOU SURE? – OCTOBER 2007

Melody watched Xavier squirm around on Trev's lap in an attempt to stave off sleep. It was amazing how much the little six-month old looked and acted like his big brother, Trevor, Jr. Xavier's big eyes kept focusing on her and she swore the little cutie reached out begging for her to save him.

Not able to take more and wanting to hold a little life in her arms, she walked over to Trev with her hands out. After four months of trying at least four times a week with Chris, she still wasn't pregnant and it weighed heavily on her mind. "Here, I'll take him."

Trev gave Melody a curious look, "I got him." He snuggled Xavier in his lap to the little boy's delight. "This is my other little mini-me."

"Yeah and you can play with him anytime," she replied, putting a hand on her hip like Imani. "I don't get to see him often enough." She threw her arms out again. "So hand the little cutie over."

Eyebrow arched, Trev looked her up and down. "You sure you're ready for him?"

"Oh, please," she said, "hand him over already." She rescued the little boy from Trev's arms and he promptly grabbed a fistful of her long, blonde locks in his grubby, little hands. "Uh, a little help here, please," she implored Trev.

"Naw, you're all big and bad. You handle it." Trev leaned back, getting comfortable on the couch with a huge grin plastered on his face.

Imani bustled down the stairs and into the family room, eyeing the situation as she headed towards the kitchen. "I thought you were putting the baby to sleep?"

"Ouch! Ouch!" Melody cried as Xavier excitedly yanked her hair.

It took everything in Trevor not to bust out laughing at the sight. But his valiant efforts to contain the laughter caused his face to contort like crazy.

"Trev, quit making faces laughing at me and help loosen his grip," she begged.

Ignoring her pleas, he addressed Imani instead as she returned with a baby bottle. "Yo, how's my wifey and son?"

"Erycah's resting comfortably and Lil' Trev is already sound asleep." Imani waited for Melody to sit back in her chair with Xavier before she handed her the bottle. "However, I really don't understand why Erycah insists on staying here when she's so sick."

"Well, for one, we just got here an hour ago." Trev looked at Melody and cracked up as she slowly disentangled the fingers of the baby's right hand from her tresses. Xavier kept a firm grip on her hair with his left hand while he greedily took the bottle with his right. She sighed and gave up.

Imani shook her head and grabbed a seat on the couch beside Trevor.

"Two, she'd rather fall asleep in your guest room, proud that she got out of the house, rather than suffer at home alone like she usually does. Three it's just her mid-morning slash afternoon sickness; it normally passes after a little nap."

"I still can't believe you got her pregnant again that fast." Melody shook her head both amazed and appalled. Erycah was already two months along and Xavier here was barely six months old. Somehow it didn't seem fair, especially since they weren't even trying. Maybe a smidgeon of their potent fertility would rub off on her.

"They like to keep 'em barefoot and pregnant in Jamaica, eh Mon?" Imani teased.

"Hey, I'd have a whole Marley clan if I could, minus the illegitimate ones," replied Trev with a wink. "But we agreed on three or four."

Melody wrinkled her nose. "You're on three now, which one is it, three or four?"

"If this one's a girl for Erycah, we'll stop. Otherwise, we'll roll the dice one more time."

"Poor woman, possibly stuck with four of your crazy clones running around the house, tearing it up." Imani tsked at Trev.

"Now you understand why Erycah doesn't want to go home." Trev patted Imani's arm. "Hey, when you finally start shooting out some babies of your own, there'll come a time when you'll long for date nights and adult company."

"I don't need to shoot out any babies," Imani replied as she arched an eyebrow. "You're shooting out enough for me, Melody, and half the neighborhood!"

Imani dodged as Trev tried to pop her with a decorator pillow. "Look, I told y'all I'm more than happy to watch the little rugrats one or two times a month. At least I know I can always give them back when they terrorize my house too much."

Melody snickered while Trev smirked.

Imani held up her hand. "However, that offer is only valid on the first two carpet climbers. You're going to have to deal with numbers three and four on your own."

"Gee, thanks!" Trev said before he elbowed Imani.

The phone rang and Imani half rose off the couch and then stopped. "Actually, Melody can you read the Caller ID from there? I don't feel like talking on the phone while entertaining company. Even if the company's just you two."

"Oh, please!" She stuck her tongue out then glanced at the phone on the nearby end table. "It's your Mom," she replied feeding and rocking Xavier, whose big eyes kept closing as he began to lose his fight against sleep.

"Forget it. I'll call her back later." Imani waved her hand dismissively and snuggled into the couch. "She's just going to start in on Lance again and I don't feel like hearing it."

Trevor and Melody exchanged a quick look, but it

wasn't fast enough to escape Imani's eagle eyes.

Imani studied them both, looking from one to the other. "Something y'all not telling me?"

"I'm not saying anything." Trev sat back and shook his head.

Imani knitted her brows. "But that statement in and of itself speaks volumes."

"Lance seems to have truly changed," Melody replied trying to give Trev an out.

Imani reared around towards her. "Meaning what exactly?"

She shrugged. "Meaning, maybe he's really not the same old Lance that we knew."

"What the hell?" Imani lost it. "You're the one that's been acting as his personal cheerleader and champion, asking me to give the boy a chance. Now you're talking out of the side of your face?"

Xavier squirmed in his sleep as if he innately felt Melody's discomfort. Her cheeks burned as she tried to explain her way out of Imani's line of fire. "Well, the situation was different a couple of months ago, he was always here. Now that he's broadcasting…"

"Look Imani, we all know the brother's history of playing around. Before and after he got married." Trev faced Imani and helped rescue Melody, much to her relief. "We're just saying be careful."

"Yo, guys. I don't need this grief!" Imani ran her fingers through her hair exasperated. "Things were so easy with Marco. I never worried about him stepping out or playing games." She glared at Trev. "Is there something you guys witnessed that you're not telling me about?"

"No, nothing like that, nothing recent." Trev shook his head. "But the boy just seemed shady to me when I spotted him in your bed, the day after Marco died."

"And I explained that to you already. It was innocent," Melody replied, actually coming to Lance's defense again. The constant back and forth wondering if Lance was or wasn't cheating, made her head spin. Half the time she trusted him and half the time she didn't and she hated the uncertainty.

"Well, you weren't in the room when Mrs. Jordan and I saw him, Melody. He looked guilty as hell."

"Ah, come on, Trev," Imani said as she slapped Trev's knee, trying to lighten the mood. "You know my Moms can make you feel guilty about nothing at all, with just one look."

"Yeah, that's for damn sure," Trev admitted. "I know I never want to be on the other side of her glare."

"She's definitely got a way about her looks that her daughter seemed to inherit, too," Melody murmured with a chuckle.

Imani threw her one of her famous looks just to make a point.

"Look I'm really not knocking the guy," Trev said trying to explain. "You know I've been friends with him for as long as y'all."

"I know," Imani replied while Trev locked gazes.

"And I've never seen him pine over someone like he appears to do for you. But all those years of playing around being a world-class ho are hard to ignore." He shrugged his shoulders. "I mean the history of infidelity exists. Do you really know how many times he cheated on Heather?"

"At least once that we know about for sure," Melody replied with a shudder. If Lance hadn't decided to cheat that night, maybe the 'incident' never would have occurred. Automatically her mind reversed course so as not to dwell on yet another life or death situation in her past.

"Do you really know who or what he's done since he quit talking to you after your wedding?" Trev asked.

"No, I really don't." Imani sighed. "And I know that he cheated on Heather more than once." Imani shook her head. The action looked like she did it more to convince herself than to convince them.

"This past year, he's been so different, though." Imani patted her hand against her chest. "I can feel it in my heart." Imani waved her hand. "But as to his actions prior to Marco's death, I can't truthfully comment on them. Although he swears that he only worked, exercised, and watched TV. He supposedly never went out with anyone."

"Lance? No sex for two years?" Trev let out a disbelieving grunt. "See, that's what I find hard to believe."

"Actually, Imani and I talked to him about that a couple of times and we're inclined to believe him," she replied before she noticed Trev glaring at her as if to say, 'you're not helping.'

Imani exhaled a forceful gust of air. "The last thing I need in my head is any doubt about Lance. Especially when the concerns are coming from two of my closest friends." Imani glared at them. "It's making me second guess myself, wondering if maybe I read Lance incorrectly."

"We're not saying that Lance *definitely is* cheating or playing games," she said to clarify their position.

"But with all of the newfound celebrity, the travel, the groupies in the hotel rooms, he's back in the environment where he played around the most." Trev shrugged. "We just want you to take it slow and make sure he's on the up and up. Alright?"

Imani nodded slowly; as if it helped their words burrow in deeper.

"Just be careful, Imani." Wanting to lighten the mood, she decided to give Imani a taste of her own advice. "You know a good friend once told me to demand more."

It worked.

Melody chuckled as Imani rolled her eyes.

SURPRISE, SURPRISE

Imani couldn't wait to see Lance's face. Especially after last night's phone call. He always called each night to say how much he missed her when he left to work the college games.

This week he was in Los Angeles, prepping for Saturday's game between Arizona and USC. But for the first time, he had complained about how lonely nights were on the road. For Imani, that was all it took.

With a wave, she flagged the hotel shuttle, embarked, stowed her rolling carry-on suitcase, and smiled at how well everything fell into place. On a whim last night after his call, she checked the airfares. The first search results produced a weekend getaway special at a price she couldn't refuse. So without a second thought, she decided to surprise Lance and fly from Albany, NY to L.A. to keep him company.

Tonight Lance wouldn't have to rely on a phone call. She would be there in person, helping him sleep soundly, snuggled in his arms. Reclining back into the seat, she smiled again as the shuttle ride from LAX airport to the Hilton zoomed by in a parade of palm trees, offices, and industrial buildings.

Arriving on a balmy October ocean breeze, she strolled into the Hilton like she knew where she was going. Actually, she did. Since Lance didn't suspect anything, he hadn't thought twice about giving her his room number last night so that she could call him directly. With a grin, she followed the signs to the elevator bank and pushed the button for his floor.

As the elevator ascended, her heart beat faster in anticipation of the look on Lance's face when he opened the door.

Anxious and nervous, she stopped at the signs indicating the room numbers and wiped her hands on her skirt. "Settle down," she fussed as she hurried along the luxurious hallway, her suitcase rolling smoothly behind her.

Halting at room 1207, she took a deep breath and prepared to knock on the door.

***

"May I have some more wine?" Robin asked Lance with her most bewitching smile and a toss of her full auburn hair. She was elated that their fellow commentator, Albert, had left ten minutes ago to call his wife. Now the two of them were alone in Lance's hotel room and she could finally act on her naughty daydreams.

Dreams of riding this handsome hunk sitting in the wing chair next to hers like a stallion. Thoughts of her unfulfilling sex life with her husband disappeared like Houdini's restraints, replaced by the image of her and Lance in the throes of passion. It could be their little road trip secret. No attachments, no commitments, just unadulterated, hot, steamy sex.

She'd heard of his Ladies Man reputation back when he played professional football and now that he was divorced, Robin figured that he wouldn't mind obliging her needs. Giving her a little test drive on his "Lancer."

With a suave move, she hitched her mini skirt up further and crossed her legs seductively to showcase her alabaster assets fully. Mary Hart couldn't hold a candle to her legs.

"Sure thing," he said before he refilled her glass with a wink.

Unfortunately he leaned back, took a sip of his wine, and mentioned *her* name again—this Imani chick that he kept putting the moves on back at home.

Boring, Robin thought, eager to switch the topic. She wanted his full lips and mouth speaking only her name. In fact, if he mentioned Imani's name again, she would simply silence Lance by putting her mouth on his. That thought brought another smile to her face.

Wrestling with the best way to seduce him, she decided to lean in and let her cleavage do the talking.

Lance's eyes began turning her way. In mere milliseconds they would recognize the prize she offered and he would be hers—the knock on the door made her jump.

Pissed at the interruption, she glared at the door, then returned her gaze to Lance's chair to prevent him from answering, but he'd already jumped up.

Damn, he moved fast!   Thoughts of how fast or slow he moved intrigued her and she smiled again. It would be nice to find out soon.

***

"Did Albert say anything about coming back?" Lance asked Robin as he went to check the peephole. They hadn't ordered any more room service. And normally the fans bothered the players versus the newscasters, but you could never be too careful.

The image of Imani in his peephole—sexy yet professional in a black, crepe suit—made him fling open the door to ensure she wasn't a mirage.

"No way!" he said scooping her up in his arms while he kept one foot in the door so that it wouldn't latch locked behind him.

Twenty questions zoomed through his head. *What was she doing here? How? Why?* But realistically, he didn't care. All that mattered was Imani standing here now, wrapped in his arms, her vanilla and cinnamon scent intoxicating his nose.

As usual, her tender lips sucked all resistance from his body like a vampire. When she finally released him from her spell, he managed to remember they were still out in the hall.

"Welcome to L.A.," he said unable to contain his big grin, "please come in." He bumped the door open with his butt and held it ajar, never once taking his eyes off Imani, afraid that this fleeting dream would disappear as unexpectedly as she appeared.

***

Imani licked her lips as she passed Lance, ready to take his greeting further—when a woman's voice stopped her mid-stride.

"Did you get rid of whoever that was?" The reddish-brown haired cougar finally looked up to see Imani just as she started to sip some wine.

Inconspicuously, she spit her wine back into the glass mid-sip so as not to choke. Her scarlet red lips pursed into a little "o" as she set her wine glass on the table. With a polished move, she adjusted in her chair, erased the guilty look, and yanked her skirt down from crotch-level to right above her knees in one clean motion.

Somehow Lance didn't notice a thing as he locked the door and came up behind Imani. His hand slid up her back before he finally noticed her stillness. He followed her stare over to Robin and stood up straight.

"Oh, where are my manners?" Lance intertwined his fingers with Imani's and brought her over to the woman, who dared to stand up and act like nothing happened. "Imani, you remember Robin, right?" Lance beamed at the two of them, painfully oblivious. "Robin, speak of the devil, here's Imani."

Robin gave Imani a bright smile, but she could feel the contempt radiating off the heifer. "Of course I remember. We met back at the studios in

Connecticut." The conniving cow didn't dare extend a hand to shake hers after observing Imani's narrowly slit eyes and set jaw.

Instead Robin decided on a quick, friendly pat on the shoulder before averting her attention to her watch. "Oh, wow, look at the time. I should probably call my husband before he retires for the night. You know the three-hour time zone difference puts a real crimp on communication." She almost snuck over to the door when Lance called out.

"Are you sure, Robin?" He pointed to her wine glass. "You didn't finish your refill."

"No, no," Robin replied with a nervous smile, eager to depart from the lethal daggers flying from Imani's eyes. "I'm good, catch you tomorrow…for work," she added to appease Imani although she couldn't for a second believe that crap worked.

The door couldn't close fast enough behind Robin as she scurried out of the room.

As soon as the door clicked shut, Imani tore into Lance. "What the hell was that?"

***

It took a moment for Lance to realize that Imani wasn't kidding. Imani physically fumed. *What now?* His back stiffened in an automatic response to her accusatory tone.

"Did I interrupt something?" She glared and matched his stiffened stance.

"What in God's name are you talking about?" His

eyes narrowed trying to see where things went wrong this time.

"A little wine before you jumped in the sack with that trollop?" Imani spit out as she waved at the glasses.

"With Robin?" he asked incredulous. "She's married."

"Like that ever stopped you in the past!"

His jaw clenched from her unwarranted attack.

"Exactly how many times did you cheat on your wife?" she asked as her hand flew to her hip.

At first each word stung like a needle prick that drew blood, but halfway through her tirade he grew tired of the pain. Now her jealous outburst only fueled his anger. This evil, sniping side of Imani looked ugly and detestable. *Seriously, what more must I do to gain her trust?*

He stared at her and she dared to glare back indignant. It sent him over the edge and his nostrils flared. He'd been more open than a book—and for what? So she could throw past mistakes that didn't even affect her back up in his face?

This whole ridiculous diatribe tested his patience. His hand squeezed his head rather than rubbed it. "I've told you time and time again, that was in my past." His eyes narrowed. "I wouldn't cheat anymore."

"Why not when you have opportunity and plenty of women still throwing themselves at you?" she screeched, each arm gesture more emphatic than the last. "Robin sitting here with her skirt hiked up to her puss, cootchie calling, titties peeking out of her flimsy blouse which plunged damn near to her navel, wine sloshing about."

"If you hadn't noticed, there were three of us here tonight sharing a drink," he growled, pointing towards the three glasses and chairs setup around the table. "Sorry, but I doubt that Albert would engage in a threesome, seeing as he's happily married and all."

"Are you blind?" she screamed. "Albert was gone and Robin didn't look too happily married to me! She looked ready to jump your damn bones!"

Although he wanted his voice to remain calm, he found himself yelling back. "Are you serious? Albert was just here two minutes ago! And for your information, Robin and I were sitting here," he pointed to the empty chairs, "talking about our significant others. Especially you!" He pointed an accusatory finger at her. "God, Imani, why are you tripping? It's not like I'm even attracted to Robin in the least!"

"Well, she sure as hell is attracted to you, Lance!" She threw her hands up in exasperation. "And your dumb ass doesn't even realize that when you put yourself in stupid, awkward situations—hotel room, wine, and horny-assed woman—bad shit happens!"

"God! What do you want from me, Imani?" He balled his fists. "To promise I'll never entertain Robin alone in my room again? Fine! In fact, I'll even go one further." He threw open one hand and pointed towards the door. "I'll only have drinks with Robin in public, to ensure no indiscretions." His hands flung in her direction. "Is that good enough for you?"

Imani's hands became cemented to her hips and her neck snaked back and forth. "Well, while you're doing me favors. Let's not just limit it to Robin." One hand made a big circle. "Why don't you add in every female? Make sure to lump in all of your freaking lunatic fans and groupies, too!"

Beyond fed up, Lance grabbed Imani's upper arms. "How many more ways and times do I have to tell you that I'm never going to cheat on you?" He desperately wanted to shake some sense into her thick head, but he resisted the urge.

However his intent rang through loud and clear because Imani's eyes widened in shock.

Before her reaction could venture down either one of two bad paths—fear, from his manhandling, or anger, as she automatically fought back against the imagined threat—he released her.

Imani lost steam. Still in a state of shock, she sank onto his bed in silent deflation.

Watching her reaction, his nerves tingled with worry and the adrenaline drained from his body. "What's going on with us, Imani? We're always erupting into these crazy fights over nothing; completely lose-lose situations. Why?"

Feeling utterly exhausted, he slumped onto the bed beside her. "I'm just so tired of this." He closed his eyes and forced out a deep, cleansing breath. Too fatigued to even think, he let his body fall backwards until he lay supine. His hands rubbed over his face once and then rested there.

After a few minutes the unnatural silence worried him and he peeked around his hand.

Imani sat there with tears glistening in her eyes.

Oh, no! His heart dropped. *What if this was finally it?* He didn't want her to say the words, but he couldn't take the silence either.

Reluctantly, he sat up, then he debated whether he should touch her or not. Caution prevailed and he kept his hands to himself. He took one more cleansing breath. *Here goes nothing.* "Imani, could you please, talk to me?"

Imani twisted her body around on the bed to face him although she kept her eyes down. "If you're so damn fed up and tired, why don't you save us all the trouble, Lance? Put us out of this misery and just freaking end this masquerade already!"

"Is that seriously what you think this is? A joke? A game?" He felt himself getting heated again. "Is that what you want? For me to leave you?"

"Why not," she said suddenly glaring at him. "It's what you do."

He frowned. "What in God's name are you talking about?"

"Every single time I let you in, and then fail to react the way you expect; you leave."

Okay, now he was even more confused than before she started speaking. He shook his head and squinted. "And I repeat, what in the world are you talking about?"

Imani huffed. "You remember that 'magical

moment' after Spring Break, don't you?"

How could he ever forget it?

Imani waited until he nodded.

"Regardless of whatever caused our crossed wires," she said, not giving him a chance to argue, "during the subsequent rift I felt like I lost my best friend." Her eyes pleaded with his. "You can't possibly tell me that things didn't change."

Lance's breath caught in his throat. Although he always pretended things continued status quo, they both knew that they'd breached an irreparable boundary.

"Then after our friendship finally recovered, you show up the night before my wedding. And when I chose Marco, you left again." Fresh tears sparkled and threatened to fall. "That time I assumed you left forever."

The blinders fell off and he could see his actions through her eyes. It wasn't pretty. "And now, third times the charm, right?"

Imani nodded. "Exactly! If I finally succumb, really fall for you, what is it going to be that sets you off this time? What's going to make you walk away for good?"

Lance couldn't stand the Grand Canyon-sized gap between them any longer. He slid beside her until their bodies touched. Imani had to feel his words as well as hear them. He summoned every ounce of sincerity he possessed and gazed into her eyes. "Nothing's going to make me walk away, Imani. I promise never to leave again."

"How can you say that?"

"Are you serious?" He felt lost. *What more could he say to convince her?*

Imani nodded. She looked so uncertain, so vulnerable.

All he wanted to do now was protect her. He sighed and tried to explain.

"I'm not going to lie, Imani. Times like tonight are frustrating as hell and I hate them. Because when you're against someone, boy, look out."

He took her hand. "But when you're with someone, and believe in them," he smiled and played with her hand, "there's nothing better. I know this sounds cheesy, but when I'm with you, I feel like there's nothing I can't accomplish. All dreams are possible. The possibilities are endless. Pick whatever corny cliché you like."

Imani smiled in spite of herself. "Lord, you must have had too much wine."

He chuckled and stroked her hand. With each stroke, he replayed tonight's events until something dawned on him. "I finally figured you out."

Imani cocked her head. "Did you now?"

"Yes, I did." He locked eyes with her. "You're purposely trying to push me away and make me leave. Hurt me before I can hurt you."

Imani didn't respond and she looked lost in thought.

Lance grunted. "Which of course naturally triggers my defenses. You hurt me to push me away, I get defensive and snipe back, and you retaliate. And that starts us down this vicious spiral of fighting and arguing."

A random image of his mom fussing crossed through his mind and he chuckled. "But as my crazy mother says, 'when you know better, you do better.' And now I know."

***

The truth of Lance's insightful observations sank in and Imani shook her head. When did crazy, self-absorbed, egotistical Lance become so perceptive? Amazed, she forgot to filter her response. "Since, when did you get so smart?"

"Excuse me?" Lance's eyebrows practically rocketed off his head.

Cracking up, she managed to reach up and stroke his cheeks until his eyebrows settled back into their proper hemisphere. "I meant to say that I used to be the intuitive one. But...I didn't see this." She dropped her hand and squeezed his. "I have to admit, you really did change."

"That's what I've been trying to tell you."

"And you're *really* not going to leave me."

Lance's hand engulfed hers. "No more leaving, Imani." He shrugged with his free hand. "I'm tired of running. Of fighting this," he said, gesturing to the two of them. "I want to spend the rest of my life with you. For better or worse."

Imani studied Lance's earnest face, filled with desire to appease her. She searched her head and her heart for any doubts, but no more excuses existed. With a quick prayer, she closed her eyes and listened to her normally trusty gut.

It remained nice and quiet. No warning bells, no sirens. Only certainty, about Lance, about their relationship. And the words slipped out as natural as the sun rising each day. "I love you, Lance."

Imani didn't know what she expected. Lance had already said the same words multiple times, so he didn't need to repeat the sentiment just for her sake. Instead his entire body spoke as it seemed to tremble and soften. The love shone from his eyes so bright that it almost burned. Then his sweet, hot lips conveyed everything his voice did not.

Wrapped in his arms, his kisses searing her soul, she wanted to give herself to Lance completely. But Melody's warnings, about *premarital sex*, *being careful*, and *demanding more*, came in and planted a seed.

Although her body argued with her mind, she managed to garner enough willpower to stop. Reluctant to completely end their make-up session, her lips lingered on his until she pushed him back a breath.

"Please, don't kill me." With her willpower at such dangerously low levels, she couldn't even look at him for fear she would succumb to his immense sexual energy. "But we can't have sex right now."

Lance studied her with baited breath. Emotions swirled across his face—concern that he'd done something wrong, desire, and worst of all uncertainty that she had somehow changed her mind about them again.

"Wait, let me try to explain," she said trying to reassure him. "Whenever we've done it in the past, we've regretted it the next morning." She shook her head, ashamed to admit it. "And although I flew out here with the express intent of knocking boots, you just changed the game."

Mustering up enough confidence, she looked at him again. "If you're really serious about us, we should spend time focusing on us, without those extra emotions getting in the way."

"Sounds like you've been hanging around Melody too long," he said with a chuckle.

Imani nodded and smiled. "Yes, I have. But maybe she's got a point with the whole premarital sex, abstinence thing."

She held a hand up. "And before you even mention our earlier protests, which would have helped Melody discover her unsatisfying sex life with Chris prior to their wedding, recognize that we have a leg up on her situation. Because we don't have any questions about our excellent chemistry." She gestured between them. "The chemistry is definitely there."

"Big time," he agreed.

Although she detested adding this clarification, she knew he needed to hear it. "Plus you don't have to worry. I'm not going to pull a 'Heather' and withhold it later."

"You promise?" Lance said trying to disguise his

concern as a joke.

Imani laughed. "Sorry, your loving's too good to even pretend like I don't want to jump you most of the time."

"Mmm, really?" his deep voice tickled and tingled.

"Yes!" She laughed. "But behave. At least until we get a handle on this." Serious again, she honed in on his eyes. "Is that okay with you?"

He squeezed her hand and maintained eye contact. "I'll do you one better. I'll wait until our honeymoon."

"That long?" she gasped.

He smiled, pleased with her reaction. "Who says, it has to be a long time?" He teased her. "I could propose tonight and whisk you off to Vegas. It's a quick flight from here."

"Vegas, hm? Stop playing."

"Who says I'm playing?"

Her brows knitted as she tried to determine if he was joking or not. "Lance, be serious." His intensity didn't decrease and her heart skipped a beat with nervous fear. "Look, I'm almost ready but not quite yet. Baby steps, okay?"

Immediately, he smiled and stood up, breaking the tension. "Speaking of Vegas, we haven't partied in forever."

"What?" Imani gave him a quizzical look.

"Some of the crew mentioned that they were going to a club in West Beverly, named Pearl. You want to go? They said there's going to be live music." He grabbed the flyer off his desk. "Yolanda Johnson is playing tonight. I heard from one of the locals that she's really good."

Imani definitely agreed that the sister was more than good as they danced the night away to Yolanda's smooth, grooving R&B vibes. Listening to her sing was almost as good as sex…almost.

MERRY CHRISTMAS / MOTHER KNOWS BEST – DECEMBER 2007

"Are you sure about this?" Imani asked Lance as he parallel-parked his Mercedes CLK into a space near her parents' house in the Bronx.

With equal parts eagerness and trepidation she stared at the semi-detached, brick house. It looked deceivingly inviting. The external Christmas lights hung in neat lines along the roof and porch, and outlined the master bedroom and living room windows, ready to party later. In the living room window, the Christmas tree sparkled, its lights visible even in the bright afternoon. But she knew her parents waited inside, ready to pounce.

"You know you already asked that before we left Albany this morning." Lance turned off the ignition. Not a trace of worry marred his confident grin. He squeezed her leg. "It's not like this is the first time I've visited your parents."

"But it is the first time you've visited as my," Imani's fingers made quotes in the air, "*boyfriend*…and for Christmas. You're just begging to get skewered." Imani buried her face in her hands.

Lance chuckled. "Relax. I don't think they would have invited my mother if they planned on crucifying me."

"Then you don't know my parents very well. What better way to understand your opponent more than by going directly to the source." Imani wanted to flee. "Ugh, is it too late to go to Trevor's mom's place? She's right around the corner."

"Ah, honey, you know that Erycah and Trev's moms traveled up to Albany to celebrate with them and their crazy clan of children. And before you even say it, you know Mrs. Wilkins is also up in Albany with Melody. Plus, I see my mom's Honda parked three spots up, so come on and quit stalling."

As Lance got out and came around to the passenger side, Imani uttered a quick prayer. By the time she looked up, Lance had opened her door and he extended his hand.

The old Lance would have never bothered with anything so chivalrous and generally she was too accustomed to doing things her own independent way to allow it.

Today she beamed as she accepted his hand. Too bad her parents didn't see this side of Lance. Then, they could understand for themselves that he'd changed and matured.

They walked to the door arm in arm. Before ringing the doorbell, she took one last shaky breath. "Are you positive you want to go through with this? We can drive back to Albany or go to Brooklyn and ditch at your mother's house."

"With both of our mother's inside," he replied and shook his head. "No chance! We'd never hear the end of it." His large hands cupped her cheeks. "You're way too worried. Everything is going to be fine." He plucked her nose and rang the doorbell.

Five seconds later, her mother swung open the door, broad smile across her face, looking ready to party in a green silk dress with red accessories. "Ohhhh, my baby's home!" She almost swallowed Imani in a huge embrace, then she stepped back and gestured them inside. "Come in, come in."

"Hi, Mrs. Jordan," Lance said as he entered.

"Lance," Mrs. Jordan replied in a less than cordial tone.

Imani shot her mother a warning look and mouthed, 'behave.'

Mrs. Jordan cut her eyes and humphed.

"Thank you for the invitation," Lance continued undeterred.

Imani knew her mother believed in keeping her friends close and her enemies even closer.

However, her mother evidently decided that Christmas warranted a modicum of civility and her tone became more genial. "I'm glad you arrived safe and sound and I appreciate you driving Imani down. How was the traffic?"

"Surprisingly, it was a breeze," Imani said as she shrugged off her coat.

Her mother eyed her up and down. "Look at you, Girl! That's a gorgeous dress, and the red just flatters your skin." She patted Imani's cheek.

Imani almost blushed although she knew that the satin and velvet wrap dress caressed her body in all the right places. Lance had told her so earlier. "Thanks, Mom."

Mrs. Jordan turned to Lance. "Can I take your coat?"

"Sure," Lance replied as he removed it. Although her mom didn't compliment him, he looked suave and debonair in a black turtleneck and slacks. "Thanks and thank you for extending the invitation to my mother, too."

"Oh, our pleasure."

When Mrs. Jordan hung up their items in the coat closet, Imani noticed her wicked little smile. More like it provided her an opportunity to see how Lance interacted with his mother. Her mom held tons of stock in what the mother-child relationship could tell you about a person.

"You know your mother's here," Mrs. Jordan said closing the closet door.

"Yes, we spotted her car parked further up the block," Lance replied.

As if on cue, Mrs. Oleta Dunn flurried in from the dining room, arms open wide. The sassy, pecan-skinned woman in the sequined poinsettia sweater and flowing, black chiffon pants didn't resemble her son physically, but as soon as she spoke—loud and opinionated, you could tell the acorn didn't fall far from the tree. "Finally! Here's the cute couple!" She smothered them with hugs and kisses. "It's about time you two hooked up."

Mrs. Dunn smiled at her mother. "You know I always used to tell Lance that he should settle down and marry Imani or Melody."

"You don't say?" her mother said as she arched an eyebrow.

Mrs. Dunn didn't notice. "Oh yes, they both have good heads on their shoulders, they're about something. And cute as buttons." She smiled at Imani. "But I always thought Imani had more chutzpah, she could keep Lance in line."

Her mother could barely contain herself and Lance looked mortified.

Mrs. Dunn patted Lance's cheek, "I'm glad you didn't ruin it with all of your trolling around."

"Mom, please," Lance tried to shush her as he took her hand.

"Well, boy, please, everyone knows you saw more ass than a seat on the Coney Island Cyclone rollercoaster. But it's all good now. You finally got it out of your system. And look at both of you now." She freed her hands to pat both of their cheeks again. "Looking happy as two bugs in a rug."

Imani's mother looked smug. "Well, let me do one last circle of all the guests before I relieve your father in the kitchen." She turned to Mrs. Dunn and Lance, "please, make yourselves at home. Imani here will make sure your visit is comfortable." She smiled another wicked little grin and squeezed Imani's hand before she departed.

Unfortunately, Imani knew her mother had heard more than enough and that last little tidbit would provide her with ammunition for years. Plus her deliberate choice of the word 'visit' meant they were welcome today, but only today, don't get used to her hospitality, however lacking it proved.

Imani sighed. It was going to be a long, taxing day.

Imani flushed the toilet and washed her hands, happy for the reprieve from her parents. If she could just eliminate them from the equation, the rest of Christmas had gone smashingly well.

Walking down the hallway to rejoin the festivities, she paused at the typical wall of photographs that each Black family she knew had. She smiled as she traversed along the fleeting images in time: relatives, friends, vacations, holidays, graduations. When she reached the end of the wall her eyes lingered on a photo. Try as hard as she might to move, her eyes remained transfixed on her wedding photo.

Images and memories of Marco overwhelmed her. Each of their monumental moments occurred in this very house. The first time Marco told her he loved her. His surprise proposal.

Her hand trembled over the photograph. Maybe her parents were right. *What am I doing here with Lance? This is all wrong.* Memories of Marco reigned supreme.

As her hand fell to her side, it glanced off a picture of her and Trevor and then one of her, Melody, and Lance. She reexamined the hallway of images as her mind cleared. All of these other memories and relationships came *before* Marco. This wasn't *his* house. Life didn't end with his death. In reality, this house captured millions of memories before Marco. Like it or not, it would probably make millions more from this moment forward.

A huge weight dropped from her shoulders and breathing became easier. She kissed her fingertips and pressed them to Marco's photo. "I'll always love you, Marco."

Feeling comforted and settled, she dropped her hand and smiled at the picture of her, Melody, and Lance.

Like an apparition, Lance appeared behind her. "Hey, I was wondering where you disappeared to." His deep voice tickled down her spine as she nestled her back against his broad chest. "I hoped you hadn't bailed."

Imani grunted. "The thought definitely crossed my mind." She cocked her head back into his shoulder and glanced up at his face as best she could from her angle in front of him. "How are you holding up?"

"I don't know what's worse, my mother embarrassing me at every turn or you mother's interrogations and veiled threats."

Imani snickered. "I always told you your moms is a pure-dee trip! And I warned you about my crazy mom."

Lance wrapped his arms around her. "Well, your mom can try her best, but I'm not going anywhere. I figure if I could win you over, she'll eventually have to succumb to my charms, too."

"Yeah, good luck with that one," Imani replied

with another grunt. "You might have a better shot with my dad." She turned in his arms to face him. "I'll get his assessment soon."

"How's that?"

"It's a funny trick he has. Since I was little, my dad would ask me to wash the dinner dishes with him. It's usually when he decides to hold all of our serious father-daughter conversations. I expect he'll be along soon to tell me what he thinks about you."

"Should I be worried?"

"Actually, for once, I have no idea." Imani gave Lance a peck on the cheek. "We should get back before my mom sends out a search party."

No sooner had they reentered the dining room then her dad appeared.

"Ah, there you are Imani. Ready to help me with the dishes?" he asked.

Imani shot Lance a quick, knowing smile and then she walked towards the kitchen. "Coming, Dad."

Her father tossed her a dish towel. "I figure you'd rather rinse and dry today."

"Sounds good," Imani replied, taking up a position next to him in front of the double sink. "You did a great job on the turkey. It was so juicy and seasoned to perfection."

Her dad gave her a crooked smile and the first of many pieces of china. "Thanks, you know the old man has to help out around the kitchen. Keep your momma sane."

"Yeah, she needs a lot of help," Imani said with a smirk.

"About that," her dad said, handing her another plate, "I'm not cool with how she's acting tonight. I'm downright embarrassed for you and Lance." His hands expertly sponged the soapy water around another plate and handed it to her to rinse. "Don't make sense to be evil on Christmas Day. It's downright un-Christian."

"Well, Mom's never been one to hold her tongue." Imani sighed as she set a fifth rinsed plate in the draining rack on the counter. At least they were making good time.

"I kicked her under the table twice, but I plan on talking to her tonight after everyone leaves. She needs to hear about herself."

"You don't have to do that, Daddy. No sense in both of us being in the doghouse." Imani wiped her sleeve across her forehead to catch some errant spray droplets that bounced off the wine glass she rinsed.

"No, she's always preaching that people can change and to forgive and forget. Well, she needs to swallow an ounce of her own medicine." He handed her another glass before plunging his hands in the suds with a little too much gumption. Luckily the splash hit the backsplash instead of soaking them.

Like a treasure hunt, his hands resurfaced with another plate. "Look, I know Lance played around a lot in the past. But if she just opened her eyes and simply watched how that boy's been chasing after you, she'd see the obvious. Lance wouldn't bit more cross you than I'd ever cheat on her."

"Wow," Imani replied, not knowing what else to

say. She knew her dad could put his foot down, but she'd rarely seen him so adamant, determined, and well…pissed at her mother. And now he seemed to be working on overdrive, she could barely keep up with the constant stream of plates and glasses.

"I know you and your momma sometimes think I don't pay attention or I'm downright oblivious to goings on around her, but I see everything."

Imani decided to keep her mouth shut and rinse.

"Just most time I don't feel the need to get involved. None of my doggone business or concern. Well, this time I'm making an exception. I've been watching you and listening. Lance is the first thing that's made you happy since Marco's death."

Imani gasped. Her dad handed her the turkey platter.

"I know what gave you and your momma pause though. I ain't saying that what Lance did was right, but I understand it." His hands worked overtime trying to clean the burnt marshmallows off the casserole that held the sweet potatoes.

"Understand what?" Imani asked, still blown away by the course of the conversation.

Her dad stopped scrubbing long enough to look at her. "Look, sometimes it's hard for men to be friends with women. Y'all used to get along fine in college, but something changed after he married that harpy, what was her name? Heather?"

Imani could only nod.

"I only saw all of y'all together twice. And one time during dinner, he kept staring at you…and not like a friend. I don't know how none of you super sensitive types didn't notice it, especially you and your momma. Heck, even Marco, or that Heather chick should have seen something. But somehow y'all didn't notice even though longing was dripping off that boy like water from a faucet with a busted washer."

He handed Imani the gravy boat. "Anyhow, nobody told me anything about anything at your wedding, but I overheard the boy muttering as he stormed out during your reception."

"You what?" Imani's eyes almost bugged out of her head. "What did he say?"

"Now you never mind about that, just know the boy had it bad." He handed her a handful of silverware.

Imani half caught the silverware and then she let her hand fall limply into her empty sink. "Daddy, please!"

Her father huffed and plunged his hands in the now barely soapy water in search of more dirty dishes. "It's not like you don't already know."

He glanced over at her pained face and then decided to continue. "He hated your decision to marry Marco, although we all know it was the right one. But he also came to the realization that I told you earlier; as a man, he couldn't go back to being just friends." His hand found some more cutlery and he lifted them in triumph before he saw the two other pots sitting on the stove.

Imani felt numb.

After her father did one last check of the kitchen and captured the two errant pots, he continued washing and talking. "So, when Trevor and your momma were storming around the day after Marco died. Well, like I said, I don't agree with Lance's actions—him being so obvious and with such horrid timing. But let's just say…I wasn't surprised and I understood why." He handed her both washed pots. "He's loved you for a long time, Imani."

A Little Help

This is so wrong, Melody thought, but she couldn't help herself. She had to do it just this once. To see how it felt. To see what she'd been missing. She stood over Lance as he dozed on her couch, with one of the numerous college bowl games droning on in the background.

No use waiting any longer. Mustering up every ounce of courage she possessed, she decided to go for broke and straddle him as he slept. Her skirt swished over their legs soft and sensuous.

Following its lead, she ran her fingers over his shirt, all soft and sensuous. His hot, strong heartbeat pulsed into her fingertips as she felt his muscular chest. His rhythmic breathing continued unabated despite her fingers' journeys, and it emboldened her to go further. Her fingers explored each inch as they traveled back up his chest, his shoulders, and then she tentatively followed the tendons along his neck.

Each of her breaths became more ragged as she thrilled at her actions. Now she couldn't stop. Almost imperceptibly, she leaned down into him, her chest against his, her face nestled into his neck. Mmm, if she really sniffed, she could just smell the sandalwood soap he used, so strong, masculine.

Feeling adventurous, she let her bottom lip take a gentle trek along his neck. Each action further fed her emotions and she became more heated and sexual. Uninhibited now, she kissed his neck and cheeks until he moaned and stirred.

His slightly sleepy and aroused eyes locked on hers. "What are you doing, Melody?"

"Shh, it's okay." She felt his body began to tense under hers and she upped the passion.

"This isn't right, we can't do this," he replied, but his body contradicted his words.

"I won't tell if you don't," she said before finally allowing her lips to meet his soft, juicy ones. As she moaned from forbidden pleasure, he intensified the kiss, exploring her mouth in ways she never imagined. Her fingers stopped stroking his chest and wandered down to the treasure trove between his legs.

Desperate to explore his skin further, she undid his pants and unbuttoned his shirt. Mmm, he looked so delectable. And he tasted even better.

He groaned as she kissed him and slid his hands under her shirt.

About to explode, she moved her skirt and panties aside and mounted him. Immediately he moved in time with her. Each stroke felt divine and she almost lost her mind in all-encompassing ecstasy. Conversely their coupling seemed to go on forever and yet her body ramped up entirely too fast. She cried out as he exploded with her. Sweet spasms rocked their bodies.

"Oh my God," Chris said as he sat back with a big smile. "I'm going to have to nap on the couch more often if you promise to wake me up like that each time."

"Sounds good to me, La—Love," she replied almost messing everything up by uttering her fantasy's name. Feeling sexually fulfilled yet exceedingly guilty at the same time, she jumped off Chris to go freshen up. *Did I just go too far?*

FINALLY! – JANUARY 2008

Imani knew immediately.

Living together for six years had forced their menstrual cycles to coincide long ago. And both of them were predictably regular like Timex watches. Without fail, Melody's period always began two days after hers. In addition, lest she ever forget, Melody's unusual one day of crankiness and water retention—the day before she started to bleed—always stood as a stark reminder.

Today there was no crankiness. Instead of bloating, Melody beamed as if Thomas Edison and GE were personally bringing good things to life.

"You're pregnant," she said to a glowing Melody as Melody took a seat in one of Imani's kitchen chairs.

"Yes," Melody squealed, hopping around on the chair. "We took the test last night and I couldn't wait to get together today and tell you."

"Congratulations!" Imani sprinted over and gave her girlfriend a fierce hug. "Little Mama's having a baby." She pulled up a chair next to Melody, deciding that their Wednesday night dinner could wait a little longer. "Is Chris telling Lance?" she asked nodding her head towards the family room where both men disappeared moments ago.

"Doubtful," Melody replied. "Chris is worse than an old wife, insisting we don't tell a soul until I'm further along."

"Well, don't worry, you didn't have to tell me, I figured it out all on my own. So it doesn't count." She clapped her hands. "Oh, my goodness, my baby's having a baby! I'm so excited."

"You do realize that we're the same age, right?" Melody scoffed.

Imani pooh-poohed her with a wave of her hand, "yeah, yeah. Let's see, so it's January now. Hmmm, that means we'll have a September baby…probably a Virgo."

Melody hit Imani's leg. "Oh, no you don't."

"What?" Imani chuckled.

"You're not psychoanalyzing my child before he or she's even born." Melody jumped up and checked out the ingredients on the counter. "So, what's for dinner again?"

Imani smiled as she joined her. "I guess you're eating for two already."

Melody punched her in the arm. "I'm warning you, no fat jokes. Not a word from you, okay?"

She raised her arms in surrender as Chris entered the kitchen.

"Hey, I'm going to run home right quick," he said as he blew through the kitchen.

"Why?" Melody asked trying to stop him.

"I forgot the bottle of wine on our kitchen counter."

"We've got wine over here," Imani said mischievously, nodding towards her counter wine rack.

"Ah, no," Chris replied while shooting Melody a secretive look. "We've got a special one that we wanted to try out."

"Oh, yes," Melody said pretending to go along with Chris's charade. "Hurry back, Hon."

"Ah, even if I took my sweet time and drove like an old Sunday driver, it would take at most twenty minutes. I mean, seriously, we only live five minutes away, Melody." Chris shook his head as he left, but then he popped his head back in the door and blew her a kiss.

Melody caught his kiss and chuckled.

Imani waited until she heard Chris shut his car door before she spoke. "Hilarious that he couldn't even admit that he's going back home to get your non-alcoholic wine."

"I told you, old wife." Melody smiled as she seasoned the salmon and asparagus while Imani prepared the rice pilaf. "Hey, weird question for you."

"Yesss," she replied sufficiently intrigued.

"Have you ever fantasized about somebody else while you were making love?"

Imani raised an eyebrow but answered the question. "Not really." She noticed Melody's funny expression, so she tried to sound more understanding. "Although it's not weird or unusual, if that's what you're asking. People do it all the time. Wondering what movie stars or other famous people would be like. Why, were you dreaming about Brad Pitt again?"

"No, someone closer to home." Melody gave her a coy smile then slid the foil-wrapped salmon in the oven.

"Don't tell me you were scoping out that cute anchorman at your job?" Imani stirred the rice pilaf and seasonings into the pot as the water began to boil. After completing the task, she turned her full attention towards Melody.

Trepidation eased into her gut at the thought of her friend inadvertently treading into dangerous waters. Her voice lost all frivolity as she became deadly serious. "Fantasies like that can spawn into workplace romances." She felt her eyebrow arch. "Should I be worried?"

"Oh God, no!" Melody finished arranging the asparagus in the square griddle pan and turned the fire on low. "Plus, it's not anyone at work."

"Well then, who?" She frowned while she stirred the boiling rice pilaf once more and decreased the temperature from high to low.

Finished, Melody gave her a demure smile as she returned to her kitchen chair and half whispered the response. "Lance."

"Lance?" Imani slammed the lid on the rice pilaf pot. "My Lance?"

When Imani whipped around, Melody was busy picking flecks of lint off her pants, so she didn't immediately notice Imani seething.

"Well, technically, he's our Lance," Melody replied with a giggle. "You know how he's always saying he's there for *his girls*." With the offending lint gone, Melody looked up at Imani and her face fell, her mouth making smokeless smoke rings.

Like an out of control fire, Imani couldn't contain herself. "What the hell is wrong with you that you're always scoping on my men?" Her hand flew to her hip.

"What?" Melody looked like a fish out of water as her mouth continued to form silent *O*'s.

Her mind raced through history at Mach 1. "Don't think I forgot all those times that you joked about making a play for Marco." Imani waited for Melody to respond, but the cow was still too stunned. "Now Lance?"

Melody regained her voice. "Imani, it's not like that at all."

The hell it ain't! "Do I need to be worried?"

"No," Melody stammered, "of course not."

If they wanted to remain friends, she needed to know that her *girlfriend* understood crystal clear where her boundaries lay. "Because if you make any kind of move towards Lance whatsoever, I will personally kick your ass."

"I wouldn't!" Melody began to cry. "You know I'd never do anything like that."

Neither one of them heard Lance slip in from the family room. "What's going on?" he asked trying to make heads or tails of the scene in front of him.

Imani sucked her teeth. "You need to talk to *your*

girl," she said purposefully giving Melody a scathing look during the play on words. "Because if she ever mentions dreaming about you again, I'm going to beat her ass down." Done, she stormed from the room.

***

Melody tried to quit crying. *Where had things gone so horribly wrong?*

Lance gaped after Imani's dust. Then his head made a slow swivel towards Melody and his eyebrow rose sky high. "Please tell me what she's talking about because I'm thoroughly confused."

"It's nothing," she mumbled trying to get up out of the chair to leave.

With his ridiculous speed, Lance cornered her before she could rise two feet and he gently sat her back down. "No, Melody, it's something. I've only seen the two of you go at it like this twice before and it wasn't over nothing. Talk to me."

After she sniffled through the story, Lance squeezed her arm and called Imani back over.

Imani huffed into the room and Lance ordered her to sit down. "Look, Imani, we both know how difficult a time Melody's had getting it on with Chris."

"Please, don't use that pathetic excuse!" Imani shouted and crossed her arms.

Lance didn't bat an eye, instead he addressed Imani all calm and cool. "Regardless of how pathetic you think it is, cut Melody some slack."

Whoa, what? Melody marveled at how well Lance handled Imani. Even more surprising—she mused, daring to sneak a peek at Imani—was how Imani let him talk her down.

"She didn't mean anything by it and you know it," Lance continued, his voice firm yet calming. "She just thought you'd have something funny to bond over."

"Well, it wasn't very funny and I'm not laughing." Imani's arms crossed even tighter.

Melody's heart beat double-time. Regardless of Lance's attempts, this wasn't working and Imani still looked two seconds away from beating her senseless.

"Yeah, well she realizes it now." Lance rubbed his hand over his head. "But you know you didn't have to take it all the way there, Imani." Lance walked over to Imani's chair and squatted down in front of her. "You know she would never do anything to jeopardize our friendship. We've been through hell and back together." When Imani didn't respond, he nudged her leg. "Right, Imani?"

"I suppose," Imani mumbled.

"You can do better than that," Lance replied, chastising Imani.

With regret eating at her and hating to see her friend mad or in doubt, Melody jumped up and threw her arms around Imani. "I'm so sorry, Imani. You know I was just joking. Please forgive me," she begged as she locked eyes with Imani. "Please."

Imani rolled her eyes. "Fine! You know I can't

stay mad at you with those ridiculously sad, Puss in Boots eyes of yours." Then she squinted like Dirty Harry. "But you best keep Lance out of your damn dreams from now on. You got me?"

Eager to get this behind them, she nodded in grateful relief.

"See, share the love, group hug," Lance said with a smile and Imani punched his arm.

Chris opened the front door. "Mmm, food smells good." He stopped, with the bottle of sparkling wine tucked under his arm, and gave them a funny look as he shut the door. "Did I miss something?"

God, Chris couldn't know! With a mortified look, she beseeched Lance and Imani to keep Chris in the dark and leave her little bit of pride intact.

Imani's eyes narrowed somewhere between mischievousness and evil. Then she smiled at Chris, sweet as pie. "Nope, not a thing. Let's eat!"

YOU DID WHAT? – MARCH 2008

Chris took the stairs two at a time, in a hurry to enter their bedroom and pounce on his wonderful wife. Once they'd gotten married, he felt like the luckiest man in the world.

His buddies and family members always complained about their wives' lack of interest in sexual encounters, whereas his wife practically jumped him—every other day, no less! And lately, when he thought it couldn't get any better, it had. It was as if Melody put the intensity in overdrive, unleashing a new lioness.

All his friends warned him that pregnancy changed women even more. However, it hadn't stopped Melody one bit. Granted, she was only two months along, but everyone said the first trimester was the hardest. If that was true…

He smiled as her back was to him. Quiet as a church mouse, he began to sneak over.

"I know, Imani. I crossed the line."

He stopped, not realizing that she was on the phone.

"I just wanted to apologize and reassure you that Lance and I will never happen again."

Melody and Lance? Chris's mouth dropped. *No*

way possible!

"Thank you for forgiving me. It was wrong and I wish it never happened. I'm so sorry."

Chris back-peddled out of the room before it even registered. Everything in his vision glowed a dark, crimson red. How could that bastard violate his wife! Even though Lance was big, his outrage was bigger and justice sat squarely on his side.

Not even realizing what he planned on doing, he flew back down the steps and found himself out the door, driving the five minutes to Imani's house, and parking in her driveway. As he stormed to the door, he knew Lance would be there, he always was. The question was how to get past Imani.

He needn't have worried, Lance opened the door.

***

"Hey, Man," Lance said, greeting Chris with a smile. He leaned back and shouted to Imani in the kitchen. "It's Chris."

"Chris?" Imani looked skeptical.

Not wanting to seem rude, he gestured Chris inside. "Come on in, take a load off." Just as he rocked back to turn, he noticed Chris's fist flying towards his face. On automatic, he juked, letting his momentum take him out of harm's way. His arm grabbed Chris's as it sailed past, directed it down, and twisted it behind his back. "What the hell, Man?"

Unperturbed, Chris pivoted away from the hold, effectively freeing his arm. He stepped back, shifting his weight for maximum force, and launched another punch.

Getting pissed at the unprovoked attack, Lance stepped into Chris's path to alter the point of impact. Deftly he blocked the punch and tackled him back into the wall. A 'whoosh' of air erupted from Chris.

With Chris momentarily stunned, Lance retreated three strides. But a long-dormant athletic aggression coursed through his veins.

Although wide receivers typically prided themselves on eluding and evading tackles, there were quite a few, Lance included, that enjoyed when the tables turned. They waited, primed and ready to serve out a punishing de-cleater on some unsuspecting mark. Chris had a target tattooed directly on his chest.

Lance bounced on his toes like a boxer, anxiously awaiting the chance to lay him out flat.

"Oh my, God!" Imani appeared and positioned herself between them. As she glared at Lance, she helped Chris into a dining room chair. "Chris what in the world are you doing? Why are you here? And why are you swinging on Lance?" Frustrated she fanned the previous questions away. "Skip all that; are you freaking crazy?"

Lance bounced himself just behind and to the right of Imani, ready for Chris to make another move.

Without taking her eyes off Chris, Imani reached back in a subtle motion and placed her right hand on his arm, somehow usurping his anger. Even with her soothing touch, he remained ever wary—keeping a keen eye on Chris and praying that he recovered enough to idiotically attempt a second assault.

When Chris managed to regain his breath, he glowered at Lance while he answered Imani. "Don't act like you don't know! Lance slept with Melody."

"What?" Imani sounded more confused than pissed.

"Oh, please," Chris replied, cutting his eyes at Imani. "Drop the act! You were just on the phone with Melody not even ten minutes ago."

Imani sucked her teeth, her hand abandoned Lance's arm and darted to her hip. "So, did you listen to the complete conversation or did you just assume shit before you came flying over here?"

Chris gaped at Imani, perplexed.

"Mm-hm, I thought so, Sherlock," she replied, tapping her foot.

"What?" Chris asked looking discombobulated.

"Lance, get me the phone, please," Imani asked before averting her full attention back to Chris.

Begrudgingly he got the phone and handed it to her as she continued her tirade. "I think you need to speak to your wife and have her explain what you think you heard. Because I'm not wading any further in this sea of crap."

Pissed, Imani punched in Melody's number, hit speakerphone, tossed the ringing phone back to Lance, and left Chris staring after her as she returned to the kitchen.

With a threatening look, Lance handed Chris the phone and dared him to pull another stunt like earlier.

Chris sat motionless, apparently afraid to take his eyes off Lance now.

"Hello, hell-looo," Melody sang into the phone, "Imani are you there?"

"Um, hi, Honey," Chris looked embarrassed as he spoke into the speakerphone.

"Chris? I swore Imani's number appeared on the Caller ID." They heard shuffling as Melody adjusted the phone. "Wait a minute. I don't understand— you're downstairs."

"Uh, not exactly," Chris mumbled.

"I'm really confused here. Are you at Imani's…how, why, when did you leave?" Lance could practically hear Melody scratching her head. "What in the world's going on?"

"I should ask you the same thing," Chris said with some of the accusatory fire he displayed when he first arrived uninvited.

"Excuse me?" Melody wasn't quite mad yet, but it was fast replacing the confusion.

"I overheard you telling Imani that nothing was going to happen between you and Lance again and I came over here to confront his cheating ass and now he and Imani are acting like I'm the crazy one."

Chris' far-fetched accusations triggered an immediate adverse reaction in Lance and he struggled to remain calm. As his jaw clenched and his nostrils flared, he commanded his other muscles not to move. Melody had better set Chris straight soon.

"Oh, no," Melody wailed before her voice broke off.

Chris looked uncertain. "Are you seriously telling me that I'm overreacting when I find out my wife's cheating with her best friend's boyfriend?"

Imani crossed her arms and glared at Chris.

Meanwhile Lance managed to shake only his head and not his angering body. A bemused smile flickered over his annoyance.

"Chris, you misunderstood," Melody whispered then sighed. "I…oh God, this is so embarrassing."

"What is it, Melody?" Chris waited, wound up tight as a spring about ready to launch.

"I had a… a dream… about Lance."

"What kind of dream," Chris looked at Imani and suddenly understood. "What like a wet dream? An erotic dream."

Imani raised an eyebrow as if to say, 'good guess, Sherlock.'

"Yes, exactly," Melody replied, sounding as if she were going to die of embarrassment.

"Okay," Chris said looking perplexed. "Everyone has a funny dream at least once, what's the big deal?"

"She had it while she was wide awake riding you," Imani muttered under her breath.

Lance shot her a warning look not wanting this to escalate after he'd so successfully reined in his anger, but luckily Chris didn't hear her snide remark.

"The big deal is that I told Imani and she wasn't amused."

Chris chuckled then caught himself and glanced at Imani to make sure she kept her cool, too. "Well, I prefer if you dream of me, of course, but no harm, no foul." He glanced up again, abashed. "But now I'll have to apologize profusely for leaping to conclusions and slandering our friends. Be home soon, okay?"

"I'm so sorry about all of this, Chris. And please tell Imani and Lance, I'm sorry, too—"

"Oh, don't worry. You're on speakerphone, they heard everything."

It sounded like Melody gulped, but Chris steamrolled ahead. "Love you, Melody, see you soon." Then he hung up, walked over to Imani, and handed her the phone. "I'm such an idiot. Can you both ever forgive me?"

Lance waved it away. If he were in Chris's shoes...no telling what he would have done. "No biggie, I would have been pissed, too. However, just letting you know as a warning. If you had connected with any one of your punches, we might be having an entirely different conversation right about now."

Chris unleashed a hearty laugh until Lance couldn't help but join him. Chris clapped him on the shoulder. "Trust me, Lance, warning received loud and clear." Then Chris sprang his hopeful, puppy dog look on Imani.

Imani held his gaze without a smile. "Look, I understand your reaction because I was pissed, too, but if you ever pull any crap like this again...accusing me of some wild ass shit..."

"Understood, Imani," Chris replied and pulled her in for a hug despite her protests.

Lance studied Chris while he hugged Imani. Hopefully, they could put all this nonsense behind them. Hopefully, but he wasn't so sure.

WITHOUT A DOUBT – APRIL 2008

The musical tinkle of a child's unbridled laughter caught Lance's attention as he slid Imani's sliding glass door closed. He strolled across her deck and surveyed her backyard, his hand resting on the deck railing.

Imani rounded the corner from the side yard with an ecstatic Xavier tottering, falling, and crawling behind her. In her hands a bubble-generating toy created enormous bubbles nearly the size of the toddler himself. An unseasonably warm April wind whispered past, contorting the bubbles into convoluted shapes.

He watched in amazement. The toy was a far cry from the little, plastic bubble wands they used when they were kids.

Xavier cracked up as much from Imani making silly faces as from the huge stream of oversized bubbles. Not one to miss out on the action, Trevor, Jr. came barreling over, shrieking and popping bubbles.

Lance chuckled as he watched their humorous interactions and he didn't immediately notice Trev sneak up behind him unannounced.

"Wow, this feels like reverse déjà vu," Trevor said

with a knowing smile.

"Excuse me?" He frowned. *What was Trevor up to now?*

"I caught Imani mooning over you once, although she vehemently denied it." Trev casually turned and watched his mini-mes shriek in glee at Imani's antics. "Looks like you got it bad, huh?"

After giving Trev a careful assessment, he shrugged, and then answered with the honest truth. "Yep, I do," he replied unabashedly staring at Imani again.

Partially to counter Trev's nosy questions and because he wanted a truthful answer, he proffered a question of his own. "What's it really like being a father?" he asked gazing at the delightful, little handfuls that Trev produced.

Not expecting the question, Trev studied him for a moment. "There are extremely trying times, like teething and colic and crying forever when you have no clue why."

Trevor beamed at his sons. "But then there's the rediscovery of the little things in life, the awesomeness of seeing these little people that depend completely on you. Watching to see what traits they pick up from you or their momma or the grandparents, or weird Uncle Jessie. Or sometimes, their own unique, little personalities shine through."

As he spoke Erycah appeared from the side yard, too, with a huge, colorful, bouncy ball that actually eclipsed her humungous 8-month-pregnant belly. She waddled over to Imani, Xavier, and Lil Trev and rolled the ball to the children.

Lil Trev immediately took off chasing after it as Xavier clapped his hands. Xavier decided to join in the chase and he crawled over as Lil Trev tripped and fell over the ball, which promptly rolled over him.

The adults all held their collective breath, ready to run to the rescue, when Lil Trev bounded back up and did it all over again, giggling hysterically the entire time.

Xavier led the adults in a cascade of laughter.

As his laughter died down, Lance studied Erycah and imagined the look on Imani. "She's beautiful pregnant," Lance complimented Trev. "Pregnancy seems to suit Erycah this time around."

He faced Trev as Trev stared back in shock. "I can't wait to see Imani like that, too. All fat and glowing with my seed growing inside her."

"Whoa, man! That sounds gross." He held up his hand in an attempt to get him to stop. "And it's a big step."

Trev shook his head, all joking aside. "Look, fatherhood is a lot more than getting someone pregnant and populating the world. I told you before, it's a lot of work." Trev squinted at Lance. "Plus, pregnancy unleashes this whole bizarre hormonal thing that should definitely not be taken lightly. It's usually not all pretty and glowing."

"I know," Lance replied with a grin as warm feelings of pride swelled within. "I can't wait to massage Imani's feet or rub her back. Make the midnight run for ice cream and pickles. Put a cold washcloth on her head as I sweep her hair back from her head while she's bent over the toilet, experiencing morning sickness."

"Aw, c'mon, Man!" Trev gasped. "That's just plain sick and twisted!"

"You'd think so," he replied as his smile grew. "But that's how committed I am to her."

Although he knew the answer, he felt compelled to ask. His eyes narrowed as worry flicked through; however, his voice stayed neutral when he faced Trev. "Do you still get feelings like that for her, too? I know it was years ago, but do you ever wonder what if?"

Trevor looked at him like he'd sprouted three heads. "From the moment she kissed me and I went home and called Erycah, I never went there again." His eyes automatically went to Erycah who stood laughing as Imani and Lil Trev rolled around with the huge, bouncy ball; Xavier crawling in hot pursuit. "Sometimes God shows you what you need versus what you think you want."

"Unfortunately for me, it was almost too late." Lance took a deep, refreshing breath as another warm breeze circled past. "Luckily, he's given me another chance, one I won't blow this time around."

Trev looked skeptical. "What makes you so sure?"

"What's with you, Man?" Lance snipped almost getting irked again as he recalled Trev's bravado the day after Marco died.

"You know what." Trev didn't back down although his tone actually sounded calm as a

Jamaican breeze. Trev's eyes bored into his. "Look, I don't want you half-stepping to Imani. She's like my sister and I don't want her hurt."

Trev placed his hand on Lance's shoulder. "I know your ass is twice my size, but I'd put up a helluva fight if you did her wrong, no matter how tight we used to be." Trev cracked a grin and dropped his hand.

"There's no need for that." Lance turned and chuckled, still contemplating kicking Trev's behind just for the hell of it. He watched Imani again until he relaxed once more.

"I admit you guys had reason to doubt the old me. However, the last few years made me realize what's important. Someone who knows and understands you, encourages you, demands more from you, and stands by you through thick and thin. My stupid pride won't let me lose that again. I feel like Jerry Maguire; she completes me, Trev."

"Damn, Lance, you really do got it bad. Big-time whipped." Trev shook his head.

"I am," Lance replied with a smile as Erycah, a yawning Lil Trev, and Imani carrying Xavier, all made their way up to the deck completely pooped.

"Hey, Baby." Erycah kissed Trev's cheek as he helped her up the deck stairs. "You ready to go, yet? Your Seeds of Chucky are getting tired."

"I'm ready, Sweetheart."

Lance held the patio door open as everyone spilled inside the house.

***

"About time." Melody grinned from the family room couch where she reclined next to Chris. They were outside with everyone earlier, but she felt winded—evidently a new experience at the third month of pregnancy, so they'd come inside about fifteen minutes ago. "We were wondering if we smelled or said something wrong."

"Of course not," Erycah replied, embracing both Melody and Chris as they stood up.

"Well I didn't want to say anything," Trev teased as he hugged her goodbye. She bumped him out of the way and playfully shoved him onto Chris who gave him a pound.

Throwing open her arms, Melody waited for Lil Trev to run over. As she gathered him up, she swung him around.

Halfway through the swing, a sharp pain sliced through her stomach.

Incredibly, she managed to withhold a scream, smoothly deposit the little boy back onto his feet, and gracefully land on the couch as if she planned the movement.

Plastering a smile on her face, she waited for another pain as everyone said their goodbyes. Nothing further came.

Relieved she stood up once again and waved as the Mathis family left the family room for the front door.

As Imani and Lance escorted them out, she sat down again, unnerved.

"You want a refill?" Chris asked as he shook her empty glass and picked up his. Without waiting for her reply, he disappeared into the kitchen to refresh their drinks when the cramps came…hard.

A slight croak escaped her lips and a bead of sweat broke out on her forehead. Then, just as unexpected the pains subsided.

Concerned, she wanted to call Chris back over, but she didn't want to alarm him. *Everything's fine. Probably just ate something that didn't agree with me.*

As in concurrence, she felt the sudden urge to go the bathroom. *See, have a bowel movement and things will be right as rain.* With a big smile, she hurried over to the restroom.

***

"Thanks again for another fine time, Girl," Erycah hugged Imani after their "quick" good-byes had led to a five minute conversation. "And thanks for occupying the wild children most of the time, too. It was nice getting a reprieve."

"My pleasure." Imani planted a kiss on Xavier's fat cheek and bent down to ruffle Lil Trev's sleepy head.

The little boy smiled then reached up for his daddy to pick him up.

"Later, Man." Trev clapped Lance on the back. "I'm glad we talked."

Lance shot Trev a look, but Trev was too busy

scooping up his son and kissing Imani on the cheek to notice.

"See y'all later!" Trev waved as they walked over to their car.

"Sounds like I missed something interesting," Imani said to Lance with a wink.

Lance threw his arm around her shoulder but declined to reply. They continued to look on as the Mathis' got buckled in and finally drove off with a honk and a wave.

"Four down, two more to go," Lance said as he held the door open for her.

"Mmm, you got plans for later?" She slipped him a seductive smile and her fingers glided down Lance's back, around his side, and across his abs as she walked past.

Lance let out an inadvertent moan as he quivered underneath her fingertips.

Before he could respond, her tickling fingers turned into a stop sign and she pulled up short, body alert. "Where's Melody?" she asked as her gut alarm twitched.

Looking back towards the family room, she saw Chris pass by munching on something in a napkin. "Yo, Chris, is Melody in there?" she asked while they walked to him.

Shaking his head, he tried to swallow the brownie he'd shoved into his mouth. "She's in the bathroom," he replied, wiping his mouth.

"Is she okay?" she tried to keep the concern out of her voice.

"Yeah." Chris shrugged his shoulders. "Why wouldn't she be?"

"No reason," she replied not wanting to give footing to the uneasy feeling coming from deep inside. She smiled and patted his arm, leaving the guys standing around looking at each other, making small talk.

Casually she made her way to the powder room and tapped on the door. "Are you okay in there?" Melody would probably fuss that she couldn't even take a dump in peace, but Imani would gladly take the ribbing if it made the funny feeling go away.

Hearing muffled sounds, she knocked again and placed her ear to the door.

Whimpering and soft cries neared the door and she heard the click of the lock disengaging.

Slowly opening the door, Imani was unprepared for the sight in front of her.

Blood—wide swaths of crimson—trailed from the area on and around the toilet—where the largest pool collected—to a pathway that ended at the door, where Melody sat weeping in a daze on the floor.

"Oh my God," Imani muttered praying it wasn't what she knew deep down it was. She threw her head out the door and yelled down the hallway to the guys, "call 911 and get an ambulance here now!"

Dropping to her knees she gathered Melody in her arms and rocked her girlfriend. "It's going to be okay, Honey, everything's just fine," she soothed. But they both knew that Melody had lost the baby.

DEPRESSION – APRIL 2008

What was the point of getting out of bed? Melody sighed and threw the covers over her head. The cold, steel-gray curtain of a depressive sky discouraged any activity. Plus, the bed felt like the only remaining soft, warm refuge left.

She heard Chris downstairs, probably grabbing munchies while he watched a movie on DVD or a game. Wouldn't matter what game: hockey, basketball, football, baseball; he loved sports and could watch any team play no matter how bad.

Melody felt a momentary twinge of guilt for not going to be with him.

Chris had been supportive beyond belief. She'd heard of guys who—unable to deal with the loss of a child themselves, no less the woman's grief— checked out and distanced themselves, eventually leading to an affair or the end of the relationship.

Thank God Chris wasn't the type. He had just checked on her, thirty minutes ago. Every day he told her how much he loved her, kissed her, brought her flowers, made sure she didn't want for anything.

It didn't matter though; she sniffed and buried her head in her pillow. Nothing could erase the pain of loss she felt.

Anger surged through her body. Chris seemed to work through it alright, though! Told her that even if they never had children, she would be more than enough for him.

She sighed as the anger disappeared as fast as it appeared. His words made her feel nice enough when he said it; she just didn't share the sentiment.

No, she wanted a baby so bad it hurt.

Sometimes the only opportunity she had to flee the numbing pain was when she escaped to work. Which depending on how you looked at it, sometimes proved to be a curse in and of itself. See when you don't inform anyone at work that you're pregnant, it's a little hard to ask for time off when you miscarry.

Tears slipped down her cheeks. That was the horrid tightrope career women traversed. When you wanted to have a family, you had to decide if stalling your career track or derailing it to start over fresh again was worth it. And she had worked too hard for the afternoon anchor position to jeopardize it now without a baby to show for it.

She rolled onto her back and pulled the pillow up to surround her head. Despite the career consequences, her life wouldn't seem complete without at least one child, even if she had to adopt.

Sadly, the competitive broadcasting environment worked in her favor over the last month and a half as she struggled to move on after the miscarriage. Folks at the station mentioned how much fiercer she seemed.

Although her patented daffodils and sunshine

smile still managed to engage and relate to people, her new-found emotions translated into added intensity on the screen and to the camera. Everyone ate it up, but it was hard continuing on like nothing changed.

A harsh laugh scraped her throat; her co-workers would die if they knew she was mere seconds away from balling her eyes out each day. Especially over the last two weeks when she covered heartbreaking stories about babies' deaths.

One confused teenage girl managed to hide her pregnancy and delivery from everyone, until she discarded her newborn in the apartment complex dumpster with his umbilical cord wrapped around his neck. Another woman, a highly medicated, stressed-out, middle-class housewife snapped and shook her baby to death.

It took every bit of professionalism in her to hold it together during those reports. *Why did those two idiots get blessed with healthy babies that they neither wanted nor deserved and yet, I couldn't carry mine to term?*

Tears filled her eyes once more and she felt like calling her mom. Margaret Wilkins, the petite blond who dared to marry an African-American man even when her parents disowned her. Who dared to raise her daughter in a predominantly African-American neighborhood with little to no help after her husband's sudden death. The woman who worked two jobs to make ends meet and never complained.

Although her mom just left a few days ago after

staying here with her for a week, she missed her already. Her mom's presence, always made her feel better and it had been instrumental in learning all the fertility problems her mother experienced trying to have Melody. Their family history of endometrioses caused many difficult pregnancies, miscarriages, or bouts of infertility.

"Keep your faith in the Lord," her mother advised, "and your options open."

Her faith remained strong for now although she prayed incessantly for a healthy child.

Imani tried to help when she reminded Melody of what she said after Marco died. Something to the effect of, "we don't know why God sends us down the paths he does, but sometimes it becomes evident in the future."

It all sounded like an utter load of nonsense now. *How could losing a child help now or in the future?* It didn't make any sense and it definitely didn't help ease the pain.

Especially considering that last week she suffered through Erycah's baby shower. *Why did folks need another baby shower every damn time they got pregnant anyway?* Erycah and Trevor even admitted they were reusing most of the items from Lil Trev and Xavier. She grunted.

Just another freaking excuse for Imani to throw a party. A couples one at that, so that her and Lance could smile and act as great hosts. All the while Erycah and Trev soaked it in as their mutual friends, church parishioners, neighbors, and Trev's co-workers oohed and ahhed since Erycah's co-workers had already thrown her a shower at work!

Then there were the stupid shower games that everyone else seemed to enjoy. But really, where was the fun in guessing baby foods or disgusting faux pooh diapers filled with chocolate or peanut butter or other smashed, gross nonsense?

"Argh!" Melody flipped over onto her stomach again. *Why am I behaving like a jealous, bitter, old hag?* "I hate this!"

God, if Imani and Lance offered to throw her the same exact baby shower now, she'd be the most involved with the biggest, most genuine grin pasted over her face. *Oh Lord, how much longer before my naturally optimistic, rose-colored world returns?*

She slammed her fist on the pillow. *Stop wallowing!* People miscarry every day and they eventually get over it. And a lot of people got over it alone. At least she had Chris, Imani, and Lance to help her through.

Hell, between the three of them she never wanted for company. Imani and Lance made a point of coming over separately or together, if they could swing it, to keep Chris and Melody occupied. Lance continued their weekly lunch tradition and Imani came over on Melody's days off to drag her out of the house to numerous functions and activities.

In fact, the two most fun events had been the excursion to the King Tut traveling museum tour with the beautiful Egyptian artifacts and her second favorite was the spa day. You just couldn't stay upset after a massage, facial, manicure, and pedicure.

Yet at the same time, their cheeriness and constant company irked the hell out of her. There were times when she just wanted to cry her eyes out and be left alone, but noooo. They wouldn't allow that.

Doorbell chimes interrupted her lamenting.

Hopefully, it was a neighbor kid selling something rather than company dropping by unannounced. Her worries were warranted as she heard Chris welcoming Imani and Lance.

Moments later her bedroom door opened and Imani burst inside.

"Get up sleepyhead, we got some shopping to do," she said knocking Melody out of the bed with a push.

Reliving the Past – May 2008

"Hey, Lance," Imani whispered into the phone so her co-workers didn't eavesdrop. "I know you're probably busy prepping for this post-draft, pre-training camp analysis, so I'll make it quick."

"Okay," Lance replied sounding amused yet cautious.

"I feel like going out tonight—"

"And I feel like staying home," Lance said with a chuckle. "So, already we have a problem."

Pausing to consider her options, she smiled. "Let's compromise. How about we hit the movies tomorrow, see *Iron Man* with that crazy Robert Downey, Jr. and sexy-ass Terrence Howard? Then for tonight why don't we go to your place instead? We never go over there and that way, you're officially *home* and yet I'm still *out*. Does that work…or is there a reason why we never go over to your place?" She grinned as she let the question whirl on the waves of insinuation.

Lance almost laughed aloud. "No, I'm not hiding anything at my place. The fact is I thought you preferred your house." His voice took on a faux chauvinistic tone. "You can bring your nosy behind over at 5:30 and cook for my troubles."

"Excuse you!" Imani tried to act put off, but she sounded as convincing as his ridiculous caveman commands from yesteryear.

"Hey, I agreed to movies tomorrow. It's the least you can do," Lance replied, pushing his luck. Knowing it, he jumped off the phone before she could respond. "See you tonight, bye!"

"Ass!" Imani muttered to the dead phone in her hand. She hung it up with a smile.

"So, neat and clean," Imani said as she ran her fingers along Lance's kitchen counter. "Even smells like a model home, all warm with cinnamon and spice."

"And everything nice, huh?" Lance replied, taking the defrosted chicken out of the fridge. "Well, it's not like I'm ever here much. When I spend seventy percent of my time with you or at work, it's easy to keep clean."

Walking over, she nestled beside Lance and helped him season the chicken. Their hands flirted together as they leaned it with lemon and massaged in the garlic, thyme, salt, and pepper.

"You want this sautéed or baked?" she asked already eyeing the wild mushroom risotto and asparagus that she needed to tackle next.

"I'll sauté it if you prepare the side dishes," Lance replied as they washed their hands.

"Sounds good," she said stopping him for a quick kiss.

Lance's eyes lit up after their lips parted and she

noticed the extra pep in his step as he whistled on his way to the stove.

Smiling, she turned her attention to preparing the risotto. Amazing how comfortable and cozy things felt between them now. She hummed along to his random whistling.

"So," Imani began as she wandered into Lance's family room after dinner, "can I ask you something that you're not going to want to answer?"

Lance stopped halfway between the kitchen and family room. Eyebrow cocked up towards the heavens.

Noticing his expression, she clutched her stomach laughing and collapsed onto his black leather couch.

"Ohhh-kay," he replied giving her an even stranger look.

When she regained enough composure, she managed to speak between chuckles. "I'm sorry, but at a quick glance—with your muscles popping from under your black t-shirt, your stance, and your eyebrow raised to kingdom come—you looked like Dwayne "The Rock" Johnson's cousin. I kept expecting you to say, 'Do you know what the Lance is cooking?'"

Lance smirked, trying not to laugh. "I'll tell you what I'm cooking," he said preparing to give chase.

"No, no, no," she shrieked making sure to keep the couch between her and him as he raced after her. "Okay, okay," she said waving her hand in surrender as he pursued her around the couch for the third time.

"I promise no more jokey-jokes, just don't tickle me."

He stopped and crossed his arms. "What do I get instead?"

Imani couldn't help the playful look she knew she exuded. "Wasn't cooking dinner enough?"

"Really?" His eyebrow cocked again as he waited for a better offer.

"Well, what do you have in mind?" she asked, coy smile piercing through.

"Mm, I know what I'd like, but since we can't do that yet… how about a massage later?"

She tapped her toe twice while thinking, then smirked. "I guess that would be acceptable," she said not disclosing how pleasant it would be to see and touch his shirtless, muscled torso. "So can we sit now?" she asked as she plopped down on his couch without waiting for a response.

As Lance approached, she hoped he'd sit near the opposite end because she felt like curling up with her head in his lap. Lately he tended to run his fingers through her hair and each time the sensations left her feeling nice and relaxed although she'd never admit it to him.

To her delight, Lance obliged and he barely settled in before she tucked her legs up and nestled her head in his lap. Not five seconds later she felt his fingers slip through her hair. Warm tingles played tag across her scalp.

"So what were you going to ask me?"

"Hmm?" she asked finding it hard to concentrate with his fingers.

He shot her a look. "You said something about asking me a question I wouldn't want to answer?"

"Oh, yeah." Hating to interrupt his fingers at play, she nonetheless flipped onto her back to look up at him. "You have to promise not to get mad, but I need you to answer this and answer honestly."

"I'm not going to lie," he replied as his fingers stuttered to a halt.

Frustrated at her timing, she popped up and gazed around the whole room, her hand sweeping out in unison. "Although I've looked all around this place, there's not one single trace of Heather anywhere."

"Why would there be?" His face scrunched up in distaste. "We divorced two years ago."

"Not one single picture from your elaborate wedding or marriage? Not a single knick-knack?" Heather had bought goo gobs of furniture and decorations during their short marriage, yet Imani didn't see anything here except for items she had personally picked out with Lance.

After his career-ending injury, he'd suddenly left his NYC home and moved up to Albany. In fact, she helped him whittle the final four selections down to this house.

A lovely home, she thought again with pride. Very similar floor plan to her own place actually. Except whereas hers had three bedrooms and two and a half baths, his place boasted five bedrooms, four bathrooms, and a lavish finished basement replete with a pool table and bar. Not that he ever really used them.

"Why would I keep anything?" Lance's deep, calm voice brought her back.

Imani placed her hand on his arm. "It's like she never existed."

"She didn't," he replied all matter-of-fact.

"See, that's not what I wanted to hear." Sadness made her wilt back, she removed her hand and looked away. "If you completely removed her, why wouldn't you eradicate me?"

Lance sighed and rubbed his head. His head dropped back and rested on the couch, hands covered his face.

Imani snapped her head towards him. "Sorry if this seems like I'm rehashing old news, but my momma always says, 'if you don't learn from the past, you're doomed to repeat it.' And I'm not trying to repeat history with you." When, he still didn't respond, she touched his leg.

That seemed to rouse him because his hands dropped, his right covering hers, and he rolled his head over to face her. "Fine, you're right." His eyes took on an honest, vulnerable quality as if she could see into his soul. "As I've told you before, Heather and I were never friends. So, when the promised passion didn't materialize, we were left with nothing to keep us together."

Sitting up fully, his hands locked around hers. "You and I are the best of friends." His gaze held hers strong and steady. "If you must know...that 'magical moment' as we like to call it now, really was. Believe it or not, you somehow imprinted on my soul."

He let out a sad grunt. "Much to my dismay, and despite my best efforts, I couldn't shake free." His voice softened. "Then, eventually, I didn't want to, although you gave me no choice after you picked Marco over me."

During his confession her throat dried to sandpaper and she forced two wet swallows before she could speak. "If Marco…" She hesitated, reluctant to uncover more although she had to know.

His eyes probed hers and when she tried to speak her voice cracked.

Swallowing again, she managed to spit it out. "If Marco were still alive, would you have ever come back…to at least renew our friendship?"

A sigh, deep as the ocean, washed over like a tsunami. "No. I don't believe so."

"Why?" her question sounded like a desperate plea and her heart stopped a beat.

Sadness settled over his features. "It ate at me like piranhas, Imani. Seeing you so happy with him. Part of me felt happy for you as your friend. But that imprinted side burned like acid; you should have been mine. I just couldn't take that constant interior battle, eating away at me, poisoning my soul. It made me angry and bitter."

"And, God forbid, this doesn't work," she asked as her breathing slowed. "Will the bitterness return? Will I lose my friend again?"

Much to her surprise he smiled and the sadness receded. "I've actually thought about that," he said almost bragging. "Nope. I realize now what I'd missed all this time."

Readjusting in front of her, he held her face between his large, warm hands. "Our friendship is priceless to me, Imani. Whatever happens, I don't want to lose it ever again."

Lance pulled her into his arms and she melted, basking in his strong, feverish heartbeat. "Although this time I swear nothing's going to tear us apart."

ANOTHER SPECIAL DELIVERY - MAY 2008

Melody couldn't believe they were here again.

"Push!" the delivery nurse yelled to a puffing Erycah.

"I see the head, Sweetheart!" Trev gave Erycah an enthusiastic smile. "You're in the home stretch, Little Mama." He rubbed her foot in encouragement as she adjusted it in the stirrups again. Then he resumed his position between her side and the doctor who posed waiting for the forthcoming child to emerge.

"You're doing beautifully." Imani squeezed Erycah's right hand.

"I…I'm going to wait outside," Chris blanched as the blood drained from his face.

"He's still not into blood and pain," she explained as Chris stumbled from the room.

Sniffing back angry tears that she tried to play off as tears of joy, she almost went outside to drag him back into the room. *Why would he leave me now to support Erycah when all I want to do is cry? This should have been me in a few months' time, delivering my own baby.*

However, that wasn't happening now and it ripped at her empty womb. "Almost through," she said not entirely meaning Erycah and her delivery, but rather how much longer she needed to be strong and supportive. Sighing, she patted Erycah's left hand.

***

Lance soaked in everything from a position behind the doctor. It was one of the only free spots left in the room since Trev and the nurse were at Erycah's legs and the girls were situated at her arms. It was definitely the best seat in the house as he could watch all the action unfold.

"How…much…longer?"   Erycah   breathed rhythmically.

"Almost there, Erycah," the nurse answered. "You're doing so well, looks like one more push and you're home free."

The doctor nodded as the next contraction came and the shoulders appeared to be in the correct position.

"Alright, Erycah, push!" the nurse ordered.

"C'mon, Girl," Imani said, supporting Erycah's back.

"Arrrhhh," Erycah grimaced, strained, and pushed.

"You did it!" Trev whooped as the baby slid out slippery as a greased pig.

"It's a boy," the doctor announced with a smile as the big, beautiful baby took his first breaths that lead to a healthy, lusty cry.

A warm, overwhelming sensation of love and wonder overtook Lance as he looked back and forth between the baby, Erycah, and Imani. This was what he wanted, this beautiful, life-changing experience. He beamed at Trev who followed the doctor's instructions on cutting the umbilical cord.

"He's as gorgeous as you, Sweetheart." Trev grinned from ear to ear.

"Oh God, I need to tell Chris the good news." Melody wiped tears off her cheeks and raced across the room to leave.

"I can't believe this little boy decided to come a week early," Imani said. "Your mom and sister are going to be so mad they couldn't change their airline tickets in time. They've missed each delivery."

"I know, and they can blame the baby because he came so quickly," Erycah said happy but tired. She looked over at Trev who waited for the nurses and doctor to finish all the initial tests, so that he could hold him. "What's it been, only three hours after my water broke? Versus twelve hours for your first little knucklehead to arrive and six hours for Xavier!"

"Guess this one couldn't wait to get out and run after his big brothers, Sweetheart," Trev replied before accepting his son from the nurse. "Oh baby, he's so good-looking," he cooed walking back over to Erycah's bedside.

"Snap, let me get my camera," Imani said making a move for her purse.

"I got it, Baby," Lance said, grabbing it before she did. "Everybody say 'cheese' on three."

Right after he finished taking a few pictures, Melody returned with Chris who looked much less green.

Lance made room for them to pass. *Poor guy!* What was he going to do when he and Melody conceived again? No way would Melody ever let him bow out of their delivery room from queasiness.

Chris came around the side of the bed and looked at the baby. Then he congratulated Erycah and Trev.

Erycah exuded a proud countenance as she cradled the baby.

Meanwhile Trevor hovered over Erycah, almost worshipful as if Erycah were a Black Madonna.

The love between them radiated throughout everyone in the room and again he realized how much he wanted this life, these experiences.

As in reply, the box in his pocket burned his leg, practically demanding to come out of hiding. Slipping his hand inside his pocket, he patted it. He'd bought it the day before and he planned on scheduling something memorable and befitting Imani's high standards.

Tales of surprise romantic getaways, rose-filled rooms, sonnets and soliloquies, and elaborate dinner proposals crossed his mind, but he hadn't decided on any specific plan yet.

Maybe all the hoopla, pomp and circumstance didn't matter. He wanted more than anything to let the mood sweep him along and determine the time and place. And this felt right. The loving atmosphere, the possibility of hope and new beginnings, surrounded by friends.

He hesitated until Imani caught his eye. Pure joy radiated from her face. She winked at him, rubbed

Erycah's shoulder, and elbowed Trev on her way over to Lance.

When Imani stood before him, her loving gaze blazing full steam, he couldn't resist. He palmed the box out of his pocket and dropped down on one knee.

Imani's eyes bugged and her hand flew to her mouth.

Trevor was the first of their friends to notice. "Ah, hell no!"

Erycah followed Trev's stare and sat up as far as she could with the baby on her chest. "Ohhh, do that thing, Boy!"

Trev shook his head violently. "No, no, no! What in the hell is wrong with you, Man? Why must you insist on being the King of Awkward, Inappropriate Timing? I know you see we just popped out a baby. So why would you even take away from our special day by upstaging it with this shit?"

Erycah slapped Trev's hand. "Oh hush, Baby, it's not even like that. Go on, Lance!"

Melody stood quite still and quiet, reserved even, but Chris waved him on.

"Imani, you taught me what love is."

"And she needed to teach you a lot!" Trev muttered. "Bet you didn't even ask her parents' permission first!"

Erycah hit Trevor's leg.

"Love is unconditional. It's appreciating each other's strengths and working together to fortify the weaknesses. It's filled with honesty, trust, respect, and communication. Just knowing that we'll stand beside each other through thick and thin, makes me the happiest man in the world."

"You have shown me the man I could become and I'm eternally grateful. You know I have loved you for years. Imani, would you please do me the immense honor of marrying me, Baby?"

Imani nodded, tears in her eyes. "I will."

Like butter melting over hot corn on the cob, the two-carat, emerald-cut diamond ring slid onto her left ring finger.

"Oh my, God, it's so beautiful," she cried while pulling him to his feet. "Almost as beautiful as you," she said before sealing the deal with a breath-stealing kiss.

LIVING ARRANGEMENTS – JUNE 2008

Melody entered Imani's house and immediately her stomach growled at the smell of good food cooking. She gave Imani a quick hug and followed her nose.

It wasn't until she settled in the kitchen and prepared to open the oven that she noticed Imani still holding the front door open wide.

"Um, Imani? What are you doing?"

"Hello, what do you think? I'm waiting for Chris to hurry up and come inside."

"Well you can shut the door. He's not coming."

A strange look rippled over Imani's face as she joined her in the kitchen. "You guys fight or something?"

"Noooo." Now it was her turn to reciprocate Imani's strange look. "Why?"

"He's always with you now like white on rice, excuse the pun." Imani shooed her away from the oven, reached past her, and opened the refrigerator. In one fluid motion, Imani pulled out a serving bowl of freshly tossed salad and handed it to her to place on the dining room table. "So something's wrong."

"I'm not sure what gave you that absurd idea, but that's not true." Melody set the salad down and returned to the kitchen.

"Please! Ever since your 'dream' he's more underfoot than a puppy." Imani handed her the potato salad. "If I didn't know any better, it would seem like he's trying to make sure nothing's really happening between you and Lance."

"Oh my God! Is that what you really think?" With fumes steaming out of her ears, she slammed the glass bowl of potato salad down on the table and stomped back into the kitchen. "For someone that's supposedly so intuitive, you couldn't be any further from the truth."

Imani stopped pouring hot baked beans from the baking casserole into the serving dish and stared back incredulous. "Really?" She set the hot casserole and pot holder down and put her hand on her hip. "Then clue me in, Ms. Thang. Why isn't Mr. Hang-a-bout Chris here?"

Melody resisted the strong impulse to blurt out the answer. Even though it would give her immense pleasure at this moment to spite Imani and knock the smug expression off her face, the last thing she wanted to do was hurt Lance.

She made sure Lance wasn't within earshot and then she dropped her voice to a whisper. "For your information, although Chris likes Lance, he loved Marco." A sliver of sadness seeped through her bones and settled into her voice. "Guess he feels a little strange that our parties went from you, me, Marco, and him…to no more Marco, and now Lance all up in the mix." Her gaze softened as she looked at

Imani. "It's still a little awkward for him."

For once Imani appeared chagrined. "Oh, Melody…" Imani shook her head, mad at herself. "Talk about open mouth, insert foot." Imani reached over and patted Melody's arm. "I apologize for my insensitive, stupid, off-base assumption."

Imani stopped and chewed her bottom lip. "Sometimes I forget that Marco's death didn't just affect me." She looked at her, hopeful. "Please forgive me?"

Melody smiled, affront already forgotten. "Apology accepted." She grabbed the serving dish of baked beans off the stove and changed the subject before the sad memories spilled over and soured the carefree mood. "Hey, are you and Lance still insisting on getting married ridiculously soon?"

Imani snorted, aware of Melody's tactic of switching topics. "Of course we are." She removed the tray of barbeque chicken from the oven. "Why?"

"Seriously, what's the rush?" She waited for Imani to decide how she wanted to serve the scrumptious, aromatic, drool-inducing chicken.

"Frankly, what's the hold up?" Imani shrugged. "We've been acting like a married couple for almost a year now—just without the sex." Imani scrunched up her face and gave Melody a dirty look as if it were somehow her fault that they weren't getting busy.

She managed to withhold a pleased, little giggle.

Deep in thought, Imani shrugged again. "Plus, he's here all of the time anyhow. So, really it's kind of silly to keep maintaining two different households."

"So, Lance is moving in here?"

"Mmm, smells good." Lance said as he entered the kitchen, rubbing his flat stomach. He smiled at Melody as he approached. "So what's this I hear about moving?" He stopped long enough to kiss her on the forehead, and then he headed to the fridge for a bottle of water.

"I was asking Imani when do we have to help you move over here."

"What makes you think I'm moving here?" He looked back and forth cautiously between the two women before he opened the water bottle and took a huge swig.

"Well, where else do you plan on living after we get married, Silly?" Imani fussed.

Lance finished swallowing, half the water gone, and gave Imani a look. "I always assumed we were moving into my place. It's bigger."

Imani propped a hand on her hip. "No way, that's where you lived with Heather."

"Um, news flash, this is where you lived with Marco…for a lot longer, I might add. Plus, Heather took the little bit of stuff she had with her after the divorce. And lest you forget, you helped me pick out the house and most of the furniture. So, technically it's more your house than it ever was Heather's."

Imani stood speechless for a moment. "Okay, all that's true, but…"

"But what?" he asked waiting for her to come to his conclusion.

"I don't know. For whatever reason, your house feels cold to me. Don't get me wrong, it's pretty. In fact, it's magazine feature-story pretty." Imani looked perplexed. "But it doesn't feel lived in." Her hands shrugged an apology. "It just doesn't feel like *home*."

"So what are you saying?" Lance asked. "That you can't do a Luther Vandross and turn my house into a home?"

Melody giggled and Imani laughed in spite of herself.

"No, I guess not," Imani replied looking uncharacteristically stumped.

"So, not only do I have to help you plan a super speedy, destination wedding at some distant, exotic location, but now you're telling me that I have to help you find a house, too?" Melody felt a warm, delightful tickle start to build inside at the prospect.

She could finally help Imani after all the times Imani had come to her rescue. And despite what the magazines warned, nothing could be more fun than planning a dream wedding and decorating a new house with her best friend.

Imani and Lance exchanged looks.

Slowly Imani shook her head. "Yep, I guess that's what we're saying."

Real Magical Moments – August 2008

The warm, tropical breeze rustled Lance's thatched beach umbrella. *This is crazy.* He sat back and reclined on the wooden chaise lounge. *How can my first marital fiasco and this ridiculously wonderful experience both seem so reminiscent and conversely divergent at the same time?* He ran his hand over his head then relaxed as he watched Imani dive through the lightly cresting, crystal clear, turquoise waves.

Not unlike his first marriage, the engagement period was quick, three months this time instead of two. But at least he knew Imani for years, and this felt more than right. This time he knew what he wanted.

He sighed. Although he detested spending brain cells even recollecting his first marriage, the wedding images sprang to life.

The first time around, he felt like a stranger at his own party because Heather's family used the occasion to host one of the social events of the year. Of the three hundred guests that attended, only fifty comprised his guest list. Oddly enough, he snickered, nine of those favored few made it to this go round, too.

Last time, Heather insisted that only family

represent them at the altar. She hated his friends. So along with her siblings and cousins, who he never really knew or cared about, his half-brother and sister acted as groomsman and bridesmaid.

With a smile, he recalled their intimate ceremony on the beach five days ago. Although he loved his half-brother and half-sister, Brian and Donna, dearly, he much preferred having his father, the man who first told him that Imani was the woman for him, standing beside his side. And of course, next to Imani, stood Melody, their one true friend—bonded by blood, through thick and thin.

The small audience of sixteen that presided over their nuptials consisted of his step-mother, Diana, and his half-siblings, Brian and Donna. His crazy mother, who clucked about here and there, making sure everyone knew how proud she was. Imani's dad, who made him feel like a welcome part of the family, and her mom, who at least showed up and acted civil.

Also in the group, Trev and Erycah, who behaved like newlyweds, using the time away from their brood as a well-deserved second honeymoon. Big Tony, one of his best buddies on and off the college football field, made the trip up from the Tampa Bay Buccaneers. Joining him was a hot tamale from Miami who looked like she might be the one to cure his perpetual resident bachelor status.

Another football friend and frat bother, John, came with his wife, Krystal, who just happened to be one of their college friends and Lance's old booty call buddy. Lance chuckled. Needless to say, their convoluted relationship created more than a few tense moments in the past, but all that was ancient history.

Finally rounding out the mini brigade of extended family and friends were Chris, Lance's aunt, and Melody's mother. Along with Imani's parents, none of the latter was privy to his first marital shindig.

Hmm, wonder what the others thought when they compared the two events?

Out of the corner of his eye he spotted their personal butler, from the all-inclusive Sandals Grande St. Lucian resort, approach with their drinks. His black pants, colorful vest, crisp white shirt, and gloves played a stark contrast to their multi-colored mixed drinks.

"Your drinks, Sir," he said with a smile as he set Lance's Bahama Mama and Imani's Sex on the Beach on the side table between their chaise lounges. In a flash, he disappeared leaving Lance and Imani alone again with the nearest couples at least forty yards away.

Lance adjusted his sunglasses, sipped his drink, and set it down next to Imani's Sex on the Beach. This time there was no ironic smirk, only a satisfied smile. When Heather had ordered that same drink on their honeymoon, he swore she did it just to mock him. Especially considering she had refused, all week long, to have sex with him again even once after their wedding night.

With a contented sigh, he gazed at his wife of five days swimming in the brilliant, sparkling water.

Imani couldn't be further from Heather. Not only

did they enjoy sex on the beach, two nights ago at midnight with the gentle waves lapping over them, they'd been making love like rabbits since their wedding night.

He leaned back, already aroused just remembering their wedding night. After the simple, romantic ceremony on the beach and the fun-filled dinner party reception, he and Imani slipped off to their Beachfront Rondovals cottage suite.

That first night was what dreams were made of. For three hours they explored each other, taking one another to the brink and back before finally succumbing to ecstasy. It didn't end there either; round two took place in the beautiful bathtub, round three on the patio right as the sun begin to rise.

Even though they were exhausted, she did insist on doing one thing that Heather did…excursions. They experienced the Pitons, volcano, snorkeling, rain forest, sulfur springs, rum distillery, golf, Pigeon Island National Park, Anse Mamin sugar plantation, art galleries, deep sea fishing, Rodney Bay, tons of restaurants, and sprinkled liberally throughout…hot, steamy sex.

As if on cue, Imani broke from the water. *Mmm, mmm!* His mouth dropped. She almost looked like a coffee and cream-colored Halle Berry in James Bond's *Die Another Day* with her fully-filled, barely there, orange bikini. He could see her mischievous smile from here on the beach.

With a beguiling finger, she beckoned him to join her in the water.

Lance didn't even bother to take off his sunglasses.

Imani laughed and walked backwards into deeper water.

As he followed, the warm water welcomed him as he strolled in—cascading over his feet, then his shins, knees, up to his thighs, waist, and finally to his chest.

"I missed you," Imani said, her voice seductive and low. She wrapped her legs around his waist and her arms around his neck. He felt the heat emanating from her bikini bottom as she locked over his totally sprung third leg. "Mmm, seems somebody missed me, too."

Aroused past the breaking point, but attempting to show some decorum, he resisted tonguing her down under the bright sunlight. "What are you doing, Baby? Someone might see us out here in the open."

"There's no one out here except us and the fishies." She smiled sweet as molasses. "But even if there were, all they'd see is a happy couple talking in the ocean."

Although her right hand dropped down to her side, he balanced her easily.

In a flash she moved his waistband far enough to free him from his swim trunks, slipped her own bottoms minutely to the side, and slid him home. Her breath caught in a little moan as he gasped in shocked pleasure. Then she settled back into her mischievous smile as if nothing were happening below the surface.

"Remember," she said, her voice a husky song, "we're just having a simple little conversation."

Mmm-hmm. He moaned as their bodies talked the language of love. *Best. Conversation. Ever.*

WHAT! – SEPTEMBER 2008

"Does that look good?" Imani asked Lance as she finished hanging their wedding portrait over the mantle of their new home.

"Perfect," he replied taking a seat on the couch.

As she stepped off the chair and pulled her T-shirt down, a deep throbbing pain made her wince and cover her breasts. *What the hell?*

When she recovered enough, she walked past Lance and popped him upside the head.

He turned and glared at her while he rubbed the back of his head. "What was that for?"

"I don't know what you did to me last night in the throes of passion, but my boobs are tender as hell. Plus it feels like you shoved rocks inside them." As she leaned up against the couch, she readjusted the waistband of her sweatpants from digging into her stomach.

Lance quit rubbing his head and looked thoroughly alarmed. "There's no way. I'm always extremely gentle with my babies." He reached out to touch them.

Imani dodged and swatted his hand.

Lance had the nerve to look wounded. "Baby, you know I would never hurt them. I swear I didn't do anything different." He smiled up at her. "And you never complained in the past."

She hit him again. "God, you're hopeless!"

The doorbell rang.

They looked at each other in surprise.

"So, I guess you're not expecting anybody?" Imani asked as she went to the front door.

"Nope." Lance replied as he got up and followed her halfway down the hall.

Imani checked the peephole. "Oh, my God!"

"Who is it?" Lance asked as she opened the door.

"Hi, Baby!" her mother said as she bowled right on in and hugged her tight.

"Mom?"

Mrs. Jordan unhanded Imani and came far enough inside so Mr. Jordan could secure Imani in a huge bear hug. "Lance," she said with at least a modicum of warmth.

"What are you guys doing here?" Imani managed to ask once her dad released her. She noticed that Lance had cocooned her mom in a big hug against her will until her mom finally quit protesting.

"Well, Baby Girl, we were kind of in the area and your mother insisted we stop by," her dad said. "I told her we should call first or get a hotel—"

"Nonsense," Lance interrupted, "we always love having you both around."

Her mom humphed then turned back to Imani. "How much did you eat in St. Lucia?"

"Excuse me?" She was too caught off guard to even get mad.

"Well, Honey, you're as swollen as a beach ball." Her mother frowned and walked over to investigate her like Sherlock Holmes. "Wait, I thought you said you two didn't have sex before the wedding?"

Lance's eyes widened at her mom's bluntness and Imani felt like she'd been slapped.

When she could form words again, she let her mother have it. "We didn't, not that it's any business of yours, Mother!"

"Oh, Lord," her dad whispered and shook his head.

"Well, don't get all pissy at me because your contraceptives didn't work and you're pregnant." Her mom put her hand on her hip and squinted at Lance. "You know the hormones are the first thing to go haywire. Expect some moodiness."

Lance started to respond, but then he looked at Imani, shocked. "You're pregnant?"

Imani huffed and crossed her arms. "Of course not, why would you listen to a word this crazy woman says." She uncrossed her right arm and gestured. "My period starts on the fifth."

Her mom threw her head back and guffawed. "It's the seventh, Baby, and don't even try to feed me any excuses. We're both as regular as Old Faithful."

Time stood still. *The seventh? How could it be the seventh already?* Her head and jaw dropped. Her mother was right about one thing, she had always been regular. The gears in her mind spun. It would explain the sore boobs...and the tight waistband. And the one thing her mother got wrong was that their contraceptives hadn't failed…because they hadn't used any.

Their wedding night was the only time during the entire sex-fueled honeymoon that she even saw a condom. And Lance pushed it away saying he could care less if they got pregnant or not. *Well, he sure as shit got his wish!*

She looked up at Lance.

His face overflowed with pride and love as he took her in his arms. He squeezed her tight but gentle until she felt his heartbeat in her chest. "I love you, Little Mama."

Second Times the Charm

"Don't get me wrong," Melody complained as she stabbed her Chicken Caesar Salad. "I love that we keep it real by eating at places like this." She waved her fork around to indicate the T.G.I. Friday's that they were dining in. "But when are we going to frequent some really upscale establishments like the Scrimshaw Restaurant at The Desmond?"

Imani chuckled. "I'm ready whenever you are." Imani licked her lips. "Although these ribs are mighty tasty."

As Melody chewed her salad she felt the familiar yet unwelcome sticky wetness of her period. "Great," she grumbled, tossing her fork in her plate. Caesar dressing splattered across the table. She frowned. "Really?"

"Problems?" Imani asked from across the table before she tore into another Jack Daniels delectable-looking, delicious-smelling rib.

Melody growled and grabbed Imani's purse off of one of the two empty chairs between them at the square table for four. Without asking, she unzipped the main compartment and rummaged through another zippered side pocket.

After her fingers failed to connect with any plastic

wrapped pads or tampons, she sighed. "Where did you move your feminine products?" she asked while checking another section, "because you should have been flowing like crazy for at least the last few days."

When Imani hesitated, Melody snapped her head up and caught Imani paused in mid-chew, her mouth dangling open.

Imani closed her mouth and half smiled.

"Are you kidding me?" She glared at Imani. "There's no freaking way you're pregnant after not even a month of marriage?"

"Well, thanks for the congratulations, I guess," Imani replied with a smirk.

"Sorry, congratulations and all that jazz," she said with a dismissive wave. Using unneeded force, she zipped up Imani's purse so fast the zipper almost broke.

"I was going to tell you—"

"You don't have to explain," she said although in actuality it stung a bit. "I've become ultra-superstitious after my miscarriage." *That part was definitely true.* "In fact if I ever get pregnant again, I'm not telling a single soul before the recommended three months." *Also true.*

Imani wiped her hands and reached across the table for Melody's free right hand. "Don't worry. You'll get pregnant again."

Melody half tossed Imani's purse back on the chair with her left hand, then affixed Imani with a steady gaze. "Is this your amazing semi-psychic side speaking?"

Imani pursed her lips. "It doesn't quite work that way. I can't foretell the future." She shifted in her seat and forced on a reassuring smile. "But regardless, I just feel it deep in my soul."

"And what if you're wrong? What then?" she asked with a huff.

"You know all the options—fertility treatments, using a surrogate, even adoption."

"C'mon! We don't have tens of thousands of dollars for fertility treatments or a surrogate. And I know we could adopt, but I want to feel what it's like to have my child growing inside of my body."

"Trust me, it'll happen. I don't know when, but it will." Imani squeezed her hand.

She dropped her head, not feeling confident, but wanting to believe. "And what makes you so uber confident?"

"You yourself said that your mom had difficulty conceiving. You even confessed that she suffered a miscarriage prior to you." Imani released Melody's hand and patted her cheek. "So, genetically if she was able to eventually have a baby, you will, too."

Melody slumped back in her chair. "Maybe so, but it just seems so frustrating and unfair. We're trying everything conceivable in an attempt to get pregnant and you and Erycah just look at a penis and get pregnant."

"Alrighty then." Imani laughed out loud.

She glared at Imani although she couldn't suppress the smile that played across her lips. "Fertile heifers!"

Imani sat back and chuckled. "You need prayer, Melody!"

Melody giggled. "Yes, I probably do."

"Well," said Imani as she became more serious, "have you prayed on it?"

A frown emerged as she thought about it for a moment and she didn't like the answer. Uttering a resigned sigh, she replied. "I think it's more like I'm constantly complaining to God and wondering why." The admission saddened her and she covered her face in shame.

"None of us ever knows why, but God has his reasons." Imani's voice soothed like a rocking chair.

"What possible reasons could He have?" she asked desperate to know what lesson she needed to learn.

"It could be anything: patience, gratitude, endurance. That's why they say He works in mysterious ways."

The words erupted before her mind could finish filtering them. "Yeah, well what mysterious nugget did you gleam from Marco's death?"

Imani's eyebrow rocketed up into her patented arch and her tongue flicked across her top teeth.

Damn it, she wanted to apologize, but she faltered under Imani's intense stare. She dropped her head to escape the heat. "I'm sorry, Imani. That didn't come out right. It was a low blow and you didn't deserve it. Especially when you're just trying to help."

To her surprise, Imani's soothing tone returned. "It's okay, Melody. It was a fair question."

Melody couldn't stop her head from popping back

up. *Huh?*

"There were a lot of things Marco taught me about love, preconceived notions and judgments, prejudice by both whites and blacks." Imani chuckled, her eyes dreamy and far away. "Love…myself." She played with her hands.

"Plus, if you want to be really warped, I guess it gave Lance a chance to mature." Imani's gaze sharpened and focused on Melody. "But I still don't know why God took Marco. At least not before he could leave some kind of legacy; a child to carry on his lineage…"

"I'm sorry." Now it was her turn to take Imani's hands. "You're right. It's not up to us to question God. Especially with all the things we have to be grateful for. He's blessed us with so much: our lives, our loving husbands, our careers." She stopped and squeezed Imani's hands. "Each other."

True to form, Imani grunted, pulled back, and picked up her fork. "And this food!"

RANDOM CALL – NOVEMBER 2008

Lance adjusted his tie in the hallway mirror. He needed to hurry if he wanted to catch his plane. Actually, there was no real danger of him missing his plane, but he liked to be early. When he arrived simply 'on time,' he felt as if he might as well be late.

"You look fine," Imani said with a chuckle before she ate another spoonful of oatmeal.

Lance's ringtone came on as his phone started to vibrate across the kitchen island.

"Could you get that?" he asked as he undid his tie again.

Imani arched an eyebrow but grabbed the phone with her left hand. Her lips twisted a bit as she checked the caller ID. "It's a Helene?"

Lance frowned and looked at her in the mirror. "I don't know a Helene."

A bit of her old attitude emerged and her eyes flashed. "Well evidently, you do know a Helene because her name's appearing on your phone. Not an unknown number but her *name*." She took a breath and her voice calmed down. "Is it someone you work with?" She took another bite of oatmeal.

"No," he replied going back to his tie. "Besides Robin, there's only two or three other women I work with and none of them are programmed into my phone." He paused as the phone hit the middle of his ringtone. "Is it a Connecticut area code?"

"No, it's 631." Imani swallowed her bite. "Isn't that Long Island?"

He turned to face her. "I thought Long Island was 516."

"Regardless," she said setting down her spoon. "It's a NYC number."

"Well some of the folks commute in to Connecticut," he began, but then he reconsidered. They both knew it was probably some old fling from his past. Although he didn't get calls on his cellphone often, it wasn't as if he ever changed his number either.

The phone stopped ringing.

As Imani set it aside, she actually smiled. "Call the ho back on your way to the airport and tell her to quit calling you." She came over and finished off his tie. "You're going to be late."

"You're not irrationally mad or jealous?" he asked, half surprised, half impressed.

She wrapped her arms around his neck. "You know which side your bread is buttered." Her lips teased his.

"I don't even know what that means, but it sure sounds good." He ached for her kiss.

"It is as long as you make sure you don't get any more random calls," she whispered before her kiss made him forget all about Helene…and almost his flight.

CHRISTMAS TIDINGS – DECEMBER 2008

Melody released her mother's hand and slid past Chris into the aisle. Pastor's words beckoning her to answer his altar call.

When she practiced Catholicism, she would have never dreamed of willingly marching to the front of the church to confess her sins or sing God's praises. That's what confessionals were for, hidden little shadowy alcoves of shame.

She tsked and checked herself. It wasn't like she was alone, at least twenty other parishioners were coming forth to kneel at the altar and unburden themselves.

As she knelt—hands steepled, head down, and soul open, she felt the weight of jealousy and guilt wash away. With a light heart, she praised God again for answering her prayers.

Funny, how He worked. It seemed that as soon as she prayed for God to take away her anger and jealousy of Imani and Erycah—wallowing in how unfair life seemed that both of them would get pregnant within a month of each other when that's all that she desired—she'd gotten pregnant.

Now they were all going to celebrate motherhood together with Imani's expected mid-May delivery,

Erycah's in mid-June, and her own in early July. And in an extra romantic turn, all three decided against finding out their baby's sex.

Erycah didn't want to get depressed if the little girl she prayed for was yet another Trevor clone. Lance because he kept insisting that he and Imani had a bet, when they really didn't; Imani could care less if it were a boy or a girl. And well, Melody just felt it was fun and romantic to get surprised by God's gift.

Feeling inner peace at last, she praised Him again for blessing her with Chris, her mother, the baby, and her friends. The mere thought made her miss them. Selfishly she wished again that Imani and Lance had stayed in town for Christmas rather than spending it in NYC with their families.

She looked heavenward and shook her head. *Sorry God, baby steps.* She chuckled and bowed her head again. This time she prayed for the health of Imani, Erycah, and herself, and the babies growing inside of them. In Jesus' precious name. Amen.

WHAT'S IN A NAME – JANUARY 2009

Lance revved his CLK until it purred and melded into the light Thursday evening traffic on from I-287 after the I-87 interchange. Even though the car was four years old, he still loved the way it handled. The sleek, beautiful machine could sense his every driving instinct, the wheel perfectly attuned to his commands. Sensing a speed trap ahead, he begrudgingly eased off the accelerator.

"This is so ridiculous."

"Hmm?" Lance glanced over at Imani in the passenger seat. She seemed to glow under the freeway lights, a perfect vision of love and impending motherhood. He smiled and placed his right hand on her firm, tight belly with the smallest hint of a protrusion.

"I know it's way too early to even think about this," she said, "but I can't stop mulling over baby names. None of the girl's names are appealing to me right now. Sorry, but there's no real way to feminize 'Lance' and I'm not feeling any of our mother's suggestions either."

"Well, you don't have to worry about that because this little package," he said rubbing her barely there baby bump, "is a boy."

Imani smiled. "And if it isn't?"

"I'll be ecstatic either way, if that's what you're asking." He glanced over at her again before returning his eyes to the road. "A beautiful baby girl like you? Yeah, I'm ready for her to wrap me around her little finger." She patted his hand.

"But he's not. Just like Trev, this is my very own mini-me," he said beaming with pride.

"I already figured you'd want a Lance, Jr.," she said chuckling.

"We could switch it up, change the middle name if you wanted to honor your dad."

"Actually," Imani replied with a slight hesitation, "I was considering Marco for a middle name."

In an instant his hand slid off her lap and he glanced at her, his eyebrow cocked back like a gun. He quickly refocused on the road and swallowed to prevent the, 'ah, hell no,' from escaping his lips.

Watch your reaction! Mustering his pre-game concentration techniques, he forced his body to inhale and exhale deeply to provide an opportunity for his voice and demeanor to remain calm and cool.

Feeling more in control, he glanced over at Imani. "Please don't take this the wrong way...because I'm not trying to sound unreasonable. But as your current husband, it feels a tad bit *uncomfortable* when you ask me to name my child after your previous husband."

Imani chewed her bottom lip and he could tell that she was attempting to temper her response, too.

Whatever the outcome, at that moment, he felt

extremely proud that they'd come so far. To be able to hold a normal, civilized conversation over a potentially volatile topic instead of their normal verbal jousting and landmines, made him want to kiss her. His hand found hers again and he squeezed it.

Keeping her head down, she stroked her thumb along his palm and held his hand. "It wasn't meant like that." She glanced up at him. "At one point in time, you thought of him as a friend. And I don't know…I just feel bad that his lineage ended with him. Outside of Maria, the Cabrettes are just dead and gone. Like they didn't exist."

He thought he heard her sniff back a tear, but when he glanced at Imani, her face remained hidden as she looked out the passenger side window.

"But I see how that must sound from your vantage point," she continued, her voice sad and soft. "Sorry, I brought it up."

"No, no," he exclaimed as he removed his hand to turn on his signal and take the Empire Plaza exit. His heart tumbled at seeing his normally strong wife so vulnerable. "Don't you dare apologize for speaking your mind. We have to be able to communicate about anything, okay?"

Imani nodded as he pulled up to the Egg Center for Performing Arts underground parking and waited in the short line. Anxious to enter and park so that they could continue their discussion, his thumbs drummed the steering wheel until it was their turn.

After he forked over the requisite parking fee to the lot attendant, Lance squeezed Imani's hand once.

Then he followed the flag and hand gestures from the other parking lot attendants.

As he rounded the bend, they spotted Melody and Chris in the crowd, walking to the elevators, dressed to the nines for the Joshua Redman Double Trio concert. He tapped the horn and Imani waved as he drove past the waving couple to find a parking spot.

Once he parked and turned off the engine, he shifted towards Imani and caressed her smooth face. "Thank you for explaining what you were thinking."

She melted in his hands and he yearned for her more.

Leaning over, he kissed her sweet lips until he knew that they were fine. "I'm so proud of us..." he said staring into her inviting, expression-filled, espresso eyes, "of you. I love you, Mrs. Imani Dunn."

"I love you, too, and I'm proud that I'm carrying Lance Joseph Dunn, Jr."

No Air – February 2009

Hot. Stifling. Suffocating. Imani panicked as she realized she couldn't breathe.

Gasping didn't help. There was simply no air. Something constricted her air flow and strangled her.

Almost hysterical, she clawed at the area around her neck…but each swipe came up empty.

She tried to scream, but nothing came out. Helplessly she felt herself losing consciousness from lack of oxygen.

"Imani!" Rough hands shook her and she slapped them away although they didn't relent. "Imani, what's wrong?"

She needed to escape and she launched herself back away from the hands. They slipped for a second and she felt her body freefalling. Automatically, she reached out towards the hands to catch herself, but the hands found purchase again and secured her tight.

"Imani, wake up!"

This time the voice connected and she inhaled sweet, fresh air. Her breath came back in ragged clumps. Searing hot streaks of delicious pain flew down her throat. Imani's eyes flew open. Somehow, she hadn't noticed they were closed.

Their low lit family room jumped into focus.

Lance's face an anguished mask of apprehension and alarm.

His hands were somewhat brusque on her forearms. "Are you okay?"

She couldn't nod yet and she really didn't know.

"Is it the baby? Should I call an ambulance? What happened, Imani?" Lance's questions tripped over one another, his eyes shimmering with concern.

Not able to make heads nor tails of his questions, she asked her own. "What happened?"

"I don't know. You were laying here with your head on my lap. Watching the news with me, I thought. Maybe you dozed off during the broadcast. I don't know. I was stroking your head. Then all of a sudden, you seized up, straight as a board, and I swore you just stopped breathing. I tried to wake you and you started fighting back." His hands cupped her face now. "Are you okay? You scared the shit out of me."

Imani noticed his use of profanity and full-heartedly concurred.

Then the icy dread slithered down her spine and settled in her gut. *Oh my God, it wasn't me; it never was. Someone else is dying!* She leapt off the couch and Lance followed suit.

"What is it, Imani? Talk to me!" he demanded as he paced behind her.

She grabbed his arms, face contorting as she tried to focus. The feeling faded fast and it seemed so faint and indistinct. The few wisps of familiarity retreated. *Think, Imani, think!*

The only vague image she could pull was of…Trev? Maybe it was Trev and Erycah? It was yet it wasn't. *Oh God, I don't understand. What is this premonition trying to tell me?*

Tears fell as she got around to answering Lance. "I don't know!" Frustration crippled her. Why couldn't she understand? "I just don't know!"

Then one last, feeble punch hit her straight in the gut before it disappeared. Her eyes widened. "Call Trevor, now!"

Lance only hesitated for an instant, not wanting to leave her even for a second to retrieve the phone, but he did. The line was ringing as he handed it to her.

"Imani?" Trev's voice sounded half-worried, half-skeptical. "It's after eleven at night. You okay?"

Imani heard Erycah in the background. "Why's she calling so late?"

"Trev, please don't panic, but are Erycah and the baby okay?"

Imani heard Trevor sit upright in bed, trepidation peppered his voice. "Yea, she's fine, she's right here next to me. You want to tell me what's going on?"

Imani's mind scrambled to make sense of her lost premonition. *Could it be?* She prayed it wasn't, but she had to ask. "What about the boys?"

Trev breathed more heavily as she heard him jump out of bed and run down the hallway.

Erycah cried out in fear as she ran after him. "Trev what's going on? What's Imani want? Trev, you two are scaring me!"

Imani couldn't bear to listen.

Lance studied her face, grabbed the phone from her hand, and put it on speaker.

She leaned against Lance's rock hard chest, afraid if she stood on her own any longer, she would collapse.

He held her tight with one arm, his chin half-resting, half-nestling on the top of her head.

Trev's shaky voice came over the speaker. She could sense him checking each child one by one. "Trev, Jr. is fine." An audible exhale escaped him. His voice seemed to get stronger as he checked the next child. "Xavier's fine, too."

Erycah gasped. "No! Damn it, no!"

"Kingston's blue. I'm calling 911." Trev said before the line went dead as he disconnected.

"Oh, my God." Lance clicked off the phone and let it drop on the couch.

Imani broke down in Lance's arms. The sobs slow to subside.

The phone rang five minutes later and Lance put it on speaker. "Trev?'

The wails from the ambulance were unmistakable. "We're on our way to the hospital. They just don't know."

Imani found her voice. "We're on our way, we'll see you there."

Imani wasn't sure how, but twenty minutes later they jogged into the emergency room. They spotted Trev at once.

He hurried over to them looking dazed yet

grateful. "Thank you guys for coming," he said pulling Imani in for a long hug.

His body shook against hers and she squeezed him back, hoping to give him some of her returning strength. "How is Kingston?"

Trev released her just enough to look her in the eye. "We're not sure. They think it was something like SIDS, but he's breathing again." His eyes dropped. "They just don't know how long his brain went without oxygen."

She wanted to cry again. "I'm so sorry, Trev."

Lance placed a reassuring hand on Trev's shoulder.

"Noooo! What the hell is she doing here?" a shrill voice screamed.

All three turned to see Erycah flying over like a bat out of hell.

Some of the nurses and other patients gave her a wary eye.

Imani and Lance stepped back shocked.

"What kind of witch are you?" Erycah sneered at Imani as she barreled forward.

Trev grabbed Erycah by the waist and pulled her to him. "What are you doing, Sweetheart?"

Erycah turned on him. "How can *she* sense my kids in danger from miles away, Trevor? They're *my* fucking kids! Not hers! I'm telling you, she's somehow responsible for this."

"Erycah," Lance started to protest, but Imani stopped him.

"It's okay," she said as she patted his arm.

"No, it is not *okay*!" Erycah screeched.

"Erycah," Trev said, trying to console her.

Erycah glared at Trevor. "No! It's me or her, Trev. Your choice, but you better choose wisely because I'm tired of sharing you."

Trev looked confused as he struggled with an answer. "You know Imani's just a friend. There's nothing to share, Erycah—"

"No!" Erycah cut him off. "I'm serious, Trevor. Either she has to go or you do, because I'm not leaving my baby here alone with her."

"It's fine, you two. We're leaving." Imani took Lance's hand to leave although he looked ready to protest.

Trev caught her eye as he turned to walk Erycah back to the far end of the waiting area. "I'm sorry, I'll call you later," he mouthed.

But Erycah either felt him or overheard. She wheeled around, face flushed and contorted in fury. "No, you won't! She's not welcome here anymore."

Lance stood there glaring at Erycah in disbelief.

Trev shook his head in warning.

Imani could tell Lance wanted to say something, but she took his hand and managed to walk out the sliding glass doors with her head held high. However, as soon as they reached his CLK, she broke down and cried like a baby in his arms. *What have I done?*

DAMAGE ASSESSMENT

"How are you feeling?" Melody asked as she bum-rushed past Imani into her house.

Imani arched an eyebrow. "I'm fine. Why aren't you still at work?" Imani closed the front door and followed her since she was already down the hall and almost into the family room.

"We wrapped early, so I came right over." She looked around the empty family room. "Where's Lance?"

Imani gave her another odd look. "Although football season's over, they're preparing for the draft. He left this morning. Why?"

She took a seat on the couch, eager to share the good news. "Kingston's fine"

Imani flopped on the couch beside her. "Kingston's okay?" she asked, her eyes tearing up. "I've been praying non-stop."

"I know," she said hugging Imani. "Miraculously there's no brain damage. All his motor functions tested fine."

"Thank God." After a minute Imani released her and pushed back. "Wait, how do you know about Kingston?"

Oh crap! Her face fell. She needed to tread

lightly here because eggshells could transform into landmines in the blink of an eye. "Erycah called and told me everything."

"Erycah called you?" Imani's face hardened. "Wait, does she want you to choose between me and her, too?"

Ah hell, forget the eggshells; things were as bad as Erycah thought. Deciding to come clean, she reached out and held Imani's hand. "Please, let me assure you that nothing could be further from the truth."

"Erycah's so sorry, Imani. She completely lost it and she feels horrible." Melody wrinkled her face. "She wanted me to figure out how best to earn back your forgiveness."

Imani processed that a moment. "And where was Trevor during all this?"

"I asked her that, too," she replied with a giggle. "Evidently, Trevor was knocked out cold asleep after the doctor gave them the good news."

"Humph, figures." Imani pulled her feet up Indian-style. "I guess you can tell Erycah that I can't stay mad at her."

Imani studied her while she tried not to look too obvious as she exhaled with relief. Erycah would be delighted to know that Imani hadn't actually decided to become a witch and cast a spell on her after her tirade at the hospital.

"I mean," Imani continued, "it probably feels a little weird to have someone call you out of the blue to warn you that you're child's dying."

That's the understatement of the year! Melody

kept a straight face and rested her hand on Imani's belly. "Especially when you've carried that little life inside you for nine months. You sort of assume that you have some special connection that no one else in the world has."

Imani covered her hand. "Yep, I get it."

"You do realize that was Erycah's first time experiencing your premonitions personally," she continued. "You sort of freaked her out a bit. That's all."

Imani smiled. "Guess I have that effect on some folks, huh?"

"Yes, you do!" Melody snickered. At least the worst seemed over now.

ANOTHER CALL

Lance's phone buzzed. He removed it from its holster while he finished reading the last line of the *NY Times*' sports article. Assuming it was Imani checking on his flight status, he almost didn't notice the name on the caller ID.

Helene.

Helene? Why did that name sound familiar? Then it dawned on him. The mystery woman from his past that he was supposed to get rid of earlier. He rubbed his head. It would help if he could at least remember who in the world she was. As he debated how best to tell her to bugger off, his finger trained in on the "Connect" call button.

"Lance! Albert! Are you both deaf?" Robin hissed at them. Her right hand rested on her carry-on positioned behind her, ready to roll, and with her left hand she pointed to the ceiling as if the overhead public announcement system were a real person. "Let's get a move on it. They just announced our flight's boarding."

She didn't even wait for them to stand up before she pirouetted around.

Albert rolled his eyes at Lance and sighed.

Yep, this was going to be a fun flight. Robin was

in one of her moods.

Absentmindedly he holstered his phone.

Crap, the missed call! Well, nothing he could do about it now.

He made a deal with himself as he followed Robin's clacking heels from the lounge to the gate, Albert puffing beside him. If she left a message, he would call her back. And if she didn't…well, maybe she would get the hint and leave him alone.

MISGIVINGS – APRIL 2009

Imani adjusted her work backpack on her shoulders and pushed the lobby door open, bracing for the cold, brisk wind.

Mother Nature, not one to disappoint, whipped her cold fingers around Imani's ankles and then gust up her pants legs and out through her coat's neckline.

Shivering for a second, Imani tightened her scarf and snuggled deeper into her coat.

With her head down to help plow through the wind, she headed across the plant's almost empty parking lot.

An odd tingling sensation shimmied down her spine and she stopped mid-stride.

As her heart began to pound, she scanned the desolate parking lot.

The parking lot lights illuminated connecting pools of light across the dark asphalt. Swollen, gray clouds hung low overhead threatening rain. Otherwise, nothing moved aside from the dirt, dead leaves, and natural debris that the wind shooed along.

Whirling around one hundred eighty degrees, she looked back at the office lobby area.

The General Electric sign glowed a welcoming greeting.

Unsettled, she turned back towards her car, ready to jog the last hundred feet, eight months pregnant or not—when she felt something on her hip.

Jumping about a foot, her heart beating faster than a hummingbird's wings, the engaging melodies of her ringtone knocked her back down to earth. Exhaling fear and embarrassment, she excavated her cell phone from her pants pocket.

"Hello," she mumbled, still too unnerved to carry on a proper conversation.

"Imani?"

"Yes?" she replied with a frown, unable to decipher the caller's voice.

The voice on the other end brightened. "Hi, this is Lisa Moffett, how are you?"

She relaxed, finally recognizing their realtor's cheery voice. "Fine, Lisa, how are you?" she asked, wondering why Lisa was calling. They'd been in their house for months now and settlement had taken place without a hitch. Plus, they weren't planning on moving again anytime in the foreseeable future.

"I can't complain. And Lance?"

"Great," she almost snapped wanting Lisa to cut the frivolities and get to the point.

"Well, you're probably wondering why I called."

"Um, yeah, the thought had crossed my mind." Imani tried to keep the impatience and sarcasm out of her tone. It wasn't Lisa's fault that she was running late and acting unnaturally jumpy.

"Well, it's a little odd and I'm not quite sure if it means anything…"

Imani frowned as the tingling sensation returned full force to augment the creepiness she felt from Lisa's cryptic phone call.

"I found out today that both your and Lance's old homes were vandalized."

Her mouth dropped open as she stopped in her tracks.

"You know, the kids nowadays are doing silly things when they're bored," Lisa continued, trying to minimize the news by downplaying it. "Spray-painting graffiti, tee-peeing houses, knocking over mailboxes, that sort of thing," she rambled on.

"Where any other houses vandalized?" Imani began walking to her car fast, her head on a constant swivel as she surveyed the parking lot for the tiniest movement.

"Well, I'm not exactly sure. I just remembered both your addresses since I sold them and I thought it was such a wild coincidence."

Using her key fob, she unlocked the car. "Do you know what they did to the houses?" After checking the backseat for unwanted visitors, she jumped in and locked the door behind her.

"No, I'm not sure. I guess I could call around and find out."

"No, no, that's not necessary." She started her Toyota and the engine roared to life. "Like you said, it's probably nothing. Thanks for calling, Lisa. We'll talk to you later."

"Tell Lance I said hi," Lisa replied as Imani hung up and peeled out of the parking lot.

A BLAST FROM THE PAST

Lance checked his watch. *What in the world's keeping Imani?*

Annoyed yet concerned, he grabbed his cellphone off the kitchen counter. Maybe she called and left a message while he changed out of his suit and into jeans and a sweater for the *Fast and Furious*.

Melody had already called to let them know that she and Chris were on their way.

His phone indicated two new messages. Quickly, he linked to his voicemail.

The first call was a work-related message from Robin; he breezed through it and deleted it. The second was from Bobby.

He half-listened, expecting Bobby to confirm their gym time for tomorrow.

"Hey, Man," Bobby's smooth voice rang out. "You won't believe who called me yesterday. I meant to call you then, but I'm sorry, I got busy and forgot. Anyhow, it's a definite blast from the past and she was asking about you. Can't wait to catch up and see how that went. Hit me back or I'll check you at the gym tomorrow."

Lance frowned and hung up. *Odd!* A mysterious message from Bobby about some old bimbo and more importantly, no message from Imani. Something else bugged him...*wait a minute...*

Checking his phone log, it showed three missed calls although he only received two messages. Relieved, he scrolled down expecting to see Imani's number, but instead the missed call showed **Helene**.

Crap! Lance frowned and rubbed his head. He really needed to call this chick back to make sure she got the hint. He glanced at his watch. It would have to wait until he figured out what happened to Imani.

As he prepared to call Imani's phone, he heard the garage door open and her car pull in. *Finally!*

He greeted her at the kitchen door as she hit the Genie button to close the garage door. "You ready?" he asked as he shouted over the rumbling garage door.

Imani left a quick peck on his cheek and pushed past him. "I gotta go bad and then I'll be right there, I promise."

As he followed her down the hall, she disappeared into the powder room but kept talking. "I noticed you parked in the driveway. If we take your car, you can make up the time in two seconds flat. Sound good?" she asked before she flushed and washed her hands.

He chuckled in spite of his impatience. "That's fine my cute, little preggers." He rubbed her Buddha belly once she emerged, then took her hand and hurried her to the front door. "You know I hate being late, especially to a movie."

"I know, I know," Imani replied on the front stoop while she waited for him to lock up the door.

"Especially when it's a movie about a whole bunch of tricked out cars going fast. Hmm, throw in Vin Diesel and I'm sorry, I was late, too." She smiled for his benefit. "It's just that my project's at a milestone and I want to make sure nothing goes wrong."

Imani hesitated as Lance helped her down the front walk. Lately her footing and balance were a little less than ideal. "Plus, I got a weird call from our realtor."

"Mm-hm," he mumbled distracted. They were almost at the car and they could just make it if he hurried.

That's when he heard a rustling noise. Not far from the car.

He turned away from Imani and surveyed the driveway and then the front yard. Nothing.

"Did you hear what I said?" Imani asked, tugging his arm. "Both of our old houses were vandalized this week."

Lance turned to hurry Imani along; they could finish the discussion in the car on the road. But when he looked, Imani had her hands on her hips, not moving…and she wasn't alone!

Marco stood behind Imani, plain as day. No hazy, ghost-like mirage or ethereal presence, just a solid, living, breathing person. Marco's hands were on Imani's upper arms; it almost appeared as if he were restraining her.

Lance's jaw dropped. He stared, unable to speak. A strange déjà vu seeped through his bones.

Marco had restrained Imani once before, while Lance stood in between Imani and Melody trying to prevent a catfight. It was a night he refused to recall because his failings had almost led to Melody's demise. A cold eeriness crept over him and shuddered up his spine.

Clear as a bell, Marco spoke to Lance. "I've got Imani. You take care of Heather."

Confused, it took him a moment to realize that Marco didn't cause the eerie sensation. In fact, Marco didn't look threatening in the least. His brain finally processed Marco's warning words. ***Take care of Heather.***

Wait...Heather? Why the hell would he need to take care of Heather—then he felt someone behind him.

Turning around, he found himself directly in the path of a silver streak flying towards his face.

Instinctively, his head veered back although his body's momentum carried him too far forward to completely dodge the blow. A long, sharp sliver burned from his right ear lobe up into his hairline as the knife glanced along his skin.

Imani screamed and Lance panicked as he realized that it was the first time during any of their dangerous encounters that he'd ever heard her scream in fright.

The pain and shock barely registered as his fight instinct kicked into overdrive. He spun around to confront his assailant.

Out of the corner of his eye he saw Marco pull Imani back to safety.

With one less worry on his mind, his full attention focused on their attacker. His mind still couldn't assess whether it was male or female, no less Heather.

Whoever it was, they didn't bother to give him time to right his bearings. They were fast and charging at him again.

Zoning in on the gleaming blade of the arcing knife, he blocked that blow and shifted his weight to throw the attacker off balance.

This time the assailant zipped past close enough for him to see the stringy, unwashed blond hair; blotchy skin; and gaunt, sunken jaw of a wild woman. An odd smell of cat urine surrounded her.

Disgusted and alarmed, he pushed her in the back as she flew past, sending her sprawling towards the ground.

Amazingly she managed to windmill her arms for three faltering steps and regain her balance. With an annoyed snarl, she stopped her momentum and turned to face them.

Lance's jaw dropped again.

There was no way in God's green earth that this wretched creature in front of them could ever have been the chaste, preacher's daughter he once knew. The elegant, beautiful woman his friends and their co-workers had appropriately nicknamed, "The Ice Princess."

She screeched at them, exposing a black maw of rotting teeth. With her right hand, the one holding the knife, she nervously scratched her cheek, leaving behind fresh, red marks on an already acne-patched minefield of ravished skin. "Why?" Heather shrieked.

He couldn't answer; his mind refused to let him believe the unfolding events.

This was not his ex-wife, no way, no how. The model-like beauty, her immaculate, platinum blonde chignon, her manicured nails…all gone.

She raised her hands, preparing for another assault and he saw the sweaty pools under each armpit of her stained, gray sweatshirt. In fact she seemed doused in sweat and caked in grime.

He recalled how pristine her flawless, designer suits fit on her thin yet fit frame in the past. Now soiled, tattered rags hung off her emaciated body. She looked like she'd lost thirty pounds off a body that could only afford to sacrifice maybe five to ten.

Heather screamed at Imani, "I always knew you coveted Lance for yourself!"

Wisely, Imani didn't respond. Lance swore that Marco still ensconced her in his now shimmering, protective bubble. Although somehow, Imani seemed utterly unaware as she adopted a protective stance, shielding her pregnant belly from any imminent threats.

However, Heather wasn't interested in Imani. Heather kept glaring and hissing at Lance amidst constant, distracted scratches to her cheeks. "You never loved me, did you?" She swiped the air with the knife in an attempt to point it at Imani. "I was just a diversion until you could get her, wasn't I?" she howled.

Out of the blue, Heather finally seemed to notice Imani's pregnant stomach as Imani's coat fell open. A warped smile twisted her features. "Now isn't that just grand?"

Heather snarled at him again, her fingers playing along the knife's sharp blade. "I begged and pleaded to carry your damn baby." She spit in contempt. "From the looks of it, you joyfully knocked her ass up before you even tied the knot." Heather wiped her nose with the back of her knife-wielding hand and pierced Imani with a lethal look. "I should cut that growing tumor from your slutty gut."

Imani swallowed hard, but held her ground, daring Heather to try.

Marco's force field shield seemed to brighten around them, but Lance barely noticed. Heather's words propelled him forward, determined to defuse the threat.

Too late, he realized his mistake.

Heather moved deceptively fast and she appeared just as determined to inflict serious damage. She dodged an inch under his impending tackle, the blade almost slashing his abdomen wide open.

Careful! He chastised himself. *That was too damn close.*

Heather's half-crazed gleam made him shake off a deep shudder. There was no mistaking it; she wanted him dead and Imani, too.

Now, totally unimpeded, Heather darted towards Imani.

Knowing he needed to move, he took two giant steps and kicked out his leg in a large sweep to trip Heather.

As she fell flat on her stomach, the knife clattered to the ground.

In an instant, he redirected his momentum and lunged for it.

Like a lithe lizard, Heather slithered to it, their hands connecting at the same time. With her free left hand, she clawed at his face and turned onto her back, all the while wriggling the knife free from under his clasp. In a move borrowed from a beached beetle, she bicycled her legs about until she flipped herself over and scrambled upright onto her feet.

Lance leapt to his feet to avoid making himself an easy target on the ground. Wary and surprised by her speed, he repositioned himself between Heather and Imani, watching her like a hawk. He had to disarm her fast. The longer the situation continued the more dangerous and out of hand it became.

"Why are you doing this, Heather?" he asked trying to distract her.

Heather barked out a sharp laugh. "Are you seriously asking me such a nonsensical question? You can do better than that, my love. Like how I found you two," she teased as they played a dangerous game of cat and mouse.

Lance refused to ask because he didn't want to know the answer.

"I'll let you know it wasn't easy. Especially when your own sister betrays you and tries to keep all the incriminating evidence hidden."

"What in the world are you talking about?" Lance couldn't help but ask as they circled each other like birds of prey.

"Don't act coy, Lance! My evil sister made sure they destroyed all of the papers in that hell hole, but I saw one." She glared at Imani again taking her eyes off Lance for the briefest of seconds. "The picture in the newspaper of the happily engaged couple, the week before your wedding." Heather stopped moving and scratched her cheek vigorously.

Lance wanted to attack, but the way Heather's eyes twitched back and forth, it kept him at bay. Somehow he'd have to make her commit first.

"They almost made me forget about you in that life-sucking institution." Heather hit her head with the back of her right hand, the blade gleaming under the street lights. "But I remembered and when I escaped, I revisited all the places you used to live and work."

Oh my God, it all made sense now. The cryptic call from their old co-worker, Bobby; Imani's strange call from their realtor about the vandalization of both of their homes; the warning calls from *Helene— Heather's sister*!

Heather snarled out an evil, black-mawed grin as she circled again. "I finally struck gold tonight when I spotted Imani at GE and followed her home. The discovery and delayed gratification of killing her proved excruciating although rewarding since it led me directly to you."

Heather cocked her head sideways. Somehow sensing she was gaining an advantage, she charged, stabbing the knife out in front of her like a fencer parrying his foil.

Lance braced himself. It was now or never.

Watching her every move carefully, he timed her stabs and found a shallow opening. As soon as Heather committed forward, he closed the gap to meet her, his arm deflecting her arm and the knife out to her side.

The sudden countermove caused Heather to fall into his unyielding body with a look of surprise. He took the opportunity to grab her wrist and employ a spin move. The maneuver carried him out of harm's way and he wrenched Heather's elbow up behind her back until she screamed and dropped the knife.

"Nooo," she wailed as she struggled against his hold, but he only tightened his grip.

This close she looked and smelled terrible. "What happened to you, Heather?" he asked not really expecting an answer. From far off he could hear an approaching siren and he wished it would hurry.

Heather stopped struggling and squirmed in his hold trying to face him. "What happened? What happened! You did you black bastard! You defiled me, Lance! You told me you loved me. Promised that you would always be there. Convinced me to marry you until death do us part!" Her body shook with anger. "I would have done anything for you barring divorce. That never figured into my plan or God's plan. And now I'm ruined for anyone else."

Her shoulders sagged as she began to cry. "No one else could ever desire a pathetic divorcee. And why would they, when all I ever crave or pontificate about is you? The perfect man that no one else can live up to." Heather arched her body subtly. "The perfect man that insists on bestowing my love on that Imani bitch."

Heather tried to spring out of his hold towards Imani, but he was prepared and she remained locked in his stronghold.

Now that the police car was visible down the block, a neighbor cautiously approached. "Is everything okay?"

Lance could tell the pudgy, bald yuppie was trying to make heads or tails of a burly, black man holding a white woman in an arm lock while a pregnant, black lady looked on frightened.

That was until Heather bared her remaining rotten teeth at him. "What are you looking at you prick? You out to get me, too?"

The man jumped back repulsed by Heather's words and disheveled appearance. He eyed the nearby knife. Then he eyed Heather and Lance with suspicion.

"Kick it further aside," Lance said encouraging him to help without impeding the upcoming police investigation. He needed to realize that the weapon belonged to Heather, not him, lest any confusion arose.

The man obliged, wanting to complete his civic duty. Then he stepped back and let the two policemen take over. "This crazy woman here attacked my nice neighbors with that knife," he said helpfully, pointing out the weapon. "I saw it all from my living room window."

As the police nodded and came to relieve Heather from Lance, his neighbor added. "Watch out, I think she's high on methamphetamines or something."

One of the cops gave the man a skeptical look.

Their neighbor puffed up. "My wife and I recently watched some television shows about addiction. She's exhibiting a lot of the signs."

Lance came to his rescue as the second cop eyed Heather. "He's right, I knew her two years ago and since then she's lost an enormous amount of weight, her teeth are rotten, her attire and appearance are completely disheveled, and she's become irrational and violent."

The second cop nodded to the first. "Yep, she looks like she's on meth."

Heather bucked in Lance's arms and shrieked. "Keep your filthy hands off of me you stinking pigs! I didn't do anything. This is harassment! I'll freaking kill all of you dirty—"

In a blink of the eye, the second cop disengaged Lance and took Heather down, cutting off her commotion mid-tirade. He had her cuffed and back up in one smooth motion as a stunned Heather complied. With his partner's help, he shoved her towards the back of the patrol car, all the while stating her Miranda rights.

With Heather securely in the officers' custody, Lance exhaled and then stumbled back towards Imani, his feet feeling a bit unsteady. "Are you okay?" he asked as she rushed into his arms sobbing.

Imani nodded vigorously and squeezed him tight trying to make sure he was intact.

"Where's Marco?" he asked.

A second later she leaned back and looked up at his face. She stared at him like he was the one strung out on drugs.

He shook his head. There was no way on earth that uber-clairvoyant Imani missed Marco. "Don't tell me you didn't see or feel him, Imani." Her face went blank and he frowned while he gestured. "Marco was right there protecting you the whole, entire time."

Imani looked alarmed then worried as she reached out to where he realized his face felt like it was on fire.

A searing slash throbbed from his right ear lobe and jaw line up to his temple. He recognized that his face felt wet…really, really wet. Against his will, his right hand reached up and touched the area.

It came back bloody.

As he sank to the ground in slow motion, he saw his anxious neighbor saying, "it's okay there, Buddy," while Imani helped him down, concern etched deep into her face.

Two paramedics appeared out of nowhere. Somehow it bothered him the most not to have seen or heard the ambulance approach. Yet there it sat parked behind the police cruiser, lights blazing.

In a haze, he answered their curious questions and let them take over.

THE RECOVERY – MAY 2009

"Stop beating yourself up, Lance. You did great," Melody repeated for what seemed like the umpteenth time. She kicked her feet up on the ottoman and sank back into Imani's overstuffed chair.

Imani smiled at her from the loveseat, where she sat nestled next to Lance.

Odd, Melody thought, Imani had maybe uttered three words during the past hour. Instead her hands were in constant contact with some part of Lance.

Erycah snuggled into Trev on the couch and rested her hand on her swollen stomach. "I can't imagine how scary that whole episode was."

"What I want to know is why you never called Helene back until after the fact," Trev said hitting straight to the heart. "Maybe if you would have returned Heather's sister's call, you might have been better forewarned."

Lance shook his head. "Simple stupidity." He covered Imani's hands. "We were joking around, thinking she was an idiotic conquest from my past and I never even bothered to call her back."

"Well, it's not like you could have known that Heather had escaped from rehab to come dole out some vengeance," Chris said as he came in from the kitchen, drink in hand for Melody.

As he handed her the lemonade and perched on the arm of the overstuffed chair, she continued his line of reasoning. "Yeah, it's kind of hard to consider someone's escaped from rehab when you didn't even know that they'd started using drugs in the first place."

Trev was having none of it. "But you would have known that she was struggling with drugs and obsessing over you six months ago if you'd called Helene back. I mean even Lance's boy, Bobby, and your freaking realtor of all people, tried to warn you that there was a crazy person on the loose looking for you at your jobs and vandalizing your old pads."

Erycah patted Trev's hand in an attempt to get him to ease off of Lance.

Melody glanced at Imani, just knowing that she'd fuss at Trev and make him back down, but Imani seemed to take Trev's comments in stride.

Lance, however, obliged by brow-beating himself further. "I know. You're right, Trevor." He absently ran his finger up along his jaw line over his healing scar. "I wish every day that I could turn the clock back to that instant and have Imani pick up the phone."

"We would have known that one of Helene's old dealer buddies thought it was a good idea to give Heather some crystal meth to 'lift her spirits' and deal with post-divorce depression." Lance shook his head. "The doctors say crystal meth is instantly addictive. Poor Heather never stood a chance."

"Yes, and Helene could have left a message after any of her three phone calls," Melody said trying to get them to squash the conversation. "You can play should of, would of, could of all day long and it doesn't change a single thing."

She glanced around the room singling out Trev with a scowl and then resting her sympathetic gaze on Lance and Imani. "What we should all be is grateful of the fact that Lance and Imani are here safe and sound while Heather's locked up, hopefully getting the treatment that she needs."

"Here, here," Chris replied raising his glass and half-hugging her shoulder from his awkward, elevated angle.

"Here, here," Erycah repeated as she grabbed her drink and Trev's off the coffee table for them to toast.

Trev stopped his constant heckling long enough to join the toast.

Imani raised her lemonade and nodded but didn't speak.

Lance raised his beer. "Thanks, guys. I really appreciate the support." He locked eyes with Imani. "Melody's right. Heather could have attacked Imani at her job in the parking lot. However, she waited and followed her to the house. Luckily, she wanted both of us and we were able to stop her."

While they sipped their drinks and mingled, Melody rested her hand on her belly over her active baby as she watched Imani and worried. She skirted another glance at Lance. He would be fine, he always bounced back. In fact, he and Chris were deep in conversation while Imani just sat there. It even looked like Lance and Chris were actually bonding.

She checked Trev and Erycah, but they remained an island on the sofa ignoring everyone else. Frustrated, Melody wondered why no one else seemed to realize that something was off with Imani. Taking another sip, she debated the best tactic to get Imani alone.

Eight minutes later she found her chance when Imani excused herself to use the restroom.

Jumping up, she followed Imani down to the powder room and squeezed inside before Imani could shut and lock the door.

Imani gave her an odd look, eyebrow half-cocked, but then she resigned herself to the intrusion and prepared to use the bathroom. "You know, Melody, I kinda prefer privacy in the loo."

"And we lived with each other long enough that you know I never really cared. We're good enough friends that we can, and have, talked to each other anywhere."

She leaned against the pedestal sink while Imani relieved herself. "So, are we going to talk about what's going on with you?" She rubbed her hand across the baby as he or she somersaulted inside.

"Nothing's go—," Imani started and then stopped when she saw the skeptical, 'yeah-tell-me-anything' look on Melody's face. "Fine!" Imani rolled her eyes. "But you have to promise not to repeat a word of this to a single, solitary soul."

Melody nodded and waited eager for Imani to

wipe and flush.

"I'm not even sure what I think and Lance won't talk about it either," Imani said when she finished.

"Talk about what?" She moved aside so that Imani could wash her hands.

"The night that Heather attacked us. Lance swears up and down that he saw Marco." Imani's eyes shimmered between disbelief, confusion, and what looked like remorse.

"Marco?" she repeated feeling the air get knocked out of her. To drive home the point, the baby kicked her as solidly as a soccer ball. Melody leaned against the wall to catch her breath, too befuddled to know what else to do. It definitely wasn't what she expected Imani to say.

"Yes, he says that Marco was standing right behind me, vowing to protect me from harm. That he actually moved me backwards when Heather dodged my way."

"So what's wrong?" she asked, unsure of where Imani's head lay with this.

Imani pierced her with her chocolaty, eagle eyes. "I know Lance believes he saw Marco…and I believe that he did see him." Imani looked crushed. "But *I* didn't feel a single thing, Melody! My dead husband comes back to save me and I don't even notice?"

Imani shook her head and covered her mouth with her hands. "How could *I*, of all people, not feel him? What's that even mean that Lance saw him and I didn't?"

Melody placed her hands on Imani's shoulders. "I

don't know."

"How horrible of a wife was I?" Imani grabbed Melody's hands and clamped them to her shoulders. "Is Marco mad at my choices? Why couldn't I see him?" Imani's voice rose and if Melody didn't know better, she'd think Imani were bordering on hysterical.

Gently she pried Imani's hands from their death grip on Imani's shoulders and shook them until they relaxed and dangled between them. "If Marco hated you or thought you were horrible, I doubt that he'd come back to protect you."

Imani processed that nugget while her hands wrung Melody's.

Then another thought hit her and she stared into Imani's eyes and hoped her friend would listen. "Did you ever consider that maybe Lance needed to see Marco? Finalize some type of unfinished business."

Feeling more confident, she powered on. "And maybe seeing him would have messed you up, confused you." She dropped one of Imani's hands and cupped Imani's chin. "To you, Lance was the one that saved you, not Marco. Maybe Marco wants you to move on with Lance. Not stagnant fixating on him."

Imani looked crestfallen and then hope crept in with slow but sure, plodding steps. "You really think so?"

Melody nodded her head. *It was as good a possibility as any.* "I do."

Relief crashed over Imani and she pulled Melody

in for a breath-constricting hug as their pregnant bellies bumped each other. "That really sounds like a lot of your romantic hokum, but since I'm not sure what else to believe, I'll take it. Thanks, Melody."

She hugged Imani back and hoped it worked.

BREATHING EXERCISES

Imani laughed at the ridiculousness of the scene. Her and eleven other third-trimester women, including Melody and Erycah were reclining on yoga mats on the classroom floor while their partners held their ankles and or hands making chimp-like, "oo-oo-oo, hee-hee-hee" noises.

Lance hit her leg to make her behave and she managed to hold the subsequent laughs halfway inside.

Meanwhile Melody gave her a dirty look while Trev rolled his eyes in agreement.

In a flash she looked away from Trev because his sarcastic antics would have her rolling on the floor busting out laughing.

Trying to concentrate, she narrowed her eyes and refocused on the high-energy, chestnut haired instructor.

In reality she had no one to blame for their predicament but herself. When Melody first suggested all three couples take Lamaze classes together, Trev and Erycah basically laughed her out of the room.

Trev's exact response was, "we've been through this so many times, we could damn near teach the class." And then he proceeded to ask Melody if she'd like to pay them for lessons instead.

Needless to say, Melody wasn't amused and that's when Imani messed up and stepped in to smooth things over.

Imani suggested they give the class a try although she expected Lance to protest or fuss about how non-masculine the whole concept was. But he surprised her and his enthusiasm won over Erycah, which in turn, suckered Trev in against his wishes.

Now as they practiced breathing, she watched Lance in awe as he sat there, huffing and puffing in unison. Hell, if Lance could make it through and not feel ridiculous, then she could, too. Taking a quick glance over at Melody, she almost busted out in raucous laughter again.

Melody seemed to relish in her romantic, fairy tale environment. Imani swore she could almost see little cartoon bluebirds circling and tweeting around Melody's head, carrying forest wildflower garlands in their beaks. And all the while Melody beamed with radiant pride at Chris as they "oo-oo-oo, hee-hee-heed" together.

Imani looked at Chris and when he caught her eye they exchanged smiles. She was proud of Chris, too, but for a completely different reason. Despite their awkward beginnings, Chris and Lance were actually talking, finding commonalities, and becoming friends.

Maybe the fact that their wives were best friends finally got them to realize they needed to cut the tension and get along. Regardless, it couldn't have been easy for Chris, what with Marco being his best friend and silly Melody revealing her wet dream about Lance. Imani shook her head. *Yep, seeing Chris and Lance hanging out together and enjoying themselves was truly a miracle.*

***

Chris returned Imani's knowing smile. She'd just told him last week how happy she was that he and Lance were getting along now.

He grunted along with Melody to the breathing exercises. He'd reflected on Imani's comment all night long, but he knew at once why it took so long for them to gel. When he first met Lance, way back during Imani and Marco's wedding, Lance stormed off before they even had a chance to talk.

He mentioned the odd occurrence to Marco later, and Marco explained then that Melody, Imani, and Lance had some strange relationship that he eventually just came to accept. For a year, he never worried about it again because Lance never returned.

Chris glanced over at Trev and Erycah huffing and puffing. They also mentioned something similar over a year ago when they all played Pictionary that one night and hidden secrets were revealed. Memories of that night replayed in his mind and he recalled yet another reason why he disliked Lance.

Lance almost attacked him when the lunk incorrectly assumed that he would abuse Melody. Between that night and the fact that Lance had conveniently substituted in for his best friend, Marco, as Imani's husband, well there were more than enough reasons not to like the guy.

Melody squeezed his hand and beamed at him, proud that he was participating so fully. He smiled back between puffs and remembered he wasn't totally blameless. Who could forget the day when he totally misunderstood Melody and charged over to Imani's ready to beat Lance down.

He grunted under his breath, in time with everyone's crazy breathing exercises, and dared a glance at Lance. Guess too much testosterone flowed when the two of them were together in the past.

They stopped the breathing exercises and he zoned out as the crazy brunette, Lamaze instructor rattled off some statistics.

Although all those reasons were more than enough, that's ultimately not what prevented them from bonding. Marco was right. The three of them, Lance, Imani, and Melody, made you feel like an outsider sometimes, never intentionally; it was just a comfortableness they exuded around each other.

Melody squeezed his hand and he tuned in again, smiling to show her he got whatever nonsense the woman spouted.

As he glanced over at Lance and Imani, Imani noticed and gave him a big thumbs up. Yes, the three of them had gone a long way to make him feel included now. Even more so since Heather's attack. Somehow the walls crumbled and they began to confide in each other.

Chris exhaled as he tried to look attentive for the last ten minutes of class. At least he knew now that Lance didn't have any designs on Melody, or she on him.

Curious though, Marco always believed that there was never anything going on between Lance and Imani. He grunted. *I wonder what Marco would think if he were around today?* He let the image go before it could take root and make him wonder if the same thing would happen between Lance and Melody if he were no longer in the picture. But he was in the picture and so was Melody.

Melody assumed the position and beamed at him between puffs as he held her ankles and counted in time. There was no doubt that she loved him unconditionally with every pore.

Chris looked up as he felt someone watching him.

Lance smiled then nodded his approval.

WHAT'S REAL

"Hey, Girl," Melody gushed into her cell phone as she set down her fork and answered Imani's call. "Are you in Boston all safe and sound?"

"Yep," Imani replied, "just checked into my hotel room." Imani faltered a moment and sighed.

"You okay, you sound a little tired?" She knew Imani would fuss at the way she kept mothering her, but someone needed to make sure she took care of herself.

"I guess…"

Instantly she could tell something more than "jet lag" from the train ride bothered Imani. "What's wrong, Imani?" Her breath hitched. "Is everything okay with the baby?"

"The baby's fine," Imani replied at once, making sure to talk her off the ledge. Imani hesitated again and then finally confessed. "It's Lance."

Melody looked up across the restaurant and zoned in on where Lance had disappeared in search of the bathroom two minutes ago. "You know I'm having lunch with him right now?"

"Yeah, is he there listening?"

"No, he just went to the bathroom. Why? What's going on?" Melody pored over their lunch conversation searching for any hidden clues or hints. "He didn't act like anything was wrong."

Imani cut her off. "He won't because he doesn't think there's a problem."

"I don't understand," she replied with a frown.

Lance emerged from the bathroom hallway, but immediately got accosted by a middle-aged, white fan-boy requesting an autograph and picture.

"You better explain quickly though, he's coming back to the table soon."

Imani sighed. "He still won't talk about what happened during Heather's attack."

"Well, you know Lance," she replied, feeling relieved that this was all. "He's always felt the need to protect us. And when he feels like he's failed, he gets a bit moody trying to get past it. Just remind him of how masculine he was and he'll be fine soon enough."

"That's not quite it." Imani groaned. "He refuses to talk about seeing Marco. It's gotten to the point where he's acting like it never happened." Imani sighed again. "I don't know Melody. If he can't talk to me about this, what else will he hide or keep from me?"

Dang it, Imani! Melody shook her head. "Don't you think you're jumping to conclusions? You remember pastor just preached on trust last week."

"Talk to Lance about trust. This is bothering him so much that he's talking to Marco in his sleep. You might want to remind him that most major problems start with one small secret."

Lance prepared to finish up with the fan boy as he clapped the guy's back.

"Are you sure that's what you want me to say because Lance is heading back to the table?"

"No," Imani replied backing down. "Maybe he'll open up to you naturally, but don't force anything. I need to think about this more. Tell him I'll call him later. Okay?"

Before she could answer, Imani disconnected.

As Lance approached, Melody pushed her plate of mostly eaten blackened salmon Caesar salad away and wiped her mouth with her napkin.

Maybe she could broach the subject in her normal, safe, roundabout tactic. Then again, if she threw him off with a direct question it could breach his normal defenses. She hesitated, uncertain whether she should follow Imani's former or latter instructions.

***

As Lance approached the table, Melody smiled his way. Her stylish, gray tracksuit and ponytail did little to conceal her natural daffodils and sunshine radiance. He chuckled again at her pitiful attempt to "disguise" her well-known anchor look and charm. Two diners had accosted her earlier for autographs just as they had him.

He grinned as he sat down. "Sorry about that. I've got to get used to people stopping me again wanting to talk about football and get autographs." He smirked at her. "But then you're pretty used to that now, aren't you Mrs. Noon Anchor?"

Melody smiled and ignored his comment. "Your wife says that she arrived safely and she'll call you tonight."

"Ahh," Lance replied with a mile-wide smile that surprised even him. "That's who you were talking to while I was away. How is my Baby?" He picked up his glass and sipped some water while wishing Imani sat here with them.

Melody replied with a sly grin. "She's tired, but her train ride was fine and she misses you."

"I miss her, too," he said already lamenting about how empty their bed would feel tonight without her sexy body beside him. Lost in reverie for a moment, it took him a second to notice Melody's suspicious silence. As he looked up, she leveled him with her eyes.

"So, Imani thinks you're keeping secrets. Are you?"

"Whaaa?" Lance's eyes widened and his jaw almost hit the table before he closed it again. "Maybe I'll hold my bladder next time and not leave you two alone to concoct such craziness." He wiped his mouth and set his napkin over his empty plate. "Where is this coming from or should I even ask?"

"She thinks that if you're holding back and can't talk to her about what you saw with Marco that you'll start to keep other things from her as well." Melody kept her eyes on him trying to gauge his reaction.

"Wow." His hands made their familiar trek across his face and over his head before his gaze rested on her again. "And what's your take on all this?"

Melody squinted, deep in thought, then she shook her head and sighed. "Actually, I don't know what to think. Imani's probably going way overboard as usual…but she tends to have good instincts overall." She gave him a mischievous smile as she deflected back to him. "So why won't you talk to her about the incident with Marco?"

"Are you really going to keep asking me about this nonsense?" he asked, wishing she would back off. He almost felt like a con artist getting blindsided by the unassuming reporter with the sneak interrogation.

"Is it really nonsense if you're having problems sleeping?" she asked all nonchalant.

Feeling floored, he slumped back in his chair. His eyes narrowed as he looked at "sweet, innocent" Melody in disbelief. "Are you two kidding me? What other *private* moments did Imani decide to share?"

"Don't be mad, Lance. We're not ganging up on you."

"Well, it sure feels like you are." He rubbed his right hand over his head.

Melody stretched her hand across the table and covered his left hand. "You talk to us about everything, why can't you talk about this?"

Peeved at her constant assault, he jerked his hand from under hers. "Because there's nothing to talk about."

Melody's eyes widened in hurt surprise and he felt terrible about his reaction.

Closing his eyes, he inhaled deep and slow. *C'mon, Lance, this is just Melody being Melody, trying to keep the peace; she didn't meant to offend or intrude.* Still, her badgering struck a nerve. He reopened his eyes.

"Well, if that's the case, it should be a quick conversation." Melody withdrew her hand, picked up her glass, and sipped her iced tea.

Watching her pained response, he felt like an ass. "I'm sorry for snapping at you," he replied as contrite as possible. "But seriously, I've already told Imani numerous times nothing happened, so there's truly nothing left to say."

Melody slammed down her glass in frustration. "So, she's making up the fact that you saw Marco when Heather attacked you? And that you're not sleeping well?"

Lance bit his lip and glared, but he didn't reply.

Melody softened her tone and reached for his hand again and this time he didn't remove it although he wanted to keep his distance. "Imani feels like you're holding back. And after your defensive response just now, I'm starting to believe she has a valid point."

Melody rubbed his hand and spoke in a gentle, soothing voice. "Regardless, if you can't talk to her..." It appeared like Melody wanted to add in, "or me," to her statement, but she continued on without shining focus on how much he'd just hurt her. "Look, if you can't talk to Imani about this, she's afraid of what else you'll keep from her in the future."

"Are you serious?" He sighed and it took all his

willpower not to remove both hands and rub them across his head in frustration and annoyance at their overreaction.

"Well, think about it, Lance." She patted his hands. "You know she values open, honest communication."

"I know," he replied. "But it's not like I lied—" He stopped without even needing to see Melody's look of disapproval. Just because you didn't mention something didn't make it any less of a lie in Imani's book. Omissions equaled lies.

God, had he really talked in his sleep and been so transparent after he tried so hard to forget that night? He shook his head and sighed as his shoulders slumped. "I guess I thought I could handle this on my own...I didn't even realize that I did anything to make her notice."

"Are you kidding?" Melody looked aghast. "This is eagle-eyed, damn near omniscient Imani we're talking about."

He dropped his head embarrassed from the lameness of his excuse. "I know."

"And if this is bothering you enough that you're talking to Marco in your sleep...well, you can deny it as much as you want, but she's going to assume that you're hiding something."

He didn't reply this time, although her words sunk in as Melody stroked his hands.

"And if she feels she can't trust you..."

"I know, I know," he mumbled dreading the consequences. If Imani developed trust issues about him now, all their progress could dissipate as fast as a snowflake melting on a defrosting windshield.

"Imani noticed and she wants to help you. We both do." Melody squeezed his hands until he returned her concerned gaze. "Even if it means recommending someone for you to talk to. You know I can personally vouch for a couple of doctors."

Lance stiffened under her hands at the thought of talking to another quack. The wasted time he spent in marriage counseling with Heather proved enough for two lifetimes. Luckily Melody didn't appear to notice his reluctance.

However, she seemed to realize she'd made her point because she relented at last. "Look, I'll leave you alone, but could you at least consider talking to Imani when she returns?"

He gazed at Melody again and appreciation washed over him. Although he hated this whole ordeal he was glad that she cared enough to broach the subject, even if she did it against his wishes. "I'll seriously consider it. Thanks"

She smiled and opened her mouth to reply when their waitress stopped over.

Now why didn't you stop by and interrupt us three minutes earlier? He smirked. The waitress could have saved him a whole world of grief.

"Can I interest you two in some dessert or coffee?" the waitress asked.

Lance gestured towards Melody. "It's up to you. I'm good."

Melody grimaced. "I really want some ice cream."

She rubbed her pregnant belly, "however, I really don't need it."

"If you want ice cream, order some. The baby will love the extra calcium," he replied with a chuckle. His phone vibrated in his side holster and he retrieved it with a practiced flick of the wrist.

"And what about the extra sugar and fat?" Melody asked.

"This is from work," he said as he finished reading the text. "I have to go, but feel free to add it to the bill." He glanced at the waitress and pulled out his wallet, "I'll go ahead and pay now, if you don't mind?" He handed her his credit card.

"Sure thing," the waitress replied taking his card.

"Well, that settles the ice cream issue, nothing for me, thanks."

The waitress grinned and hurried off to tally their check.

"Thanks for lunch, Lance," Melody said looking rather pleased.

"My pleasure," he replied as he holstered his phone. "Unfortunately, we don't get to go out as often as I'd like. Even with all today's craziness, I still miss our lunches."

The waitress returned in a flash with the bill and he reviewed it, signed the charge slip, and pocketed his receipt.

"You ready to go?" he asked as Melody nodded and grabbed her purse.

In a flash he leapt from his seat and helped her out of her chair. He continued to walk beside her until they reached the exit door, which he held open for her.

Melody laughed. "Imani's right. I never would have imagined in college that you'd become the consummate gentleman."

"The two of you really need to stop talking about me." He raised his eyebrow. "I might just get a complex."

"Ha! Doubtful," she said with another laugh.

With a half chuckle, half grunt he scanned the parking lot until he spotted her bright yellow VW Bug and gestured for them to proceed.

As they walked over, he waited for her to unlock the car and then he opened her door.

Just before she got in, he stopped her. Wanting nothing more than to sweep her up into a giant bearhug, he decided at the last second to settle for a tight hug so as not to squish the baby. "Thanks again, Melody."

She answered with her face still pinned against his chest. "That's what friends are for."

He withheld a belly laugh while recalling snippets of the video with Dionne Warwick, Elton John, Gladys Knight, and Stevie Wonder.

A sudden wave of overwhelming gratitude washed over him and he hugged Melody even tighter. "I'm such a lucky man," he said, thanking God for sending both Melody and Imani into his life. Even when he preferred to ignore his problems, they always had his back and helped him through the tough times.

He leaned down placing his mouth close to her ear

to ensure she heard him. "You know I really love you, right?" Squeezing Melody tight again, he kissed her forehead for an extra second, and then he released her.

As soon as he let go, she swayed a bit, so he placed his right hand under her elbow to steady her until she slid into her driver's seat.

While she settled in, his phone buzzed in its holster. Knowing that it was work, he gave Melody one last smile and wink before he shut her door. With a half-wave, he hustled over to his car, his mind already focused on work and football.

LANCE?

Minutes after Lance peeled off, Melody sat in her car breathless and motionless, unable to believe what had just occurred.

Lance? She shook her head trying to remove the thought. He never hit on her before but... The words he said, the way he said them, the way he touched her—skip that—embraced her. The lingering tingles from the electrical shocks coursing through her body, all unmistakable confirmations.

What felt worse was that she really wanted to act on the feelings. Succumbing to his kiss, letting his strong hands squeeze more. She hit the steering wheel. *Damn it, snap out of it!*

Using extreme concentration, she forced out two deep inhales and tried to physically shake it off.

Once she felt composed enough to drive, she started the car.

Only after pulling into her driveway did she realize that she let the car drive itself home. She half recalled vague sightings of familiar freeway exits and street names before she arrived home. Instead her mind contemplated Lance's farewell salutations, his behavior, his actions...and her body's intense reaction.

God, she wanted to talk to Imani so bad. But there

was no way in hell that could ever happen. Not after the last time.

Before she could turn off the engine, Justin Timberlake declared he was "bringin' *Sexy Back*" on the radio. *Oh God, that's the last thing I need to hear!*

Absently, she killed the engine, grabbed her keys and purse, and then her cell phone rang. She answered it without checking the caller ID. Maybe in hope against all hopes it would be Lance calling to explain himself.

"Mel-o-dy," Trev half sang her name in a funky Patois reggae beat.

Melody tried to mask her disappointment. "Oh, hey, Trev," she said as she got out of her car and kicked the door shut.

"Nice to hear from you, too," he replied with thick sarcasm.

God, she really needed to do a better job of hiding her emotions. "No, no, I didn't mean—"

"It's alright," Trev interrupted. "I won't keep you. My wifey just wanted to know when you were expecting us to come by next Saturday for Chris's birthday party."

"Five pm is perfect. We'll serve appetizers and get cooking." Readjusting the phone between her shoulder and neck, she fumbled with unlocking the front door.

"Alrighty, I'll let you get back to whatever I interrupted."

"No, no, you didn't interrupt anything, Trev, I

promise. I'm sorry. I just got home and I'm not as adept at juggling my phone, purse, and keys as I'd like." She dropped her purse and keys on the table and locked the front door behind her. "But I'm fine now. Let's start again. How are you, Trev, really?"

Trev laughed. "How am I really? I'm absolutely fine. And how are you, Melody?"

She wanted to reply in all honesty that she was horny and confused but thought best of it. "I'm fine. I just have a lot on my mind—"

"And you really wanted to talk to Imani, but you forgot that your girl was traveling on business?"

'That's only the half of it,' she wanted to say. "Ah, yeah," her voice faltered and she wished again that she could lie easier.

An awkward silence settled over their conversation for a moment before Trevor broke it. Melody knew immediately that she hadn't slipped a thing past him.

"That didn't sound too convincing." He paused. "Plus, I'm sure she's already called you to let you know she arrived safely. Especially if I already got a text."

Melody didn't reply as she stomped up the steps and that seemed to spur Trev on further.

"So what's going on that you couldn't talk to her about it?"

Damn it, she hated how transparent she was to everyone else. She sulked over to the bed and slumped onto it with a sigh. "Can you keep a secret?" she asked already knowing that he could. She'd been able to confide in him in the past even though he was closer friends with Imani.

"Of course," Trev replied, his tone dead serious.

"Lance and I just had lunch." She hesitated, still debating if she should tell anyone. "And, well...I swear he hit on me as we were leaving." Her voice dropped as she found it difficult to admit her assumptions out loud.

"Lance?" Trev sounded skeptical. "Like your Three Musketeers, Lance? His voice deepened. "Like Imani's husband, Lance?"

"Yes," she whispered.

"Whoa, Melody, back up. Tell me step by step what happened because, don't take this the wrong way, but you tend to over romanticize everything."

She half-grunted and fell back on her bed. "No offense taken. I'd actually love if you can convince me otherwise." She exhaled before continuing. "When we were saying our goodbyes in the parking lot, he embraced me for like two to three minutes. Then he kissed my forehead soft and sweet and he whispered that he loved me in my ear."

"Okay...let's start with the first item. So he hugged you a little too long—"

"No, we hug all the time. This was so much more intense and intimate. Suggestive even," she replied feeling the heat rising throughout her body. "Plus he kissed me—"

"On the forehead—"

"Yes, I know it was just on the forehead, but his lips lingered there for longer than he's ever done before." The remembered feel of his lips on her skin forced her breathing to become shallow. "Plus he said something about being a very lucky man. And you're forgetting that Lance told me he loved me."

"Well we all know he's become a lot more expressive over the years. Even I've heard him say, 'I love you,' to both you and Imani."

"Not like this." She hugged herself with one arm remembering the sensation.

"So what are you going to do?" Trev asked cutting right to the heart of the matter.

What am I going to do? She sat up and crossed her legs. "That's the problem. I honestly don't know."

Trev sounded like he bolted straight up. "What do you mean, you don't know?"

She tried to back down from her statement. "You know I'd never cheat." *I wouldn't, would I?* The mere thought scared her.

"But?"

"But, what if Lance—"

"Melody, stop it right now! Even if Lance did mean it, you know Imani would kill you, not to mention your husband, Chris."

"I know, I know." She sighed coming down from her irrational, romantic high. "Don't worry; I'm not going to act on it." She closed her eyes and concentrated on removing the images from her head. "Thanks for talking me off the cliff."

"No problem," Trev replied sounding quite relieved. "You know I'm always here if you want to talk some more. Okay?"

"Thanks," she replied with a resigned sigh. Before he could say anything else, she disconnected and tossed the phone on her nightstand.

IT'S OVER

"Who were you talking to?" Chris demanded more than asked.

Melody jumped two feet in the air as his voice bellowed from the bedroom doorway. "Oh, my God, you're home early."

"Yes, I knew you were off today and I wanted to take a half day vacation and surprise you." Chris fought to modulate his voice when all he wanted to do was shout at the top of his lungs. "Guess I got surprised instead."

Melody's fake smile faltered as she tried to figure out how much of her illicit confession of desired infidelity he'd overheard. "How long have you been there?"

"Long enough," he replied watching his guilty wife clutch her hand to her heart while her mind whirled wondering what to do. He didn't bother to disguise the contempt and anger emanating throughout his entire body any longer. "You never answered my question. Who were you talking to Melody?"

Her face fell and she scurried back onto the bed, almost trying to burrow into the headboard. "Trevor," she replied in a confessional whisper.

"Trevor?" his voice cracked as he cocked his head to the side. His eyes widened. "You just confided to another *man* that you wanted to cheat on me! With fucking Lance?" He took a threatening step forward and his eyes narrowed so that all he could see was red. "Why?"

"I don't know why," she cried dropping her head. She pulled her knees up to her chest looking to make herself as small of a target as possible.

He didn't buy it. Each step he took forward infuriated him more. His heart hammered loud enough through his veins that it almost drowned out every other sound.

When he reached the bed, he towered over Melody, his hands flexing open and closed into fists. With a concerted effort, he opened his right hand and lifted her chin up so that she faced him.

Her distraught expression wrenched his heart and he felt his face contort into a desperate, pleading snarl. "Don't you know that I love you more than anyone else on this earth?"

She nodded through the tears.

Why would she do this to me? His hand slipped from her face down to his side where it recommenced opening and closing. "But I could never forgive you if you committed adultery!"

Fresh anger surged through his gut and erupted up through his nostrils. "I guess what they say about nice guys finishing last is true, huh?"

She whimpered but didn't reply.

He bit his bottom lip then shot it out with a snort.

"Maybe Trevor, Imani, and *Lance*," he spit his name out like venom, "were right." He leaned in close. "Maybe you can only love men that beat you."

Melody straightened and shot forward full of fire and fury. "No!"

Chris backed down a minuscule amount. He would never hit Melody although he was still too pissed to divulge that little tidbit to her. A wall maybe...but not her, no matter how mad he got.

Desperate for answers, his anger flared into frustrated confusion. "Then what do I need to do, Melody? Because I've done every single thing you've ever asked me."

He slapped his right fist into his left palm and the loud "smack" made Melody jump again. "I've already charged over to Lance's house to beat him down once before. Do you need to have men fight over you?"

She shook her pathetic head back and forth.

"Then what, damn it?" His fury rocketed. He needed answers before he started hitting things. "Do you like seeing me make a fool of myself?"

Melody slumped back again in a torrent of tears.

He slammed his hand down on her nightstand. "Come on, Melody! You need to tell me something now. Because I can't guarantee that I'll ever listen to your lies again."

Her body shook with tears. "It's so hard to tell you this," she blubbered.

"But you could easily blab it to Trevor?" He glared at her and wondered what planet she'd just arrived from.

She looked even more sorrowful if that were possible. Her hands clasped together in front of her, pleading. "It's the sex."

He didn't follow. "Ours...or you and Lance?" His eyes bulged open wide as his worst fears materialized. "Are you telling me that you and Lance actually had sex?" His gaze fell to her pregnant belly. "Is that baby even mine?"

A pained wail erupted from his gut and he clenched his fists, ready to pummel the nearest wall.

Melody reached out and grabbed his arm.

Snarling, he snatched it away.

But she didn't relent, her head shaking back and forth wildly. Her eyes were as honest and earnest as he'd ever seen them. "Of course the baby's yours. Lance and I, we've never," she couldn't even say the words. "Not even close." Her head and arm dropped in shame. "I'm talking about sex between you and me."

Grabbing two handfuls of his hair, he threw his head back wanting to scream again.

"How is that even possible?" His hands flew down and started emphasizing his words. "We screw damn near every other day, Melody! Stupidly, I always thanked God that I was so lucky to have a freaky wife that initiates sex all the time while my buddies constantly complain about how their wives shut it down after their honeymoon. And especially after they have kids."

"So what is it?" He leaned forward and screamed

in her face. "Are you a freaking sex addict?"

She buried her head in her hands. "No! It's not the frequency, it's the duration." She sobbed, then blurted it out. "No matter what I do, you rush in with minimal, frenzied foreplay, and then it's over five or ten minutes later."

Like a deflated balloon, his deep exhale left his body limp. "Are you serious?" Stunned, he shook his head in utter disbelief. "And all this time I thought I was doing you a favor."

Melody's head popped up, a mask of confusion.

"Listening to my buddies talk, their wives just want it over with quick. Their weekly 'duty' fulfilled." He laughed, short and bitter. "And you never said anything different. So I thought that's how you liked it!" His hand went up in a question. "Why didn't you ever tell me what you wanted?"

Her gaze softened with regret and shame. "Because I thought it would embarrass you or hurt your feelings."

Wrong answer! His fury reignited. "More embarrassing or hurtful than hearing you tell Trevor how much you want to fuck Lance? God, I'm so mad I could—" Without even thinking he grabbed her sweatshirt zipper and yanked it down so hard that it whipped unzipped and flew open exposing her tight fitting, pink T-shirt.

Melody's eyes widened in fear and surprise...and then desire?

Oh my God, maybe she does like it rough. Not his preference although her reaction aroused him and following his instincts, he focused on her V-necked T-shirt. Grabbing it with both hands at the neckline, he pulled expecting it to stretch and deform.

The flimsy cotton ripped straight down the middle.

They both gasped and her eyes locked on his.

"I'm so sorry, Chris." Her hands were in his hair and she pulled him toward her waiting lips.

He wanted to resist, but she looked so sexy and sweet.

Her chest heaved, allowing her pink, lacy bra to peek from beneath her ruined, tattered T-shirt. And her eyes begged for forgiveness while her hands combing through his hair demanded it.

Unable to refrain any longer, he succumbed to her lips and the fire between them exploded into inferno-level flames.

Then the oddest thing happened, she *swooned* into his arms.

In the past, he always thought the romance books she read were ridiculous with all of their heaving bosoms and swooning women.

Now he understood and it turned him on even further.

Kissing her non-stop, deep and slow, he climbed onto the bed and straddled her, careful of her pregnant belly. As she melded against him, his hands slid up her back, slowly tickling her spine. Somehow like magic, her bra unfastened on the first try with a simple flick of his fingers.

Melody moaned and slid down to lay beneath him, never breaking their kiss.

Finally he broke their lip lock long enough to refocus his attention on her beautiful, pregnancy-enhanced breasts. If she wanted long, non-frenzied foreplay, he'd gladly oblige.

Taking his time he set to work on her swollen nipples, determined to kiss every square inch of her rosy skin. Her constant stream of ecstasy-filled groans made his job both easier and harder at the same time. The sounds spurred him on to new areas to explore, but they also made his member want to finish taking care of business pronto.

Resolute, he continued down over her taut belly, stopping long enough between kisses to whisper, "I love you," to their unborn child.

Melody's moans intensified as he neared her puss and the hot kitty purred to him in a manner he couldn't ignore. His tongue traversed tender terrain—teasing, tantalizing, tingling—until she trembled and twisted.

"Oh God, Chris," she cried, clawing at his arms and shoulders trying to pull him up. "Enter me now, please," she screamed.

Happy to accommodate her wishes, he entered her, but he eased in as slow as possible.

Her hands grabbed his ass, begging him to go faster.

However, he leaned back far enough so she could see him teasingly shake his head, 'no.'

She slapped the bed in fevered frustration and thrust her pelvis up to grind against him, hoping to force the issue.

Smiling, he took control of the rhythm, slowing it even more. All the while driving her and him wild.

In time Melody stopped resisting and joined him on their slow journey to ecstasy.

Thirty minutes later, neither one of them could wait any longer. As he rocked them faster, he felt a shudder start deep in her belly. The shudder grew and soon consumed them both in its intensity, making their orgasm powerful enough to register on the Richter scale.

Utterly exhausted, he managed to roll off her three minutes later and onto the bed beside her.

She smiled at him with the most wondrous look of love.

He chuckled. "If that's what it's like to fight and make up, we're going to have to fight more often."

WELCOME HOME

"How does that feel?" Lance asked as he turned off the bathtub faucet. He slipped his hand under the cover of bubbles into the warm, inviting bath water.

"Delicious," Imani replied stepping into their Jacuzzi tub.

He held her hand until she settled into the aromatic, frothy mix.

"It's just missing one thing," she said sending him the most sensual invitation he could imagine. As she released his hand and let it drop, she shrieked and rocketed her arm away from the water's surface.

"My watch!" She unfastened it and gave him a mischievous grin. 'We don't want it to get wet, now do we?" she asked looking sultrier by the second.

Frankly, he didn't care; he'd buy her ten more watches. He just wanted to jump into the tub behind her and properly welcome her back home from her Boston business trip.

Imani smiled, reading his mind. She held up her hand to stop him, her unfastened watch dangling from her fingertips. "Could you be a dear and put this in my jewelry box for me?" she asked sweet and smooth as French Silk pie.

Whatever he needed to do to get into that bathtub

with her, he'd do it. Snatching the watch, he left the master bathroom for their bedroom.

"I know you're in a hurry, but could you set it in there nice and neat next to the others?"

He grunted. That was the last thing on his mind however, he knew how borderline OCD she acted when certain things were out of place. 'Will do," he replied as he opened the top of her jewelry box.

Like bejeweled soldiers, her watches stood at attention all in a tidy row except for one empty spot. Chuckling, he folded her watch and prepared to insert it into the empty space when a sparkle caught his eye.

Curious, he used two fingers to fish it out, trying not to disturb the surrounding watches.

His fingers snagged the object and he let it drop into his palm as he extracted his hand. When he opened his hand and examined the item, his breath caught and he rocked back a step.

Imani's wedding ring sparkled on his palm, catching the sunlight streaming in through the nearby bedroom window. Not the wedding ring he gave her, but Marco's.

"You find the right place?" Imani asked sweet as honey. "They're located in the top section."

"Found it," he replied snapping out of it. With one last glance, he dropped the ring back where he found it and set her watch in place. He closed the jewelry box with a frown. "Coming," he said, giving it one last parting look.

CHRIS'S BIRTHDAY PARTY

"I love you so much, Chris," Melody said throwing her arms around his neck.

He ran his fingers through her blonde curls, then he pulled her head close and inhaled her sweet scent of roses and lilacs. "I love you, too." He leaned back enjoying her face during afterglow. "I guess I should help you off the kitchen counter."

She glanced at her watch and alarm erased the afterglow. "Oh my God, folks will arrive any minute."

"We still have time," he said lifting her off the counter and setting her onto the floor.

"Your sisters promised to arrive early to help settle your parents in when they landed. Plus you know that Imani and Lance always come early, just to help set up." She scrambled and grabbed a paper towel and 409, cleaning the counter they'd just soiled.

"True," he said cleaning himself in the kitchen sink.

Melody turned and caught him. "Eww, gross!" She swatted his butt. "Go do that in the powder room, not in here where we prepare the food."

He chuckled. "That's not what you were saying mere moments ago."

"God, you're so incorrigible!" She tried to swat him again as he escaped to the powder room with her following in close pursuit.

As she pushed him aside and relieved herself on the toilet, he finished cleaning up in the powder room sink.

When he finished drying himself and fixing his pants, he leaned back against the wall and watched her try to clean herself with Kleenexes.

Hard to imagine that only one week ago she confessed to wanting to sleep with Lance. It felt like they'd experienced a year of real conversations and daily, mind-blowing sex since then. Their relationship had flourished and grown by leaps and bounds. Yet it had only been a week.

And today was the first time that he would see Lance since his huge altercation with Melody.

He caught her eyes in the mirror's reflection. "Are you still attracted to him?"

Confusion creased her brow and she turned around to face him. "What?"

"Do you still have feelings for Lance?" His eyes narrowed although he remained perfectly calm.

Melody shook her head, her eyes sad. "No, nothing whatsoever." She rubbed his arms. "You have to know things between us have changed so much recently." She struggled to find the words. "You are the only person on my mind."

Reaching up, she held his face between her gentle hands. "Now and forever more. I love you, Chris. You and only you."

Exhaling the breath that he didn't even realize he held captive, he felt the tension release from his body. Innately he knew it however, he still needed to hear the words.

Nonetheless, it took two to tango, and if Lance still harbored feelings… "You might have changed your tune, but what about Lance?" He gazed at her with complete composure as he held her hands.

"Look, Melody. I can confront Lance, however, nobody will like it if I do. And I don't want Trevor strutting around here tonight acting like he knows some big secret either. Therefore, I'm trusting you to speak with both of them to make sure this is never an issue, ever again." He tenderly squeezed her hands. "Because if you won't squash this thing with Lance once and for all, I will. Do you understand?"

She nodded. "I understand and you don't have to worry about my love ever again." She lunged into his arms and hugged him as tight as she could.

With his remorseful, loving wife in his arms, her fragrant floral scent enticing him, he felt his heart melt and forgive. Although he never told Melody, it was love at first sight when he met her at Imani and Marco's wedding. Deep in his heart he believed she felt the same undying love for him also.

But sometimes he wondered if he loved her too much for his own good. As he kissed her loving lips, he hoped this wouldn't come back to bite him in the ass.

And then the doorbell rang.

***

Melody prayed it was Chris's sisters and parents, but when she flung open the door with Chris standing by her side, she found Imani and Lance standing on the doorstep grinning.

Imani almost bowled her over as she stepped forward and hugged Melody.

A twinge of guilt flooded through Melody as she realized how close her wayward thoughts from a week ago had come to making her even contemplate ruining all of their marriages and friendships. Especially considering everything Imani had done for her over the years.

In reality, she never would have cheated, but temptation could take root after sowing just one little mustard seed of doubt. Feeling truly remorseful, she returned Imani's hug and embraced her tight. "I love you."

"I love you, too," Imani whispered in her ear. When Imani stepped back and relinquished Melody, she gave her a quick once over. "Girl, you look good!"

Meanwhile Lance greeted Chris. "Happy Birthday, Man," Lance said trying to give Chris a pound with his free hand.

"Thanks," Chris said as he ignored Lance's gesture and instead grabbed the casserole dish that Lance balanced in his left hand. "Let me get that for you."

Melody tensed and she noticed Imani's eyebrow raise, but Lance seemed oblivious as he gathered her in a bearhug and Chris leaned in and kissed Imani's cheek.

"Hey Imani, do you want to help me arrange the food?" Chris asked.

"Sure thing," Imani replied as she followed Chris into the kitchen leaving Melody and Lance momentarily alone.

Once Lance set Melody down, his eyes followed Imani and a lusty smile emerged.

And just like that she realized once and for all that her crazy, pregnancy hormones had gotten the best of her because there was no way that Lance wanted anyone except Imani. She smiled with relief. "Guess things have improved with you and Imani since our talk last week at lunch?"

"Indeed they have," he replied, his eyes still following Imani's every move. "Thanks again for always being there," he said finally turning to look at her. "You and Imani are the best friends a guy could ever have." Lance threw his arm over her shoulder and side-hugged Melody as he kissed the top of her head like a big brother. "Thank you."

"My pleasure," she replied, sincerely meaning it and then the doorbell rang again. Pulling back, she gestured for Lance to join Imani and Chris in the kitchen so that she could let in their guests.

"And the party begins," she said going to answer the door.

For the next twenty minutes she welcomed Chris's crazy sisters and parents, about twenty of their co-workers, and a couple of neighbors. Just as she was about to join the party, the doorbell rang again and she opened the door wondering how many more people were coming.

A harried Erycah smiled and hugged her while a patient Trevor waited. "Sorry, we're so late," Erycah said with an apologetic look. "Just wait 'til you have kids, you'll understand."

As if on cue, Trev, Jr. and Xavier bowled past Melody's legs almost knocking her over. Erycah gave her an embarrassed smile as she hurried after them. "Boys!"

Shaking her head in amusement, Melody turned to greet Trevor, but something hit her legs. Looking down, she saw Kingston hugging her shins, his head buried against her knees.

Sensing her bend down he looked up with a big, drooling smile and after he received his welcome kiss from Melody, he toddled off after his brothers.

Finally free and alone, Trev gave her a huge hug. "Everything okay?" he asked as he released her and his questioning eyes insinuated much more than his innocuous question.

"Chris and I are the best we've ever been. Please, let's just pretend that you were never privy to the rambling thoughts of a delusional, hormonally unbalanced woman ever again, okay?" she asked, hoping he could forget.

Trevor broke out his huge grin and the fingers from his right hand practically danced across his forehead. "Erased and forgotten," he said making his fingers flick the imaginary gathered thoughts in the trash.

"Oh, Lord, you're so nuts," she said ushering Trev inside. With the weight of the world lifted off her shoulders, she shut the door and breathed a sigh of relief.

Chris caught her eye as he laughed at some joke Imani and their co-workers shared. On the surface, he looked happy, but she sensed the underlying currants of uncertainty.

How Much Longer?

"Whew, I can't wait to get this beach ball out of me," Imani complained as she stopped walking up the pathway to the Pointe long enough to catch her breath. She frowned as the baby took her reprieve as an opportunity to practice kickboxing inside her stomach.

Lance smiled and rubbed her lower back while Melody walked past and punched her arm.

"Please! At least you two cows had an easy pregnancy." Melody frowned as she patted her belly. "I'm still experiencing morning sickness daily from this little monster!"

Chris rubbed Melody's Buddha belly and tsked her. "Now, now, Honey, that's my little angel you're talking about."

Trev laughed as both he and Erycah overtook them. "That's what you're calling the baby now. Just wait until he or she arrives!"

Imani planned on offering a rebuttal, but then Trev's three monsters ran past screaming and chasing each other up the hill. Lil Trev and Xavier led the charge as they raced about, weaving in and out. Poor little Kingston, who was just learning to walk, tried to wobble and toddle along as fast as his unsteady legs could carry him. With a pensive look set in place, you could see how determined he was to hang with his brothers and not get left behind.

Trev looked at her and smirked. "See what I mean?" He scooped up Kingston in one arm and kept his other hand on Erycah's waist.

Lance laughed as Melody and Chris darted out of the way.

"Well, notwithstanding your little curtain climbers, I've already paid my dues," she said shaking her head. "I'm a week past my due date and this little sucker shows no signs of wanting to come out." She rested her hand on her bloated belly. "In fact, it's so bad my OB/GYN said I'll need to get induced if this continues much longer."

Erycah stretched and followed the kids up the hill. "Well, like Melody said, I feel great! I'm in the home stretch with only three more weeks to go and this pregnancy's been an absolute breeze." She shot Melody a warning shot before she could say anything snide. "But don't forget, I suffered through three hellacious pregnancies already, so I was due for some love!"

Melody shrugged, "yeah, I guess you have a point there, but I still have about a month and a half left to go and this little baby is kicking my butt."

Trevor laughed. "Not as romantic as you envisioned it, huh?"

Imani and Lance laughed as Melody frowned and tried to hit him, but Trev easily skipped away while Melody shook her fist.

When they crested the hill, they entered the garden oasis of the Pointe.

Erycah stretched and inhaled deep, soaking in their luscious, bloom-filled surroundings. "Hey, Melody, thanks again for suggesting we walk around up here. I really needed the exercise."

There was a moment of awkward silence as Lance, Melody, Chris, and Imani tried to let Erycah's reference to needing exercise slide. No one wanted to tell her that she'd put on weight.

Trev whipped his head around to see what was going on while Erycah laughed.

"I know it's true, you guys don't have to pretend for my sake," Erycah said. "Even chasing after three little ones isn't enough exercise to keep from piling on the pounds."

"Well, when someone insists on keeping you barefoot and pregnant for years, that's sometimes an unfortunate consequence," Chris said, making Trevor's jaw drop at his bluntness.

Melody jumped in and backed up her husband. "Well, Trev, my Honey's got a point. Poor Erycah has suffered in an almost constant pregnant state for five years. Chris gained about twelve pounds with me. The least you could do is gain some sympathy weight with her." Melody smiled, happy to give Trev a dig.

Erycah joined in then. "I do agree there. Trev can eat a horse and still not gain any weight. It's ridiculous as I just look at food and gain ten pounds. I mean seriously, I've gained ten pounds with each pregnancy."

Erycah threw Lance and Imani an evil look. "I mean look at Mr. and Mrs. Universe over there. I used to have a cute figure like her, but I went from a size 8 to a 10 to a 12 and now…well, I never imagined I'd balloon up to a 14!"

"Don't drag me into this," Imani said wagging her finger. She wanted to add on that Erycah could always spend a bit more time in the gym like she, Lance, and Bobby did. Especially since they designed water aerobics classes for pregnant women nowadays! But she refrained not wanting to hurt Homegirl's feelings.

Trev smiled and hugged his wife. "I'll always love you and find you beautiful no matter what size. In fact—" he swatted her full, round bottom, "I think you're even sexier with more curves."

"Okay, okay, enough of that," Chris said watching the boys race past again. "That's how you have three little ones now and one more on the way."

"Agreed," Melody said as she started them walking along one of the paths again after the boys.

Lance chuckled as he took Imani's hand and walked beside her. "How are you feeling?"

Although she could tell it wasn't his intention, she found his question and tone, sexy as hell. She stifled an overwhelming urge to drag him into the nearby bushes and get busy. *Damn, pregnancy hormones were dangerous!* They'd enjoyed an almost daily dose of sex…hot, passionate, primal sex.

"Good," she replied, fanning herself and looking

away on purpose to take her mind off jumping his gorgeous, sexy bones.

As they passed some rose bushes, she took a deep inhale and let their fragrant blooms expand her diaphragm and lungs. "It's nice to get out of the house for a while," she said enjoying the feel of the sun kiss her skin. "And not have my crazy mother hounding me about going into labor."

"How long were your parents here?" Erycah asked.

"Two weeks," Melody replied for Imani.

"Two *long* weeks," Imani said with a sigh. "I love my mom, but she has an old wives' tale for everything. Plus she kept pestering me to have the baby before they left for their cruise. As if I had any control over that!"

Lance chuckled. "She was mad at you for not delivering before they left and she was mad at your dad for not canceling the trip."

"Please!" Trev said shaking his head. "If I had a choice between watching my daughter give birth or going on a seven-day Caribbean cruise, you know what I'd choose. Your mom would just have to be pissed off at me, too."

"Hmm, maybe that's what we should all do next year," Melody said in a dreamy tone. "Let's all take a cruise together."

"Someone please stop Ms. Romantic before she gets started," Imani said with a groan. "I'm not ready to even think about making baby number two yet."

Everyone except Melody laughed.

"Skip you!" Melody stuck her tongue out at Imani and grabbed Chris's hand. "Next year, you can deal with your mom while I'm getting romantic on a cruise ship with my man."

"Mm, I like the sound of that," Chris said as Melody dragged him along the path, ahead of the group.

The three couples laughed and then paired off as they walked past the lookouts to downtown Albany and hooked halfway around the paths until they looked out over their old college campus. They all gathered together and gazed at the distinctive library, dorms, and the domed stadium.

"We had some fun times down there," Lance said as he swung his arm over Imani's shoulder.

"Yes indeed we did, our little slice of heaven," Trev said squeezing Erycah to his side until the boys raced past. Alarmed, he immediately gave chase. "Xavier, put that stick down now and quit trying to hit your brothers."

Everyone broke out laughing, or so Imani thought, until she noticed that Melody and Chris weren't really engaged.

Imani sobered up. D'oh! This place held haunting memories for Melody. In fact, she was both amazed and proud Melody even suggested the location. But then it dawned on her why Chris seemed aloof. Chris attended Rensselaer Polytechnic Institute; their college meant nothing to him. She excused herself and slipped away from Lance to ensure Chris felt included.

Chris looked surprised and then pleased. "Hey there."

Imani placed her hand on his shoulder and pointed him towards the northeast. "And way over to the north is Troy. You can probably just make out R.P.I. if you squint just right."

He threw his head back and laughed. "Doubtful, but thanks for the attempt." He bumped her hip and draped his arm around her shoulder.

"Thanks," Melody mouthed and turned away.

Imani swore she saw tears shimmering in Melody's eyes before she strolled off alone.

SHOWTIME

"Hey, Mom. How's Jamaica?" Lance asked Mrs. Jordan as he placed the kitchen phone on speaker. With his hands free, he finished arranging the bouquet of a dozen yellow roses in the crystal vase

"We're just getting back on the cruise ship now, but it was beautiful. Poor and proud, but beautiful. Thanks for asking. How's my daughter?"

"There's no change." Lance looked up from the florist's display-ready bouquet as he heard the door from the garage to the kitchen open.

Imani entered and he gave her a heart-felt smile then a wink.

"The doctor plans on inducing her in three days. So you guys will make it back from the cruise with one day to spare."

"Good, good, tell her to keep that baby inside a little while longer," Mrs. Dunn replied.

Imani set down her purse and keys on the counter and carefully stepped around her packed labor suitcase that played alert sentinel by the garage door for the last four weeks. She inhaled the bouquet, smiled at him, and gestured for the phone.

"You're in luck, Imani just got home. I'll let you tell her yourself." He picked up the phone and handed it to Imani, but she stopped mid-reach.

An embarrassed, confused look crossed her face and she reached between her skirted legs. "Oh my God, I'm peeing on myself."

Lance's jaw dropped before he managed to bring the phone up to his ear and speak. "Um, Mom…you and Dad might want to tell the ship's captain to hustle back home now." He held Imani steady with his other hand. "Your daughter's water just broke."

A bunch of excited screams emanated from the phone and Lance held it at arm's length.

"I told you we should have cancelled this trip," they heard Mrs. Jordan yell at Mr. Jordan.

"Listen, woman!" Mr. Jordan fussed back. "I told you to buy trip insurance and you wouldn't do it. And there's no way I'm losing our money. They don't need us in the delivery room anyway, we'll see them and the baby soon enough."

"Umm, we gotta go, we'll call you later," Lance shouted at the phone, but then they heard a click and the dial tone as Mrs. Jordan hung up. Shaking his head, he dropped the phone on the counter and held Imani with both hands.

Imani still looked shell-shocked as the water continued to spurt and then trickle from her. She appeared uncertain, sad, and disgusted all wrapped into one. "I can't get it to stop."

Lance chuckled and scooped her up in his arms. "It's okay. I got you, Baby." He whisked her to the powder room and helped her get situated on the toilet. "Will you be fine while I go call the doctor?"

She nodded, so he took off back down the hall and grabbed the kitchen phone, beaming from ear to ear. His beautiful wife was having their baby and he couldn't wait to get the show on the road.

COMPLICATIONS

Melody raced into the hospital.

"Do you need any help, Miss?" the information desk attendant asked as Melody breezed past.

Melody glanced back. "No, thank you. I already know the room number." She followed the signs to the elevator bank and repeatedly pushed the up button. "Come on, come on," she said tapping her toes.

An elevator to her left dinged and whooshed open.

In her haste to enter, she almost bowled over a little, old lady trying to exit the elevator.

"Sorry," she said with a half-smile as she waited with impatience for the woman to leave.

Once the path was clear, she jumped onboard and pushed the floor for the maternity ward. When the doors reopened, she exhaled a sigh of relief as she saw Lance walking Imani around. Feeling suddenly very pregnant and unwieldy, she wobbled over to them as fast as she could.

"Hey, Girl," Imani said spotting her. "That was quick. I swore Lance just called you."

Melody hugged her. "You guys have great timing, I just finished up with work when you called and I sped right over." She released Imani and stepped back to examine her. "How are you feeling?"

Imani shrugged. "So far, so good. The contractions are getting more intense and closer together, but I keep moving from the bed to the bouncy ball to walking the halls." Her eyes bulged and her face tensed.

Just as she was about to ask her if she was okay, Imani reached out with a grip of steel and clamped down on her arm.

Imani's hand inflicted excruciating pain and Melody's mouth and eyes flew open. She bit her lip so as not to scream in the middle of the hallway.

Lance nodded at her and grimaced as Imani held him captive with her other hand. "Yep, the contractions are getting more intense and frequent." He looked at Imani. "Let's not forget to breathe like we learned in Lamaze class. Okay, Honey?"

"Yes, can you breathe with us, Imani?" she asked praying that Imani would release her hand soon before her bones shattered.

Imani raised her head and glared at them with fury-filled eyes.

At that moment she swore Imani's head was about to spin around ala *The Exorcist*. "Or not," she replied through gritted teeth while praying for the torture to end.

Imani's grip tightened around her hand, if that were even possible and then Imani's entire body relaxed and she released them to Melody's extreme relief.

"Ow, so not cool," she said backing away from

Imani. Ever so gingerly she rubbed her bruised hand, trying to regain blood flow and circulation to it.

"Whew, sorry about that, y'all," Imani said as she popped upright like nothing happened.

"It's okay, Honey," Lance said in a soothing tone as he rubbed Imani's back. "Do you want to head back to the room for a while?"

The hell it is okay! Wincing she wondered what she'd agreed to by coming here.

The elevator dinged and Chris burst out of the opening doors. A relieved smile washed over his face as he saw them standing in the hallway. "Great, I'm not too late and I promise this time not to pass out."

Chris pecked her on the cheek, nodded at Lance, and addressed Imani. "How are you doing?"

"Don't ask," she muttered under her breath.

Imani gestured back and forth with her hand. "It comes and goes, but unfortunately I'm only dilated four centimeters."

Chris looked confused.

Melody enlightened him. "That means we have six more centimeters of hell to go before she even starts to push."

Lance chuckled and led Imani back towards their room.

As soon as Imani settled into the hospital bed, she grabbed Melody and Lance's hands again, her face a mask of agony.

"Look, if you're going to permanently mangle my hand, the least you could try to do is breathe like we practiced in class," she demanded loud and firm enough that Imani took notice.

Imani nodded and followed Melody's lead. Then Chris and Lance joined in, too.

They continued breathing and adjusting Imani's positions from the bed to the ball to walking around the hallways between checks by the doctors and nurses for the next two hours.

When they returned to the room from their latest jaunt down the hall, Melody plopped into one of the two reclining chairs to catch her breath. She grabbed a tissue from the end table between the chairs and dabbed the sweat from her forehead. *Whew, I'm getting as much of a workout as Imani!*

As Lance helped Imani settle into bed again, Imani frowned at her. "You okay, Melody?"

Chris and Lance swiveled their heads around to check on her.

Melody managed a weak smile. "Yes, of course, I just wish you'd dilate and push out this baby already."

Imani relaxed and leaned back. "You and me both! How far along did Dr. Mike say I was this last time?"

"Six centimeters," Melody, Chris, and Lance replied in unison before they broke out in raucous, tired laughter.

Imani ignored them and looked at Lance. "Oh, did you call Trevor and Erycah?"

Lance gave Imani a funny stare. "I know the memory's the first to go during pregnancy, but do you seriously not recall talking to them on my phone just ten minutes ago, right before our last trek around the corridors?"

Imani popped herself in the head. "I did, didn't I? That seems so long ago already." Then Imani's face contorted in pain again and Melody jumped up to resume her position by her side.

As Melody led them in their breathing exercises, she felt fine beads of sweat pop out on her forehead again. Ignoring it, she continued breathing, but each breath became more strained and difficult.

To make things worse, Imani squeezed her hand again and this time she did it so hard that Melody swore she felt sympathetic pains course down her lower back. With a grimace she braced against the hospital bed railing waiting for Imani's contraction to subside.

Imani screamed out in agonizing pain and it was only after Melody looked up into their surprised faces that she realized the scream hadn't come from Imani, it had emanated from her!

Shocked, she covered her mouth and slid down towards the floor as her body crumpled and her knees buckled.

Chris appeared behind her in a flash holding her steady as she felt her body tense and weaken.

Lance's jaw hung down as he stared at her while Imani's face looked ashen.

Imani immediately switched into the mothering role although she still had to be writhing from her own contractions. "Melody, are you okay?"

"Yes, I'm fi—" she jolted in Chris's arms as

another slash of pain streaked through her lower back and then slumped against him as the pain slashed around to her belly and settled in her pelvis. She cried out as her hands went to protect the baby.

"Nurse," Lance yelled into the intercom. Melody hadn't even realized he had pressed the call button. "Please hurry!"

Two nurses burst in before he even finished his request. The first one, Nadine, looked at Imani, but the second one, Mary, noticed Melody.

"How far along are you?" Mary asked as she helped Chris get her to the reclining chair.

Frantic, Melody shook her head so hard that it hurt. "No, I'm not due for another month."

"Nadine, get the baby monitor," Mary said as she whipped on a pair of gloves. "What's your name, Honey?" she asked looking at Melody again.

Melody wanted to speak but couldn't. Between the whir of activity, an impending sense of doom, and the unrelenting pain engulfing her back and pubic area, apprehension clammed her mouth shut.

"Her name's Melody," Chris replied as he squeezed her shoulders trying his best to keep her calm and optimistic.

"Alright, Melody, we're just going to check you and your baby." The two nurses had the contraption attached to her in what seemed like a few seconds flat.

Mary exchanged worried looks with Nadine. "Get the ultrasound unit in here and page Dr. Mike."

"No, no, no!" Melody cried, as a heavy blanket of

dread cloaked her body. She grabbed Mary's arm. "Please, no, it's too early."

Mary patted her arm. "You're fine, Melody, we're going to take good care of you. You just sit back and relax. We need to keep you and that baby as comfortable as possible. In fact, let's get you ready. Can you unbutton your shirt for me?"

Dr. Mike charged in with Nadine and another person who wheeled in the portable ultrasound machine.

Dr. Mike examined her as they prepped her belly with the cool, slimy ultrasound gel. "Now Melody, you know we were supposed to be here for Imani today," he said trying to lighten the mood. "Your turn's not supposed to occur for at least another month."

Melody tried to smile back, but she found it difficult to breathe.

They were done with the examination lickety split and Dr. Mike jumped up and clapped her back. "I need you to stay calm and strong for me. However, the baby is in distress. We're going to need to perform an emergency C-section." He nodded towards Nadine and she raced off to start preparations.

Imani's voice cracked. "Is Melody going to be okay?" She wiggled off the bed and Lance held her steady.

Dr. Mike nodded, then turned his attention to Nadine and the ultrasound technician as they returned with a gurney. He glanced at Chris and Melody.

"Okay, let's get you on here."

"Right now?" Melody asked her voice shaky.

Chris, Nadine, and Mary assisted her onto the gurney. Her eyes never left Dr. Mike's face and she didn't like the worry she saw residing behind the fake, everything-will-be-okay smile. She felt someone squeeze her left hand and she realized Imani was next to her side with Lance positioned just behind her.

Then she experienced a weird sensation as the cloak of dread slipped off her shoulders and beautiful relief washed through her body starting at her head and flowing down through her tippy toes.

She smiled at Imani then tilted her head towards Lance. She grinned and gave him a wink before she redirected her attention back to Imani. "Promise me that you and Lance will watch after Chris and the baby."

Imani gasped. "Don't talk like that Melody. You heard Dr. Mike; you're going to be fine. Just fine!"

"I know," she replied feeling angels wrap their wondrous wings around her.

Imani and Lance slipped away as the team of doctors and nurses rushed her out of the room and down the hall.

With each passing overhead fixture, her body seemed to lighten and the pain disappeared. She struggled to stay connected for one more minute.

With a slight effort, she focused on Chris.

The amber flecks in his gray eyes glimmered as he ran along with the team, holding her right hand. His free hand stroked her hair from her face. She could feel her once springy, blonde curls, matted to her head with sweat.

"You're going to be the best father."

Chris tried hard to look strong and brave for her benefit.

She smiled at him. "I love you so much, Chris."

"I love you, too," he said as his bottom lip quivered.

Her head lolled to the side and she locked eyes with Dr. Mike. "I'm ready," she told him as she felt herself succumbing to the call of the angels. The last thing she heard was the sound of the baby's heart monitor screaming out its warning beeps.

PANDEMONIUM

"Damn it, Melody, fight!" Imani yelled, reaching out after the mob of people as they whisked Melody away. *God, this wasn't happening!* She let her outstretched hand drop and then her body shook trying to hold in the sobs as she spun around into Lance's strong, waiting arms.

Before he could comfort her, she leaned back to look up at him and noticed a whirlwind of activity barreling down the hall towards them.

Following her newfound, quick, motherly instincts, she pushed Lance back against the wall and leaned into him to flatten them as much as possible and give the somehow familiar, oncoming flurry of pandemonium room to pass.

It took her a second and she squinted then her eyes popped open in disbelief. "Trevor?"

"Huh?" Lance turned to follow her stare.

Trev glanced up as he ran beside two nurses pushing Erycah in a wheelchair. The nurses charged into the room two doors down from hers and Trev stopped long enough to point an accusatory finger her direction. With a half-snarl, half-grin, he shook his finger. "Sometimes I wonder if my wifey was on the right track when she asked what kind of witch are you."

"What?" she asked half-offended and she felt Lance stiffen behind her.

"No sooner did I hang up with you and tell Erycah that you were in labor, when her water broke!"

They all turned and ran towards the room as they heard the nurses screaming at Erycah. "Don't push! Don't push! We're not ready yet."

"I don't care if you guys are ready or not, this baby's coming out now." Erycah growled back, her hands gripping the bed railings as she spread her legs open further and prepared to hunker down.

Imani raced to the right side of Erycah with Lance on her heels as Trev hurried over to Erycah's left. Erycah relinquished the railings and grabbed their hands instead.

"Hold on one more minute," the nurse said.

Erycah grimaced but obeyed. "I should have known this baby would come two weeks early. They're like backward ticking time bombs!"

"What?" Trev asked.

Erycah graced him with a snarl as she waited for the nurse's green light. "Trev, Jr. was a week late, then Xavier was right on time with his due date, then Kingston came a week early. So, I should have expected this one to come two weeks early and keep to the one week earlier each pregnancy timetable."

Lance and Imani chuckled.

"Push now," the nurse said as a female doctor entered the room. "She's fully dilated and the head is crowning."

"Wow, how long did you wait to come to the hospital?" The doctor asked as she took up position between Erycah's stirruped legs.

"Believe it or not, her water just broke about thirty-five minutes ago," Trev replied.

"Well, this baby's wasting no time." The doctor examined the area and then nodded at Erycah. "Okay give me one more good push."

Erycah grimaced, braced, and then summoned one loud, long moan.

"Excellent, excellent," the doctor said. "Keep it coming…Good!"

Wails erupted from the baby as the doctor and nurses went to work.

"It's a beautiful, baby girl," the doctor declared.

Erycah slapped Trevor's arm as she slumped back onto the bed in relief. "Did you hear that? It's a girl! We can finally stop!"

Trevor's toothy grin lit up the room. "My Sweetheart finally has a little Sweetheart." He leaned over and kissed Erycah's forehead. "I love you and I'm so proud of you. You did good! She's so beautiful, just like her mother."

Erycah beamed in elated exhaustion.

"Congratulations!" Imani said as Lance echoed her sentiment. "Let me rub your hands and hope that some of your easy delivery rubs off on me or transfers through osmosis."

Erycah laughed. "I have to admit thirty minutes of labor with two pushes is much more pleasurable than my first time around." She looked at Trev. "Would you like to share with them how long your first little knucklehead took?"

He shook his head and sighed. "Twelve hours of labor and two more hours of pushing."

Lance chuckled. "Hopefully, that's not us," he said squeezing Imani's hand.

Erycah tapped Imani's arm. ""How far along are you now?"

"I was at six centimeters before..." her voice trailed off and her head dropped as worry returned.

"Before what," Trev asked looking concerned. It took him a second to follow. "Where's Melody?"

Imani couldn't answer.

"The baby was in distress, they sent her for an emergency C-section when you guys rolled in," Lance said.

Erycah gasped aloud. "Oh, my God."

"Is there anything we can do?" Trev asked as he held Erycah's shoulders.

She shook her head, hoping to fend off the doubts. "Just pray," Imani replied. "We need to pray as if her life depends on it."

As if to challenge her own resolve, a slow throb in her lower back built into a crescendo. She gripped the bed railing as another monster contraction took hold, determined to make up for lost time.

"Here you go," one of the nurses told Erycah as the nurse stepped between Trev and Erycah and placed their daughter in her arms.

"Imani?" Erycah cried, not sure who to focus on.

"I'm okay," she replied as Lance's steadfast hands

swooped her off her feet.

"I got her, don't worry," Lance said as he carried her to the door. "You guys take care of that gorgeous, little girl."

Once Erycah and Trevor half smiled and nodded, Lance whisked her through the door and back into her room. After he laid her gently on the bed, he stroked her hair.

"How are you holding up?" he asked, his chocolate brown eyes glistening with concern.

"I'm fine, I guess..." she replied letting her head droop. "There's just so much happening...and Melody."

"I know, I know," he whispered as he pulled her into his chest and kissed the top of her head.

Mary entered the room. "Alright, it's time to check on you, Mrs. Dunn."

Imani sat up straight, trepidation tingling her nerves. "Do you have any word on Melody?"

Mary looked away as she reconnected Imani to the monitors and made her lay back. "They delivered the baby. She's small, but she's doing fine in the neonatal unit." Mary remained quiet while she noted Imani's vital signs. "Okay, let me see how dilated you are."

Imani couldn't wait any longer as Mary putzed around between her legs. "And how is Melody?"

Mary finished her examination. "You're coming along beautifully. You're at seven centimeters now."

"Great," she snapped as another contraction took hold.

"Do you want anything for the pain?" Mary asked

as she glanced at her.

Imani tried not to snarl. "Yes, give me an epidural please and an update on Melody!"

Mary snapped off her gloves and tossed them in the trash can. "I'll have the anesthesiologist come right in." Mary stood at the door to leave and sighed. "Your friend lost a lot of blood; they're trying their best to save her now."

THE BLESSED TRINITY

"You can do it, Honey," Lance said as he endured another one of Imani's almost constant contractions. Thank God the epidural had diminished her labor pains drastically, so she was pretty much back to acting pleasant although they were still concerned about Melody.

"Are you pushing yet?" Erycah asked as Trevor wheeled her in with the baby.

"What are you doing up out of bed already?" Imani asked.

"Please, this time was a piece of cake. I could almost run a marathon."

"Alrighty then," Lance replied.

Trev laughed. "We won't go quite that far, Sweetheart."

Mary entered the room and went straight to business. "Let's see if you're finally ready." She examined Imani and came up with a smile. "Ten centimeters, let's get the doctor in here."

"It's about time!" Imani checked her watch. "Humph, I guess I should be happy. It's only been six and an half hours."

"Yep, I told you that we were in here with Trev, Jr. for twelve hours. Six or seven is a piece of cake,"

Erycah said cracking up.

Nadine barreled in and went straight to Imani. "I wanted to let you know I just came from the OR and it was pretty touch and go for a while. But Melody is going to be just fine. She's in critical but stable condition. She, Chris, and baby Genesis are all resting in recovery and the NICU respectively."

Imani reached out and hugged her. "Oh thank God! Bless you, Nadine."

Nadine returned her hug, then pulled back and smiled. "My pleasure."

Lance embraced Imani while Erycah let out a long sigh of relief.

"Genesis? Genesis Weaver? What do they think; that she's the beginning of the new world? I can tell you what that name is, it's the "beginning" of the end for that little girl," Trev said using air quotes. "It's the beginning of bullying and teasing."

Erycah hit Trev's leg while Imani, Lance, and even Nadine tried their best not to laugh.

"You know it's true," Trev said. "Not sure about that name but whatever. I guess we'll still let little Sierra play with her, right Sierra?" Trevor said in a baby voice as he played with his bundled daughter.

Nadine whirled around taking notice of Erycah for the first time. She frowned at Erycah and Trevor. "Did you just give birth?"

Erycah smiled and nodded.

"Oh, no, no, no," Nadine said shaking her head. "You shouldn't be in here."

Trevor protested. "But we want to introduce

Sierra to her other playmate."

"Out!" Nadine shouted.

Trevor protested. "We need to support Imani—"

"Out before I kick you out," Nadine replied shooing them out of the room as Mary followed them.

Imani laughed and clapped her hands together.

To Lance she looked more radiant and beautiful than ever. He stepped forward and kissed her until she melted in his arms. When he withdrew, her eyes simmered with love and desire.

"You might want to wait a while before we decide to try for baby number two," she joked.

Smiling, he decided now was as good a time as ever. "Imani, it took me a while to realize what love truly is."

Imani arched her eyebrow and stared at him like he'd lost his mind.

He reached into his pocket and pulled out the black, jeweler's box.

"Are you experiencing déjà vu?" she asked. "You already proposed in a hospital after Erycah delivered. We wound up getting married and now we're having a baby."

He laughed. "No, I didn't forget. In fact I finally remembered how integral all of our friends have been in our lives." He flipped open the box to expose a sparkling, diamond crucifix pendant on an 18 carat gold, herringbone necklace. "Even Marco."

Imani's eyes shot up from the necklace to him to the bouquet of yellow roses he insisted they bring, and then back to him, trying to understand.

"God sent Marco down to protect us from Heather and without his assistance," he shook his head unable to fathom what could have happened that night. "So, the princess-cut diamond in the middle of the cross," he said as he pointed to the larger, one carat diamond located at the intersection of the two arms of smaller diamonds. "Is the solitaire from the wedding ring that Marco gave you. I thought it should sit at the heart of the crucifix."

Imani covered her mouth with her hands and tears welled in her eyes. "Are you serious?" she asked in a voice little more than a whisper.

Anxiety jangled his nerves. He nodded, praying she liked it. God help him if she got pissed thinking he defiled her memories of Marco and her old wedding ring.

"It's beautiful," she said, hugging him tight.

Relieved beyond belief, he exhaled and relaxed. Sporting a large grin, he removed the necklace from the box and fastened it around her neck.

Dr. Mike came in followed by Mary and another nurse. He gave them a weary but pleased smile. "Looks like we can get this show on the road."

"About time!" Imani said bouncing with glee.

After thirty minutes of pushing, Lance finally heard the words he'd been waiting for.

Dr. Mike held up their fat, blood-covered, crying, squirming, full head of hair baby. "It's a bouncing baby boy," he said. "Are you ready to cut the cord?" he asked showing Lance where to snip.

Beaming with pride, he cut the nasty looking, long worm and then the doctor handed off his son to Mary for the battery of clean-up and tests that newborns endured.

Feeling happier than he ever thought possible he went back to his exhausted wife's side and kissed her head, cheeks, and lips.

"I knew you were carrying my own little mini me," he said bursting with pride.

She smiled and chuckled. "Hopefully, he's nowhere near as bad as Trevor's little clones. Can't you just see the three of them playing together now, Lance, Sierra, and Genesis? Just like you, me, and Melody but as babies."

"Scary to think of what they'll get into," he replied shaking his head.

Nadine brought over the paperwork. "Have you two decided on a name?"

***

Imani prepared to respond, but Lance beat her to the punch.

"His name is Lance Marco Cabrette Dunn," Lance replied with pride.

Imani's eyes shot open wide. *What?* Lance was just full of surprises today. "Are you sure that's not too long or way too much?" she asked with baited breath. "Four names is a mouthful."

He covered her hands with his. "Don't worry, it's perfect."

Overwhelmed by his unbelievable sacrifice and filled with appreciation, tears glistened in her eyes. "Thank you so much." Her eyes settled on the dreaded yellow rose bouquet behind him.

Lance never understood that yellow roses always reminded her of Marco's funeral and heartbreaking loss. But not anymore. She could finally see the beautiful roses for what they really meant, undying friendship

And that's when she saw him standing just between Lance and the roses.

Marco shimmered like sunlight reflecting off a lake, his smile of approval and unconditional love radiated out toward her, Lance, and the baby.

An immense sense of peace encompassed them and her tears fell like raindrops.

Then like a mirage, Marco slowly disappeared.

Feeling lighthearted and breathless, she stared after him for a minute, grateful for every single moment, and then she looked at Lance.

Lance smiled and nodded and she knew he had seen and felt him, too.

"I love you so much, Lance."

"I love you, too," he replied before he leaned down and kissed her with his sweet, succulent lips.

When Lance pulled back, she stared at the little bundle of love swaddled in her arms.

His beautiful mini-Lance features twisted and turned into a yawn as he snuggled into her chest, nestling next to her heartbeat.

Feeling so at peace, Imani smiled and kissed his

delicate forehead. "We love you with all of our hearts. Welcome to the world, Lance Marco Cabrette Dunn."

###

Book Club Questions

1. Have you or has someone you know ever experienced an extrasensory sensation?

2. Do you believe in the existence of guardian angels? Why or why not?

3. Would you consider Lance's behavior inappropriate or was he correct in telling Imani how he felt during her grieving process?

4. How far would you let your husband or wife go to support a grieving friend before you put your foot down like Erycah did with Trevor?

5. Chris doesn't like Lance because he feels like Imani replaced Marco with Lance. Do you think he's right? What are the differences between Imani's relationship with Marco and her relationship with Lance?

6. How appropriate is it to share your fantasies with your friends?

7. How would you react if a friend mentioned that they were dreaming about your significant other?

8. When Imani senses that something is wrong with Erycah and Trevor's children, why do you think Erycah called Imani a witch? Have you ever felt that a friend was hurting you, when they were really trying to help?

9. What scene did you find most memorable?

10. Which character did you relate to most and why?

11. In what ways could Imani or Lance have prevented Heather's attack?

12. How do you think their friendship will change with the addition of children?

GET HELP

If you or someone you love is in an abusive relationship, please call the National Domestic Violence Hotline at 800-799-7233 for assistance.

OTHER WORKS BY K. R. RAYE

The Colors of Friendship
The Colors of Love
True Colors

CONNECT WITH K. R. RAYE:

If you enjoyed the book, please let others know and **post a review** on Amazon, Goodreads, Barnes & Noble, other retail sites, or your blog. Request your local library carry a copy.

Would you like to contact the author or schedule her to attend your event? Please email her at krraye@jpadpublishing.com. Keep tabs on specials and what's next by signing up for her monthly newsletter at https://www.krraye.com/.

Thank you for your support!

K. R. Raye

BookBub –https://www.bookbub.com/profile/k-r-raye
Facebook – https://www.facebook.com/KRRaye13
Goodreads – https://www.goodreads.com/author/show/7160771.K_R_Raye
Twitter – https://twitter.com/KRRaye
Website – https://krraye.com/

OTHER WORKS BY K. R. RAYE

The Colors of Friendship
The Colors of Love
True Colors

CONNECT WITH K. R. RAYE:

If you enjoyed the book, please let others know and **post a review** on Amazon, Goodreads, Barnes & Noble, other retail sites, or your blog. Request your local library carry a copy.

Would you like to contact the author or schedule her to attend your event? Please email her at krraye@jpadpublishing.com. Keep tabs on specials and what's next by signing up for her monthly newsletter at https://www.krraye.com/.

Thank you for your support!

K. R. Raye

BookBub –https://www.bookbub.com/profile/k-r-raye
Facebook – https://www.facebook.com/KRRaye13
Goodreads – https://www.goodreads.com/author/show/7160771.K_R_Raye
Twitter – https://twitter.com/KRRaye
Website – https://krraye.com/

"The characters were well-developed and had me frustrated at times... This was a good start to the series and has me anticipating the next book. I recommend *The Colors of Friendship* to others."
– A&RBC Reviews

"I loved *The Colors of Friendship*. K. R. Raye told a story about a friendship that lasted... The story line flowed well and I could really feel the love between Imani, Melody, and Lance."
– OOSA Online Book Club

"Mrs. Raye did an excellent job of pulling readers in and keeping their attention from beginning to end. This is definitely a book that I recommend you read."
– Olivia Evans Books

"*The Colors of Friendship* by K. R. Raye is a fun-filled story about three college friends, Imani, Melody and Lance. It is entertaining and the conflicts between the characters have been developed well. As a first in the series it will be interesting to see where the plot follows on from here."
– Christoph Fischer, Author of *The Luck of The Weissensteiners* and *Sebastian*

"This first installment of a new adult trilogy follows three college friends as they grapple with romance, jealousy, and threats. A compelling series opener about friendship that will make readers want to devour the sequel."
– Kirkus